THE DANGLED ILLUSION

THE DANGLED ILLUSION

A Novel

R. A. Kuffel

iUniverse, Inc.
New York Lincoln Shanghai

THE DANGLED ILLUSION

Copyright © 2007 by Richard A. Kuffel

All rights reserved. No part of this book may be used or reproduced by any means, graphic, electronic, or mechanical, including photocopying, recording, taping or by any information storage retrieval system without the written permission of the publisher except in the case of brief quotations embodied in critical articles and reviews.

iUniverse books may be ordered through booksellers or by contacting:

iUniverse
2021 Pine Lake Road, Suite 100
Lincoln, NE 68512
www.iuniverse.com
1-800-Authors (1-800-288-4677)

Because of the dynamic nature of the Internet, any Web addresses or links contained in this book may have changed since publication and may no longer be valid.

This is a work of fiction. All of the characters, names, incidents, organizations, and dialogue in this novel are either the products of the author's imagination or are used fictitiously.

ISBN: 978-0-595-46540-8 (pbk)
ISBN: 978-0-595-70399-9 (cloth)
ISBN: 978-0-595-90836-3 (ebk)

Printed in the United States of America

To my wife, Jo, who in every way made everything good in this story possible

Contents

BOOK ONE

Chapter 1:   EXPECTATIONS 3
Chapter 2:   PERSPECTIVE 9
Chapter 3:   COMMUNICATION 13
Chapter 4:   REALITY 21
Chapter 5:   IT HAPPENED 25
Chapter 6:   OPPORTUNITY 31

BOOK TWO

Chapter 7:   WORKING AGAIN 43
Chapter 8:   TRAVEL ASSIGNMENTS 49
Chapter 9:   NEW YORK AND BEYOND 56
Chapter 10: OPPORTUNITY KNOCKS 61
Chapter 11: CRAFTING A NEW CAREER 69
Chapter 12: CAN'T MISS AT FISHCO 74
Chapter 13: TRANSITION 79
Chapter 14: CLOUDS ON THE HORIZON 82
Chapter 15: WORK TEAMS 89
Chapter 16: IMPOSSIBLE 97

Chapter 17: THE REPLACEMENT 105
Chapter 18: LIMBO 113

BOOK THREE

Chapter 19: INTERNATIONAL IT IS 121
Chapter 20: HASTA LUEGO, SOUTH AMERICA 132
Chapter 21: ALOHA PROJECT REYNOLDS 138
Chapter 22: ONE MORE TIME AND A HALF 148
Chapter 23: PROJECT FLEET—THE RISE AND FALL 155

BOOK FOUR

Chapter 24: INEVITABLE 169
Chapter 25: APPROACHING COUNTDOWN—THE PURCHASE 174
Chapter 26: TRY THIS ON FOR SIZE 177

BOOK FIVE

Chapter 27: PREPARING FOR FINALS 187
Chapter 28: THE TRANSITION II 189
Chapter 29: PREPARATIONS 193
Chapter 30: PARTY TIME 198
Chapter 31: CLOSING OUT 205
Chapter 32: PASS IN REVIEW 214
Chapter 33: WHEW! 218
EPILOGUE 221

ACKNOWLEDGMENTS

How many people impact a life or participate in the making and telling of a story? I don't know. And it seems foolhardy to even try to extend gratitude to those who helped bring this project to a conclusion, but I want to try. What follows is my feeble attempt.

First, I thank my father, John H. Kuffel, who believed in this project and, when he was 97 years old, encouraged me with his wish: "I just want to hold the book in my hands." He did get to read the manuscript—it took him two days. He's gone now. But I thank him for his support.

This story is fiction because it allowed me freedom to cobble events from various companies to say what I thought needed saying, but my family will recognize vignettes from lives and situations they knew or just heard about. So I thank my wife, Jo, for her insight and encouragement, and our daughter and son, Lisa and Craig, for their love and patience through it all—and for reading the manuscript and offering their insights.

Several friends read the earlier version of the manuscript and helped me clarify some of the concepts. I thank them: Terry Harrington and John Roufs worked double shifts evaluating it for technical merit, Mike Hinkemeyer lent a professional writer's perspective, Wally Pattock and Andy Hilger supplied a clear business perspective, Lloyd Metzger offered suggestions on directions I hadn't considered, Marilyn Fritz underlined the importance of just telling the story, the Keith Jentoft family challenged and encouraged me to complete the work and suggested specific changes that led to a stronger story, Cal Vraa shared his writing experiences and encouraged me in the project since its earliest moments, Dave Schwain helped me understand corporate thinking so I could deal with it in a non-adverserial way, and Todd Kramasz edited the final versions of the manuscript and is still involved in the project.

BOOK ONE

CHAPTER 1

EXPECTATIONS

Raef Burnham always knew he'd be a success—he just didn't know at what. Today the company would announce a new director and his boss had called to meet at 9:30. Raef squeezed the steering wheel as he slid to a stop at Lake Drive. His briefcase with the WorldFoods, Inc. logo slid off the passenger seat and pitched forward onto the floor. He let it lay as he tapped the wheel with his thumbs and waited for a snow plow followed by three cars and a school bus to snake on by. His eyes flicked right, then left as he leaned forward, his chest brushing the steering wheel. He wetted his lips and ground his teeth. His boss had called last night. His boss ... last night in the middle of a storm that probably shut down the whole state of Minnesota ... to see him at 9:30 this morning. A directorship ... opened in the New Ventures Division ... Raef was ready.

He drew a deep breath, and waited; the school bus passed. *Rats! Can't that thing go any faster?* He pulled in behind the behemothic orange crawler browsing its way between neighborhoods. The driver reined the beast to a pause, took on two piles of clothing puffing clouds of vapor, and coaxed the monster to a start. As it inched its way to the next rendezvous point, he lowered the stop arm and turned off the blinkers. Raef raised his hands and stage whispered to the window, "Why ... of all days?"

He checked his rear view mirror and flipped a switch on the dashboard. The radio blared to life. "... Wesphalia Elementary—classes delayed, Robbinsdale Spanish Immersion—classes delayed, Sonnysyn Elementary—classes delayed two hours ... expect delays, folks. It's slow out there today." The mid-April storm that dropped 10 inches of snow and just about shut down Minnesota delayed the day's opening, but it didn't bring the day to a halt.

Five stops later the bus wandered off to a neighborhood on the right. Raef slipped onto the frontage road that melted into the woodsy junction with World-Foods Drive that snaked its way up through black trees silhouetted against sparkling white snow and set against patches of blue sky to a clearing at the top where all was still—just still.

He headed for the west side of the research center and turned into the parking stall designated "R. BURNHAM". He slipped out of the car, flipped up his collar and ice-danced his way to the employee entrance. Inside he flashed his badge and smiled. "Morning, Roger. 8:45. Not bad for a day like today."

"Well, you must have a meeting 'cause there's almost no one here," the security guard drawled while he flipped a page and almost looked up.

"9:30—just trying to get a jump," Raef called back. Two steps later he caught himself when his boots found a wet spot and lost traction. "Whew. Dangerous terrain, Roger."

Raef's office on the second floor nestled between Goodwin Metcalf, his long-time friend and co-worker and Geben, their boss. In a few steps he was at the door. He pushed it open, flipped on the lights and tossed his gloves on the credenza. Before he could hang up his coat he saw Geben's note on his desk. "See me when you get in." To himself, Raef smiled.

He hung his suit coat and checked his messages while he arranged his desk and pulled his notes from his briefcase. As a final check, he walked to the men's room and stood before the mirror. Grey glen plaid suit—*neat, pressed, perfect*. Blue and silver striped tie—*excellent choice*. He adjusted his tie, straightened his gig line and tucked in his shirt so nothing gathered in either the front or back. *178—Good weight for 5'10*. He scanned once more. *Not bad for 42—or anytime*. He touched his light brown hair at the edges to remove the hat marks, straightened the tie one final time and headed to his desk.

Geben wanted to see him now. It was time to do some business. He picked up a writing pad, grabbed a pen and walked to the next office. *Okay, Boss, let's see what you got.* Raef stepped into the doorway. "The note said, 'When you get in.' You wanted to see me, Sir?"

Geben impressed—visually and audibly. At 6 feet 6 inches and weighing an eighth of a ton, he was two-thirds of a Goliath and filled most doorways with little to spare in any direction. And what his bulk didn't cover his volume did. Wherever he was in a room, that was the center of activity. During his 25 years at

WFI he'd run WFI's Cincinnati plant, the Westphalia pilot plant, and some operations in drinks and sauces and managed to become the darling of whatever vice president headed his current assignment; he was an equal opportunity suckup. Now he was the director of research for Raef's division—Frozen Dinners.

He stood and reached across the desk to shake hands with Raef. "You're in early. Have a seat, please. I didn't expect anyone until the roads got cleared. I'm an early riser and with my car—it's pretty big—I can get anywhere I want whenever I want." Geben sat down and nodded to Raef. "Oh, it's just my way. Have a seat. Sit down. Let's talk about the division's needs."

Raef nodded and sat down. Geben laid out some boilerplate beliefs, then droned on with lists of projects and needs and personal insight on progress and shortfalls and gossip about people who are doing well or poorly—in his estimation; always in his estimation. Raef, drifted in and out of contact with the monotony spewing from the other side of the desk and rocked and swayed to the cadence of the monologue. After a fourth of the sand in the hourglass had passed through its portal, he noticed Geben look down at what looked like a list, square his shoulders and look up.

What!

His hands came together in front of his mouth so that he spoke from behind the underbrush of extended fingers. He leaned forward on his elbows and dropped his voice to a *mano a mano* tone that made Raef cringe. "… and you're complacent. Myself … personally … I think you're bored. You have a 'not invented here' attitude. Your recent track record isn't very good and we have to do something … We … have … to do something."

Raef's heart leapt to his throat, his already pounding pulse started to race, his upper lip moistened. His eyes searched for a focal landing point—darted from looking at his hands to the door to the window back to hands … shoes … dark …! He closed his eyes.

Geben's voice cracked. His mumble changed to the grating staccato of an airport announcement—and the babble turned to ramble and twisted back on itself and turned to … expressionless … and then added a complexity—they widened and turned glassy—washed in fear. In one jerky motion he picked up the paper on his desk—it shook like an autumn leaf on a windy football afternoon. And like a runner finding relief in seeing even the broken tape lying on the ground at the finish line, he took a deep breath and eased out the words, "Eff … Effective imm … immediately you no longer have responsibilities in this division." He opened his mouth wide and inflated both lungs fully to proclaim, loud and full,

"Perry will move into your job—today." Then he took another deep breath, exhaled and sank back into his chair. His breathing deepened, his eyes dimmed, his facial muscles relaxed, then sagged. "Take the rest of the day off. It's Friday. Take the weekend. Absorb this information. Get your head together. We'll talk on Monday ... consider your next steps. Any questions?"

Raef stared. *What a clown. This incompetent freak! From Day One I knew this guy was trouble. He wasn't in the division 15 minutes that day five years ago when I called my section heads in to tell them that this ship was going down. Going down. We didn't have a prayer.* "We're dead," I said. "This guy is totally clueless—ignorant even of his ignorance. We won't be able to control him." *What a time to be right. Why didn't I move out of the division then?*

Raef felt the walls narrow, the ceiling compress; the room get smaller and smaller. He felt his lips grow rigid and form strange-feeling shapes. His whole being suspended itself—and he sensed ... nothing. He was a disembodied mouth moving without sound. And all the while his mind scrambled for advantage. *Think. Think. Buy time. Buy time.*

"P ... (ahem) Pardon me. I'm being demoted?"

"Yes."

"Demoted ... me?"

Geben shifted in his chair. "Yes."

Raef set his feet under his chair and leaned forward, resting his left elbow on the arm of the chair. With his open right hand he sliced the air upward. "That makes no sense," his voice grew stronger. "No sense at all." He edged forward in the chair. "I came here on a leadership fast track, became a team leader in two years, introduced a ton of new products in three different divisions, helped the company find its latest acquisition. And ... and when I came to this job I was one of the two youngest Level 6s ever. Heck, last month ... last month you gave me a 3+ performance appraisal—a 3+! That's better than satisfactory. Now I'm demoted? What changed? I don't get it."

Across the table, the two hands that had axed more than one forest grabbed the edge of the desk and pushed his chair back a couple of inches. The puppet in the chair took a deep breath and looked down again at that simple statement on the sheet of paper lying in front of him. He ran his tongue across the corner of his mouth, across the top to the other corner, and back across the bottom—all in 2 seconds. He pursed his lips, lifted his chin slightly, swallowed hard and in a thinned voice growing thinner said, "But I warned you—remember? I warned you. 'You have a not-invented-here problem', I said. 'You're too comfortable', I said. 'Too comfortable.' Those were my exact words."

Weak. Weak. Weak. What a ... Geez! How did this clown ever get his job? How can he keep a job? Careful, Raef. This is the first speech of your next campaign. You'll need this guy. This is no time to burn bridges. Settle down. Now! Settle down ... Settle down.

"That was my warning? I was supposed to understand from that ... you're kidding, right?" He thought about the implications of that failed communication. "If that was supposed to communicate something, what are you saying now? What am I supposed to understand from your little speech? Are you telling me that there are no other department head positions open in the Tech Center?"

"None that are interested in you."

Raef shook his head and looked up at Geben. "With my record? My network? None?"

"None. I tried. No takers."

No authority here. Outcome's fixed. Door's closing. No options. No support in the organization. Gotta grab some advantage—now!

"What about salary and bonus? How long do I keep what I have?"

Geben rested back in the chair and crossed his legs. "Until you leave the job."

"And that is?"

"Until you take another position."

This game is over. Make it a slow search. How do I tell Jenifer?

Geben gathered the papers on the desk and put them in the folder. "Take the rest of the day off. We'll talk on Monday."

"Do I have any recourse? ... Any?"

Geben shook his head.

Raef looked to the side. *Nooo.* Then laid his head back and stared at the ceiling. "How'm I going to tell my wife ... my family ...?" He slid back a little further; only his heels, seat and neck supported. "What happens to my caree ...?" He rocked forward and pulled in his heels; cleared his throat and wiped the corner of his eye. His voice trailed off. "Will I ever be able to ...?" He took a deep breath and exhaled slowly. Geben sat still and studied his hands.

Raef grasped the arms of the chair, lifted himself to his feet, and toddled into the empty hallway partially closing Geben's door behind him. He took a step to the right of the door and leaned back against the wall, closed his eyes, rubbed his temples and took a deep breath. The silence of the empty halls made his thoughts echo as they bounced and bounced and faded away. From inside Geben's office he heard, "It's Geben ... Yeah, it's done, Fortune ... Exactly." Click.

Like a man sleepwalking Raef gathered his briefcase, put on his coat, topcoat and boots and walked out to his car. He got in and turned on the engine, then sat and stared at the sign at the front of the assigned parking space—R. Burnham. He looked at his watch.

In the middle of January 16 years earlier, WorldFoods, Inc. at this research facility in Westphalia, MN transformed Captain R. Burnham, U.S. Army Chemical Corps into Raef Burnham, Research Scientist. Armed with bearing and attitude shaped by the military, he entered a work force whose mentality and work ethic was shaped by World War II and the Korean War. Into a company whose leaders were concerned about hair length and respect and students marching in the streets and wondering where they would find the next generation of leaders came Raef, a 26-year-old discharged Army Captain with an M.S. in Organic Chemistry: A new hire who understood hierarchy and structure and discipline—a fresh haircut who had just bought a house in the suburbs. He was selected for rapid career development almost before he signed the employment papers. And now this.

9:30 And I have nowhere to go. I can't go home—not yet. Don't feel like going to the gym. Prayer is the only thing that makes sense and I don't feel like praying.

Chapter 2

▼

PERSPECTIVE

Raef turned onto the service road and stopped at the exit. He leaned his head back against the rest and paused ... then slammed his hand against the steering wheel and pointed the car toward downtown Westphalia.

∗   ∗   ∗   ∗

Dean, the pastor of Emanuel Christian Center, watched Raef place his black felt hat on the rack, slip off his Chesterfield topcoat and tuck the silk scarf and gloves in the sleeve and lay them on the chair near the door. He saw the suit label, the shined black wing-tipped shoes.

While Raef dawdled, Dean walked over to opposing leather chairs, sat down in the one with its back to the door and planted his feet on the end table stretched out between them. Raef surveyed the bookshelves as he moved to the far chair, paused now and then to check out a title, and slumped into the leather. "I'm always amazed at how much this study feels like old Scotland: the wood, the books. It's an easy place to be."

"Used to be an Episcopal church. Lots of good architecture." Dean folded his hands on his lap. "Raef, you didn't come to discuss my bookshelf."

Raef shook his head and looked down. "... I ... I've been demoted." His voice trailed off in the final three syllables as he uncrossed his legs, leaned forward with his elbows on his knees, and lowered his face in his hands. The rest was lost in sobs. Dean placed his elbows on the arm rests, pressed the palms of his hands together and rested his index fingers against his lips as Raef's tears flowed and flowed and flowed; no words, just tears. His shoulders heaved and eyes poured their deluge and his nose dripped and ran and needed wiping. Sometimes the breathing became almost even only to start up again and then again.

"Sorry ... 42 years old and ..."

"When did you hear?"

"About an hour ago."

"Raef, I understand. No need to explain. I understand.... I ... understand.... Hey, people survive blows like these; they get better. But it takes time. Getting ... better ... takes ... time."

Dean reached for his Bible. "Raef, you'll get through this. You're capable, you have a good record, you'll find another job. Half full, half empty, you know?"

Raef wailed without sound. More tears flowed.

"But the only comfort you're going to receive today will come from the Scriptures. Two come to mind. Dean opened his Bible to Hebrews 13:5. Here's the first one. '... I will never desert you, nor will I ever forsake you.' Get it? God's promise. He's there. He's in this thing with you."

Raef wiped his eyes. "What else?"

"Well, the second one is from James. He says: 'Consider it all joy ... when you encounter various trials, knowing that the testing of your faith produces endurance.' He goes on to tell us we're to let endurance work itself out for our completion. But did you see that first concept, to consider it joy? He's got to be kidding, right? Wrong. He means just that. Know why? Because God's in charge. Somehow He's working something good here."

Raef closed his eyes, breathed deep and settled back in the chair.

Dean paused and laid his bible on the arm rest. "When this is all cleared up I think you'll find that you have grown in your faith more than you thought possible. You're going to find yourself leaning on Him more than you ever thought you could."

With this prism Dean and Raef separated the bands of dim light shining on Raef's life. An hour and a half later, Raef wiped his eyes, blinked, and tried to pull himself to full stature—tried. "I'm so ... I don't know where to start with what I'm feeling. I want to be strong, but I feel so pathetic ... so weak ... inadequate ... embarrassed ... failed. I can't believe this happened. And I haven't even come to anger yet, but I know that's coming. I want to hit something. Yeah, I do. This is so unfair. So unbelievably unfair." Raef spread his arms a shoulder's width. "I was blind-sided. I can't tell you ... if I look back, I can't tell you the last time I heard something I know to be true spoken by the people I work for ... or with. Now who do I trust? Yeah, I want to strike out. These little ... I just ..." He dropped is eyes to the floor and lowered his voice, then looked up. "I want to be a good husband in this ... good father. I'm still an example of something. I mean I have to provide for my family and I don't know if I can do that now ... and I think my career hopes are over. Director? Forget about director. I think I have the skills. I think I'd be effective at that level. But that's over for sure. At a bench level job if I even have a job and if there's a place for me at the bench ... how can I do anything significant from a Level 5? I'll be viewed as a failure. Inadequate. A dolt. How can you work in my world if you don't have a network? Who'll want me in their circle after this? I think I'll always be suspect. 'Hey, he used to be a star. Look at him now.' Used to be. All my fears before me." Raef lowered his head.

Dean sat and listened. He waited for the rest of the statement.

"Taking counsel of my fears. Not a good thing. But I see nothing good in the path ahead. Nothing good. On my way over here I started thinking about my options. You know? Put my resume out; shop around. But the job market is bad now and my skills match WFI—I'm considered to be good technically ... but my skills are team leadership, project management, problem solving—I don't think I'd market well. I traffic in human capital—my relationships are what make me good. And putting the family through moving ... I don't know ... I'm babbling." Raef laid back into the chair and closed his eyes again. "Oh, man. Well, what's next?"

Dean sat up and slipped a marker back into his Bible. "You rebuild your life. The process has already started."

"I blew my opportunity." Raef looked up. "When I started ... I mean Day One ... I wrote on the top line of my first lab notebook, 'Goal: Director.' I could have been big and I blew it. I own this one and it's humiliating. Director! I'll do well to do level 6 again." He paused. "Joy, huh?" Raef sat up.

Dean closed his Bible and laid it on the table next to his chair. "So you adjust. You can rebuild ... you will. It's going to be tough. I don't think either one of us has any idea how tough it will be. But you have to do it and you have to know that the effort will be successful."

Raef nodded and shifted his feet. "Sounds pretty simplistic and you're probably right. What's crazy is that on my way over here I was thinking that if I chose to resign now I could leave as a Level 6 with no negatives on my record. It's tempting. Where does that thought come from? AARRGGHH."

They both stood up and began walking toward the door. Dean put his hand on Raef's shoulder. "There's another point you have to consider."

"And that is?"

"Something went wrong at WFI, and you don't know what it is. This hiccup happened for a reason. If something about you is the problem and you go somewhere else now, you'll just take your problem with you and possibly have the same thing happen again somewhere else—where you don't have the network you have here. And there you start over a third time, still not knowing why."

Raef stopped. "Meaning what?"

"I think you have to figure out why you should leave and why you should stay. Then pick a direction and craft your plan." Dean helped Raef with his coat. "You have some thinking to do, but first you have to tell your family. Call me tomorrow after you've chatted with Jenifer, OK? Let this settle a bit."

Raef lowered his gaze as he touched the corner of his eye. Dean stepped closer, gave him a one-armed pastoral hug and patted him on the back as they walked to the door. "Call me."

CHAPTER 3
▼

COMMUNICATION

Raef shielded his eyes as he stepped out onto the sun-washed sidewalk. He tromped through the snowbank to get to his car, turned the ignition, touched the accelerator and headed toward the lake. The sun, reaching its highpoint in the cloudless sky, poured in the open car window and purged winter from his mind. The brisk April air cleared his lungs and sparked his life. Ten minutes later he found his exit and meandered home along Lake Drive.

Gone were the plows, the foot of snow on the streets, and the kids on the corner waiting for the bus. Present were the drifts, the glare, and the quiet left to hold the neighborhood for the day. Raef turned up the driveway and guided the car into the garage. He shut off the engine and sat there—jaws clenched, breathing a little shallow, heartbeat a bit rapid—he didn't move. He just sat there staring ... at ... nothing. Slowly ... slowly ... he emerged ... found a shovel ... and cleared the rest of the driveway.

✻ ✻ ✻ ✻

Jenifer heard the garage door open, the car pull in, a car door slam and ... the scrape, scrape, scrape in the driveway. She stepped to the mirror and checked her hair, front and right side, left side, adjusted her blouse in her slacks, and smiled. Forty years old and two kids later: not bad.

Jenifer and Raef met while they were both in college. Raef finished his undergraduate degree and moved to Grand Forks, North Dakota for graduate school. The two managed a long distance romance while she finished her elementary education degree and he finished his master's studies in organic chemistry. In 1964 they married and entered two years active duty in the U.S. Army Chemical Corps. While they were stationed in Dugway, Utah, Jake was born and in their first year at WFI, Mindy was born. Jenifer's 1962 degree in Elementary Education never really got dusted off. She had disliked "practice teaching" while in college and her experience as a substitute teacher on the Army base squelched her remaining desire to pursue a full time career in the field. The teaching was fun, but one day after a particularly difficult day with the second graders she walked in the door and declared, "That's it for teaching. When we're out of here, I'm out of the profession." Later on, they made their temporary decision permanent: they'd make it on one salary.

From her earliest years, Jenifer focused on family. Even as she pursued her education, she looked forward to marriage, a family, creating a happy home. So, Jenifer 'didn't work', she 'stayed home.' She hated those expressions because the question at every party, at every family gathering, at even every church function was, "Oh, so what do you do?" She'd learned to say, "I'm a stay-at-home mom," but the looks always told her she 'didn't work.' She 'stayed home.'

Her 5'6" 130 lb frame needed four miles of walking and a half hour swimming four times a week to keep her ready for the tennis, golf, or water skiing that their ever active social life demanded—and the marathon contract bridge events required stamina. Keeping her brown hair styled and her peaches 'n cream complexion perfect wasn't easy when challenged by the pool's chlorine—but she did it. And the kids liked her availability.

A slight chill blew into the house and she heard the door close. "Anything for lunch?"

Standing next to the sink Jenifer laid out two more slices of bread and began to spread on the mayo. "Hi. Home early?"

"I thought I'd join you—but I have to tell you about my morning." Raef walked up from the entry and sat down at the table.

"Are we celebrating something?"

He rubbed his forehead and looked down at the table. "Pretty much the opposite."

Jenifer brought the sandwiches, relishes and milk, set them on the table, and sat down. Raef shifted in his chair and leaned back, putting an arm on the railing behind him. "I met with Geben this morning ..." The rest was a tale of dreams lost and betrayal and tears. It concluded with, "I've been demoted; I don't know what's next; and I feel really crummy about it."

Jenifer listened and thought and asked questions and offered thoughts and understanding and concern. A half hour later she folded her napkin, "I'm so sorry. Are you OK?"

Raef swallowed. "I will be. Right now, I'm pretty shaky. I need a little time."

"Does this mean you're out of a job?"

Raef leaned back in the chair and opened his eyes wide and raised his eyebrows and shrugged his shoulders. "I'm not sure. I don't think so. I was pretty much caught off guard and wasn't thinking too clearly." Raef shifted in the chair. "And Geben wasn't clear on that. I think I have to shop around the company—I have to find the opportunity. I think … I don't know."

"If you stay, what happens? I mean … to position and salary? Can you get promoted back to where you are, or were …?"

Raef placed his forearms on the table with his hands together and leaned forward. "I'm demoted. That part is sure. It looks like I stay at my same salary, but the bonus is gone. That's sure. So we lose 20 percent almost immediately. But returning to a Level 6? Who knows? That's about the least of our concerns now, I think." He paused for a few moments just looking at Jenifer.

She felt tears welling up. "This is so unfair! You work so hard! Do they have any idea …?"

Raef cleared his throat softly. "I don't think that's how they keep score. But we have options. I can look outside the company. I can switch fields. None of these are easy, but all are options."

Jenifer caught her breath. "Do you mean move? Raef, what are you saying? Move?"

He raised his hands defensively. "Easy, honey. We have Cargill, Pillsbury, General Mills and International Multifoods here in town. Somebody has to have an opening. But, sure, Firmenich, and Fries & Fries and Procter & Gamble in Cincinnati are possibilities; and in New York…."

"No. I can't handle that. Not the east. In fact, I don't want to move, period. No."

"And market analysis with one of the stock firms—I talked to C.F. a couple of weeks ago. That's still a possibility."

"Sure. At about a third of your current salary and limited benefits. I think that's 100 percent risk."

"My point—we have options."

"Not if they involve leaving this area." She looked out the window and noticed the sign in the front yard. "What about the house? Do we call Tom and tell him that our plans have changed? Take it off the market?"

"Have to."

Jenifer's voice was rising as her speech became more rapid. "What do we tell Jake? And the college? Is Calvary College out? No more basketball?"

Raef shrugged his shoulders. "I got it, OK. I'll call his coach and tell him we're working through some tough stuff, but that our plans aren't changed—at least for now, OK?"

Jenifer continued off the list that wasn't visible. "And Mindy. This is going to be a shock. We have to tell them this evening when they get home." Jenifer nodded slowly as she sat back in the chair. "It's so unfair."

"My biggest concern right now is Monday: I don't know if I'll have a job! And we have to let the kids know what's going on. After supper, OK?"

"OK, but you know they can look at me and just know something's wrong."

Raef smiled. "You'll do fine. Right now, I'm pretty shaky. I need to take some time and try to get my head on straight. About all I know at this point is that the Lord knows something about this that we don't know. I'm going to take some time...."

The room was silent; the sandwiches, untouched. Raef laid his hand on Jenifer's and gave a gentle squeeze. Jenifer watched as he reached for his briefcase and walked down the steps toward his office, his step a little slow and his shoulders a little slumped. She wiped the corner of her eye and collected the plates.

* * * *

Raef closed the door and stepped into the home office—a desk, table and bookshelves—that took up about a third of the split-level's lower 900 square feet. He'd never managed to finish the space; too busy doing company work. He sat down at the three by five maple desk and looked out on that beautiful day—but before he could think of what he was going to do, tears began ... again. This time his stomach felt like it was being squeezed by a giant hand. He wanted to holler, to scream, to lash out, to blame; anything but contain this flood of anguish that totally filled him. Tears led to sobs. Sobs led to breathlessness to sobs to embarrassment to more sobs to drained energy to tiredness to resignation to ... a kind of acceptance. He wanted to go back to dawn to start the day over again. He wanted to undo, to not have this pain. He just wanted it all to go away; to just go away now; go away.

His mind wandered.
"What do you do?"
"Oh, I'm between jobs."
"Oh."

He gazed out the window. *Am I the least competent person in the technical center? Couldn't I work in the pilot plant or ... That's zero pay, but it's an income. Hold it! Enough.*

That afternoon Raef's dirigible of life floated with mooring ropes dangling, but they had nothing to tie to. As he floated, his mind grabbed no thought, engaged no problem, reached no conclusion, grasped no new reality and hours later when Jenifer called, "Dinner's ready," he hadn't moved from his chair. Raef breathed deeply and lifted himself from the chair; after a moment he moved toward the stairs.

Jenifer served baked chicken breasts with potatoes, cooked peas and rolls. It was 5:30. Raef paused as he rounded the corner, squared his shoulders and raised his chin. "Anyone got plans for the evening? It's Friday."

Jake, a high school senior with plans to play Division III basketball, answered as he sat down, "I'm playing hoops with Mark and Duggs, later." Jake began sports as a hockey defenseman, but in the seventh grade he encountered the Olympics-bound concept of dedication to the sport and decided to switch allegiance to basketball. In the four years that followed Jake had grown about a foot and now stood 6'5" and weighed about 195 lbs. Though he had visited a D-III school in central Minnesota he had selected Calvary College to play ball and major in accounting. The remaining six weeks of high school stood between him and his future.

Mindy, at 5'3", had two state championship trophies in volleyball and was looking forward to summer camp at State. She had been helping Jenifer with dinner and reached out to place the final plate on the table. "A movie with Susan?"

Jenifer said little and Raef less as they moved their food around on the plate and only occasionally picked some up and ate a little. Jake and Mindy had survived the week and were excited about the weekend. Neither seemed to notice any change in the parental moods.

Jenifer was about to clear the table when Raef said, "I've something to discuss with all of you. It'll only take a minute." He pushed his chair back and crossed his legs. "At work today, Geben called me in to tell me that I'd been demoted. What I know is that I'm not a department head any more; but I don't know much more about the situation. I'm supposed to get more information on Monday."

Jenifer sat poised, looking at Raef. Not a flinch. Not a tear. Calm and poised. For 30 seconds that seemed like an hour, neither of the kids moved.

Then Mindy's eyes narrowed, her eyebrows moved closer together, her lips parted just a little. She lowered her head just a bit, took in extra air without opening her mouth, and swallowed. "Are you OK?"

Mindy had spent her junior year challenging Raef with hair styles, the amount of mascara she wore, the clothes she preferred, the people she wanted to associate with. Raef, parentally intransigent had continued to impose restrictions—maintain the fences he would say—while they jousted. But on both sides of the discussion, respect.

Raef was taken aback for the moment by the concern. "About a 3, honey. About a 3. I may have to redefine what success is, but I'm hanging in there. Thanks … Jake?"

Jake shifted in his chair and settled back with his left elbow resting on the table. With a sweep of his right hand he paused in mid stroke. "What does this mean?"

Raef thought a moment. "I don't know, but I have some guesses."

"Like?"

"I think I'll have a job, but I'll lose some money and end up working somewhere else in the company. And we have other options."

His eye contact never wavered. "Do we have to move?"

Raef looked at Jenifer. "I don't think so. Sure don't want to. But that depends on the other options. I can also look outside the company and I can switch to other work. In both scenarios, some of the opportunities may be someplace else. Not around here."

Jake shifted in his chair and leaned forward against the table. "Is Calvary College out?"

Raef shook his head. "That's way too early to call right now. I'll give Coach a buzz in the morning, tell him my situation, and let him know that we hope … we expect to keep to our plan."

Mindy waited for the opening. "I'm not finishing high school someplace else." Her eyes filled with tears. "No. I can't do that."

Jake waited out the silence. "I'll be away next year, so any change will affect me the least—at least if we can keep the plan. But I don't think that makes much sense. I mean, to make that big a jump when you don't even know what your situation is. Makes no sense. I don't think that's smart."

After an hour of questions and answers, Jenifer broke in. "Can I get a little help with the dishes?"

Raef looked up. "Tell you what. You kids go about your plans for the evening, and try not to get too into all of this. Jenifer, I'm going to call Goody and see if he has any insight."

Mindy stayed at the table. "I don't feel like going out … I don't feel like staying home either. Geez."

"Sis. Let's go. I'll drop you off." Jake grabbed the back of her chair and pulled it away from the table. C'mon."

*   *   *   *

Raef made the phone call. "Goody … Raef … Blindsided, Man … Not so good. I didn't see this coming and I really don't get it … Zero warning!"

Goodwin Metcalf graduated from the University of Minnesota about when Raef was a sophomore in high school and joined WFI by the time Raef was midway through college. His 6'2" frame coupled with his penetrating brown eyes and hail-fellow-well-met personality, belied the seven years age difference between the two men. The only giveaway was Goody's premature gray hair, a family trait he was trying to pass on to three of his children. Raef and Goody had shared an office in the mid 70's and cultivated a friendship still strong ten years later. Goody had his own way of viewing life and Raef enjoyed his tutoring.

"… No, I'm not handling it so well.… Yeah, a little scared, actually." Raef was silent for awhile and nodded about every 10 seconds or so. Finally he stood up with the phone in his hand and walked around behind his desk. "True … But I think there's more to it than that. I think it's tied to the management conference at Key Ponte. Remember Geben's phone call in February where he said, 'You guys have nothing to worry about?' Remember? … Yeah … Well, my darling little wife heard that at the time and said, 'Something's not right. Otherwise, why'd he say that? Something's wrong. Why does he have to assure you, if there is nothing to be assuring you about? I'm concerned.'"

Raef was silent again for awhile. "Yeah … Hey, I have to accept some blame. I've played hardball most of my career here and screwed up my share of times, but over the years I think I've changed—I thought for the better. What's more damaging is that work hasn't had the right priority for me for some time. It's boring, and to a degree, pointless. So, some of this is my fault. But I deserved at least one clear warning. A demand to change. A recommendation. A suggestion. A hint. Geez. Wimps. And Geben … give me a break."

* * * *

Jenifer came into the office and sat down near the door. "What did Goody say?"

"He agrees that something happened at Key Ponte; that there's a change in direction or something and I got caught in the middle. He also thinks the rest of the building is on edge; they don't know what's next for them either; Monday or down the road. People are scared."

"What's your main issue Monday?"

Raef paused. "Whether I have a job."

"What does he think?"

"Not sure. But he thinks I should keep my outside options open and see what's available."

* * * *

Sleep evaded Raef that night while the angels of forgiveness, petition, pleading and prayer chased the demons of anger, self condemnation, self flagellation and despair. He awoke to a weekend where only the washing of tears interrupted the conflict. Tears came without warning, without reason—just tears. Private five minute cry sessions punctuated his days—cleansed him.

I blew it. I ... blew ... it. It's my fault. All ... my ... fault. I'm to blame. No one else. Me. Argghh!

Saturday Raef fixed a door, cleaned out the garage, reorganized his files, cleaned out the attic, and changed the oil on the car. On Sunday they attended church and went out for brunch. Raef read a little and took a nap. That evening, he said goodnight to Jenifer and sat up in bed to read for awhile. But as he tried to focus on the page, the loop of questions without answers serpentined its way over and under and through and around his mind again and again and again.

After awhile Jenifer rolled toward him and touched his hand. "What are you thinking?"

"I keep wondering what went wrong? What do I do next? Do I have a job? All that stuff."

She patted his hand. "You need some sleep. G'nite."

Chapter 4

▼

REALITY

Raef opened the door to his south-facing deck and stepped out with his steaming cup of coffee to drink in the new day. The warm sun and fresh spring air introduced April to spring and welcomed Raef to his new world. The morning sun glistened off the disappearing snow and patches of grass broke through the crystal cover to herald yet another victory over winter.

Jenifer stepped onto the deck with her cup in one hand and the pot in the other. She poured Raef a warmup and looked at dazzling snow. She smiled and turned toward Raef, "Well, it's Monday, you survived your winter and you're still standing. I have some things to do. See you tonight."

Monday and … I'm still standing. This world says it's ready for change—I hope I am.

Three sunrises after the cataclysmic career shock, Raef arrived at WFI's Research and Development Center ready to take on whatever came next. What he was not prepared for was Charlie, one of the technicians. Charlie came in, shook hands, wagged his head and mumbled, "I don't understand," and walked out the door. And he wasn't prepared for the administrative assistant from across the hall who stepped into his office only to have tears well up in her eyes—and leave without saying a word. Nor was he prepared for the stream of co-workers who checked in to offer their best, even if in silence, because they couldn't find the words. *Won-*

derful people. No access to these folks for years at Level 6. Now, at Level 5, no walls. What's different?

*   *   *   *

Geben sat at his desk sharpening the division's research final budget. He laid down his pencil, leaned back and scanned the room. His maple desk was clean except for the report open in front of him and the picture of him holding a 36 inch walleye that was perched on the far left corner. In front of the desk two wooden framed cloth chairs angled toward Geben. Crouched against the wall behind him was a credenza that reached three quarters of the way from the wall on his right across the room, careful to stay out of the way of the window. In the far left corner across the room stood a bookshelf filled with the engineering books of a five-year program at Georgia Tech 30 years earlier, the requisite engineering charts and tables, Weast's *Handbook of Chemistry and Physics*, various dictionaries—and it was locked. The door across the room hung partway open. He liked what he saw—neat. And began writing and calculating some of the figures by hand.

About mid-morning Geben looked up to see Raef step partially into the room. "What's a good time to get together?"

He looked at his watch. "Give me five."

Raef moved the door to its original position and Geben put down his pen. He paged through Raef's file, checked his notes from Friday, rifled through some other personnel memos, and pulled out the notes from Key Ponte. He set the budget papers aside and glanced through the packet.

The first note was the overhead from Key Ponte that read, "Research not developing new products fast enough." When it came up on the screen, Fortune Montag had looked at the directors and paused.

Montag was one of WFI's rising stars in management. Graduating with honors from Stanford and the top of his MBA class at Harvard he was wooed to WFI by the CEO, through family connections and as the object of an all out recruiting blitz in the early 1970s. He joined the marketing ranks and rose rapidly to become a vice president before age 30. Now, with broad experience in his eight years with the company he had recently completed three years in New Ventures and had been appointed the head of Corporate Growth. In that capacity he had joined the research and development leadership at Key Ponte to discuss the future of WFI's research and development organization. That's what he was doing now.

Fortune checked the monitor on his lectern. He looked back at his audience. "Any of you who have marketed a new product that has failed in its first year, include yourself here—you are responsible. Fast development that fails in the marketplace is like work not done at all. Plus … plus the cost of lost opportunity." Geben looked at the headings on the three sheets in his hand. "Doing well." "Doing poorly." Fortune had given each of the attendees three pieces of paper on which to evaluate first directors (rank them 1—14,) then department heads (rank 1-42,) then list potential leaders to be developed. The first two lists translated to promotable (top third,) status quo (middle third,) and vulnerable (the rest.)

Geben placed the sheets on his desk. *Why's Burnham on the vulnerable list? … What has he produced in the past year? … Did he do that competitor knock-off that was such an embarrassment? … I don't care if that was the marketing direction—he put it on the market, right? What else? … So, he is independent, not a team player, and you cannot predict what he will do in a given situation. Make room for Perry … I do not care if he is a 3+, that there has been no indication of inadequacy, that he has not been warned. Fix it. So he was a good Level 5; keep him for his technical ability, I do not care—but make room. Close the deal, Geben. That is your job … or are you not tough enough? May we move on? Right, Montag. Let's move on. So, why's Burnham on the list?*

Geben closed the folder and put it in the drawer. He wiped his upper lip and reached for a cigarette. A knock and the door opened. "Now's good. C'mon in. Close the door."

Raef closed the door and selected the chair that didn't provide Geben backlighting (the chair he didn't use Friday).

Geben smiled. "Where would you like to start?"

Raef looked directly at Geben. "Have I been fired?"

"What?"

"Do I still have a job?"

Geben stood up and leaned on the desk. "Whoa, whoa, whoa. Nobody's talking about firing. No, no, no. You had plenty of support around here … plenty of support … during the discussions." He sat back down. "More than one person spoke up saying, 'this guy was one heckuva good product developer'. No-no-no. No one's talking about firing."

"What discussions?"

Geben blinked. "Pardon me?"

Raef sat with his legs crossed and arms on the chair rests. "You mentioned discussions. What discussions?"

Beads of sweat glistening on his upper lip, Geben looked at the door and almost whispered. "These moves aren't made in a closet, you know. We discuss things. What else?"

Raef didn't move. "So you mean at Ponte when you called back and left the message that Goody and I didn't have anything to worry about." He raised his eyebrows and opened his eyes wide and lowered his chin. "Well, I guess it was at least half true." Raef waved a hand and shifted in the chair. "Forget it. I have to deal with the real world. What are my options? If I haven't been fired and I don't have a job, what are my options?"

Geben pushed himself back away from the desk and crossed his legs. "That's where it gets tricky. There are no Level 5 positions open."

"Oh, great. First there's nothing at a 6 and now no 5s are open? Terrific."

"Hold on. Agricultural might have some interest, and other groups also … but where you go is going to be yours to find. You have one job now and only one—to find that position. Forget about transitioning out; we can manage that. Your job is to find that job."

Raef thought a moment. "What kind of help do I have?"

"What do you need?"

"Access. I need access. I want to do informational interviews in quality control, purchasing, and a few other areas that might not be looking and, if they are looking, might not have thought of me."

Geben smiled. "Done. Let me know where you want to visit and who you want to talk to, and I'll arrange it."

"I appreciate that. I'll get back to you with my list." Raef shook hands with Geben and walked out, closing the door as he left.

✳   ✳   ✳   ✳

Geben lit up, inhaled, and reached for the phone. "Fortune? Geben … Yeah, his search starts now and I'm on it … Access … Level 5 … I sure will."

Inhaling again he put a foot on his lower desk drawer, sat back and crossed his legs. He pulled out the Perry file, read the first page, laid the file on the desk and gazed out the window.

Chapter 5

▼

IT HAPPENED

Raef divided the page into three columns and labeled them Research & Development, Quality Assurance, and Purchasing. Down the left side of the paper he labeled rows with Reasons (Why would I work in this area?), Skills (What do I bring to the resolution of the problem?), Projects (Specific activities I know they're engaged in), and Key Contact (Who do I want to interview?). On Tuesday afternoon he gave Geben a list of names.

In the day and a half before those interviews began Raef worked his own private list to explore what happened—15 minute meetings with a few trusted 6s and 7s and a session with Mitch Jordan, a good friend at the director level.

Raef's first unveiling of the demotion mystery came that noon with lunch at the Twin Lakes Country Club. Jarvis, a 64-year food broker called and asked Raef to join him at the 19th Hole. He opened the conversation at his table overlooking the 18th green with, "Young man, I understand you've landed in one of life's fairway divits. How're you handling it?"

"Jarvis, thanks for the invitation—and your concern. Divits? It feels more like one of those fairway traps in the British Open—the one's you can't quite see out of. But, I'm still here. What's your experience with this kind of thing?"

Jarvis shook his head and took a sip of water. "At least 80 percent of everyone in the workforce will encounter something like what you're going through, Raef. And it's always a surprise. Why me? Why this? What could I have done to prevent it?" He went on to share his own story of shattered trust in the brokerage business—then smiled and nodded. "Raef, this demotion—it's bad, and I know it hurts. But you'll make it. You'll do better than that. For now, you gotta get through it. But don't let'm wear you down."

Raef put two fists on the edge of the table and leaned forward. "I'm still looking for why."

Jarvis shook his head. "Don't bother. It happens. Just move on."

Raef left the lunch and headed to the business office to meet with Paul, the transportation manager for Shortenings. He caught him between meetings. Paul looked at Raef as he walked into the office. "Yup. Ten years ago I was in Sales—the U.P. in Michigan—same thing happened to me. It turned out great, but nothing about it was good while it was happening. Sit down. I've got only about five minutes."

Raef plopped into the chair near the door. "That's where I am now; in the 'nothing about it is good' part."

Paul finished selecting his papers for the meeting. "You have quite a reputation for action. What's that based on?"

"Simple. I delivered the goods. But I had a touch of ruthlessness—fired some people, closed down some careers—but I've tried pretty hard to get rid of that and I think I've succeeded."

Paul stood and stuffed the papers into a folder. "Raef, you've changed. But the 'delivered the goods', can you do it again? Without the ruthlessness?"

Raef wrinkled his brow. "Of course. It's what I do."

Paul smiled and moved toward the door. "Then do it. I have to run. Hey, don't worry, you're going to do fine!"

"Any guarantees come with that?" Raef left the office and walked down the walkway past the painting that always caused him to wonder—vibrant colors in a blend of patterns and motion and freedom that resulted in a matrices. The artist was bold, understood the need for action, caught the need for systems, yet was free. *What's the pattern in these interviews?* Without resolving the conundrum he turned and walked to his car. *Well, it happens. Move on.*

On Wednesday morning Raef cornered Todd, a process engineer who'd just picked up his MBA at the University of Minnesota and was headed to the financial group. Todd laughed at the question about what happened. "You've played hardball over the years, man. Made some enemies. I think some of those birds came home to roost. You going to survive this—politically, I mean?"

"You think this is about politics?"

"Isn't everything? Let's just say you don't always sing the corporate rouser—you've got a little independent streak that might worry some. Good luck. I'm off to finance."

Raef met with two other "advisors" that day and delayed four until later. Each person shared a personal phoenix story complete with suggestions for how to be better thought of in the corporation followed by a statement of encouragement: Raef should expect good things.

The next morning Goody walked into Raef's office and sat down. "Have you given any thought to leaving the company, finding a different situation in maybe a smaller company at say a director level? You don't really need this, you know."

Raef laid down his pen and turned toward the table. "I did that once: in 1973—considered leaving. I marched into the personnel office and announced, 'Play me or trade me—you have two options. I'm moving, either inside or outside the corporation.' It was gutsy, but it worked. I got transferred to Newman's division—the first lateral transfer of a Level 5 ever. Newman was one of the top five people in the company at the time; but, more important, he was my handball partner—we played a couple times a week then, at noon." Raef stood up and then sat on his desk, dangling his feet. "Yes, I thought of leaving … even interviewed with a West Coast paper company back then. But, have I considered it in the last couple of weeks? Well, I'm putting together my resume and I'm going to look at the food industry here in the area. Beyond that? I think I'd lose my family if I chose to move right now. They're pretty upset. And there's other work also. I'm really not a food guy, you know. I was an organic chemist once upon a time. And I like analysis—maybe the market? Who knows?"

Goody tapped a pencil on the table. "Just thought that maybe it was time to look outside again. Who's next on your visitation list?"

"Jordan."

Goody smiled as he got up and moved to the door. "That should be interesting."

*   *   *   *

Mitchell K. Jordan settled his 6'3" 250 pound frame deep into his high-backed leather chair and practiced finger pushups while his eyes roamed the mahogany landscape that reached out toward plaques and trophies, banners and advertising posters, pictures and memorabilia on walls, bookshelves, and tables. He lowered his chin, resting it on his index fingers as his stare fixed on the trophy across the room.

Mitchell Jordan/Raef Burnham
Doubles Champions 1971
Handball

After a moment he walked over and picked up the statuette with the engraved plaque.

Mitch and Raef had joined WFI the same year. One day Mitch had suggested that Raef and his family join his club, the Lakeside Sports Club. Raef's response had been instant. "I should what? C'mon, Mitch. There's no way. It's out of my league. We're a one career family."

Mitch had countered with, "You don't have to take a full membership. Do the open part; we need members. It's part of our outreach into the community. Your boy's what, 6? And your daughter's, say about 4? You'd love it. C'mon down with me Saturday afternoon. We'll get in some pickups. See if you like it."

"Any handball? Swimming? Running track? What?"

"Wait 'til Saturday. You'll love it. Bring your gang."

A quick knock and the door opened. Mitch turned. "Your call on Line 1."

He stepped over to his desk. "Mitch, here … yep. I need some specifics about Key Ponte—the conference. I need to know what happened down there—I missed it—family emergency. Give me the specifics on Burnham." Mitch doodled some footballs, some sports gear, a boat, and ran his eyes over a pile of promotion jerseys stacked in the far corner.

"I understand." He nodded, pursed his lips and searched the surfaces of his front teeth with his tongue. "Any sponsors?" Then he lowered his eyes, then his head, further, then his voice. "Thanks … No … I'm meeting with him in a few minutes and I just wanted to make sure I had some facts straight. Keep in touch."

Jordan's secretary stepped into the doorway. "Mr. Burnham is here."

Mitch returned the phone to its cradle, took a full breath, and stepped to the door. A firm dry-palm handshake later and the two men seated themselves in chairs close enough to be friendly and far enough apart to be comfortable. The engineer's eye measured his visitor. *What did I expect, a wreck? This guy's career has just been crushed and he looks unscathed. Man, if he can get caught in the wheels of this juggernaut, none of us is safe. Well, more power to … Show me your stuff, Mis-*

ter. To the door he said, "Clarice—two coffees, please." And looking at Raef, "How can I help?"

Raef didn't move. He looked straight at Jordan. "I need inside information and straight talk, Mitch. I'm pretty naïve—a little too trusting ... never saw it coming. But I think a lot of that is me—I don't read signs well. Now I need perspective. What happened?"

Mitch's face relaxed and he knew his smile had gone away; his eyes felt dry. He watched Raef's steady expectant gaze flicker just a little. "When you and I came into WFI nobody liked you, but you were hell on wheels, effective. Man, you were a star. For some of us, you were almost an idol. Now everybody likes you, and you're useless." He picked up a pencil from his desk, leaned back in his chair and rolled the pencil between his fingers. "What happened when you got religion? What ...", Mitch's hand opened up and raised to above his head, his eyes opened wide, he pursed his lips and tilted his head, "... happened? You changed."

Raef absorbed the body blow, motionless. He searched Mitch's gaze as if the answer were written somewhere deep in Mitch's eyes, and his expression didn't change. "That's probably it. I did change. How much of that answer do you want to hear?"

Mitch twisted the pencil as Clarice walked in with the coffees and laid them on the desk. "You start. If you get too windy I'll stop you. Go ahead."

Raef sipped his coffee and rested the cup on his lap. "Here's the short version. I was confronted with being afraid to die, ended up getting serious with the Lord and it changed my life. Haven't been the same since."

Mitch nodded. "But that doesn't explain your change in work ethic, loss of aggressiveness. Religion is okay, but you didn't have to quit performing."

Raef moved forward in the chair and laid down the coffee cup. "I saw a bigger picture. What I brought to work after that was a different view of how to treat people, a new priority about what's important ... what's ultimately, really important."

Mitch laid down his cup. "Yeah, and forgot that what we do for a living is important also. I mean, you get paid for this; you owe performance—I think you forgot that, a little."

Raef sat back and looked up for a moment. "Yeah, I took my eye off the ball. But, you know, my team still performed pretty well. We still delivered the products."

Mitch felt himself squint and show his disbelief. "Not really. At least not the way you did a few years ago. And in the meetings you lost your presence—you went quiet; appeared soft." He laid his pencil down. "Raef, of all of us, you had the best chance to succeed in this work. You weren't the best scientist and everyone knows you're no engineer, but you had the style and connections and you put projects on the board. Now, I don't know. I think the corporation has passed you by—I don't know what to advise you. You haven't been on the fast track for some years—now you're actually not on any track at all. And even getting considered for anything good down the line means having a sponsor—I'm not sure that anyone will take on that burden. But I do wish you well."

Raef shook his head. "Well, I asked to see you because I knew I'd get an honest response. So this is what 'Jordan candor' feels like." The slightest of smiles found its way to Raef's eyes, then the corners of his mouth. "In some ways, my friend, your words hit like a blow to the head, but I think it'll help me figure things out. I appreciate the honesty. Now let me see what I can do with it. Thanks."

Raef stood up to leave and Mitch got up with him. On the way to the door, Mitch put his hand on Raef's shoulder. "You going to stay?"

"I don't know." Raef stopped. "I think I should; I just don't know if I will."

Mitch leaned against the door jamb as he watched Raef walk out the door and down the hall. *Yeah, he screwed up, but that guy's worth saving.* "Clarice. Cancel my next meeting." He closed his office door and got out the organization chart for the research center. An hour later he picked up his phone, "… Of course I understand, Fortune … Of course I'm a team player … No, I wasn't down there, but I got the point … I want to help this guy—we go way back … I understand … I won't."

Chapter 6

▼

OPPORTUNITY

The Monday after May Day 1983 when spring bloomed full and summer seemed ready to peak through any day, Adam Irish reached for the phone. "Raef! How about lunch today? D'Angelo. I'll pick you up at the visitor's entrance … noon."

Adam grabbed his dark grey striped suit jacket, slipped it on, and checked his reflection in the window he used for a mirror—white shirt perfect, red tie aligned, matching pocket handkerchief reaching out of his lapel pocket at just the right angle, and black winged-tip Allen Edmonds shoes shining. Trim at 160 pounds and 5'10" he could have modeled for Brooks Brothers, but he settled for his ranking as the number one customer at Westphalia's Toggery For Men on Main Street. With a sweep of both hands, he brushed back his trimmed-close blond hair, settled the suit jacket to hang without draw and smiled at the almost-forty bachelor in the reflection.

Adam walked down the east stairs with the measured gait of Cary Grant auditioning for the role in *To Catch A Thief*. He slid into his 1983 black TransAm and 10 minutes later, at exactly 12:00, he pulled up to the curb in front of the visitor's entrance. He rolled down the driver's side window. "Anyone ready for some good food?"

Raef stood chatting with a young, trim black man dressed in work whites, the uniform for the laboratory. They shook hands and parted as Raef turned toward the voice. "You're buying? I'm ready."

A quick drive, light conversation about what works in restaurants and at what price, an order placed as soon as they sat down and the two were dining at D'Angelo on Delaware Avenue thirty minutes later. Over hot baked Italian sandwiches, chips and steaming coffee Adam moved the discussion toward Raef. "How's your program working?"

"Reinstatement?"

Adam took a sip of coffee. "How about re-engagement?"

Raef finished a couple of chips. "Not too bad. I tried to learn better what happened—you know, where'd I screw up?—but my advisors weren't much help." He leaned back in his chair and smiled. "Everyone encouraged me—showed support. But answers? I learned more that stuff like this happens all over the place, we're all damaged goods, and I'm going to do fine. Everyone wants to help, but I think this is all pretty much mine to deal with. One thing's sure, life will change. Oh, Mitch ... Mitch was great."

Adam's eyes never left Raef. He leaned with every voice inflection, laughed at every hint of humor, frowned with every challenge or negative statement—totally engaged in Raef's response.

Raef gulped a couple swallows of coffee. "I've lined up meetings with Quality Assurance, Purchasing and some others—informational interviews. Geben's opening some doors for me. And I'm investigating some good leads in research. I think it'll work out."

"Are you enjoying any part of it?"

Raef smiled. "I am, actually. I am. Once I got my mind off the pain and focused on the need, things got better."

Adam wiped the corners of his mouth and laid down his napkin. "Any offers?"

"No, none. And that's a little troubling." Raef looked down, but caught himself and quickly looked up at Adam. "I'm closing in on a team leader job in Shortenings—that's actually a pretty good fit for me with my organic chemistry background." He paused a moment. "It's not my choice; I've never been wild about that area ..." His voice trailed off. "It's a good job."

"Back to you. On a scale of 10?"

Raef thought a moment. "About a 4, up from somewhere between zero and one, and climbing." He paused, pushed his empty coffee cup aside and took a sip of water. "It's been interesting. I can't believe I've enjoyed taking a look at who I am, what I'm good at or thought I might be good at, and where I'd like to work. But I haven't asked those questions for a long time and I should have. Actually, I've never asked those questions of myself—ever. It's good."

"How'd you like to work for me in Restaurant Support Operations?"

Raef dropped his fork and grabbed the table with both hands as he leaned forward rising slightly from his chair. "What is this? I lay out my strategy—or lack of one. You know I'm vulnerable—and you make me an offer when I have no position to bargain from? Geez!" He pushed himself away from the table and turned his chair.

Adam sipped from his glass and picked up the napkin to dab the corners of his mouth. "No problem. One is friendship, the other is business. Are you interested or not?"

Raef drew a deep breath. Then he exhaled for several seconds, laid his wrists on top of his head and closed his eyes. "Can I sleep on it?"

"Sure. One night. I need an answer tomorrow." Adam let the response hang in the air for about thirty seconds. "This position has been open for a few weeks; the person I'd recommended wasn't accepted by the business group, so now I'm scrambling. I have to get it done so I need your answer tomorrow or I move on to my next alternative."

Adam paid the check and the two men drove back to the research laboratory. As Adam dropped Raef at the door he rolled down his window, "One more thing. I like my development leaders to attend a national technical meeting every year—it keeps everyone current—and our national sales meeting also. The Institute of Food Technologists national meeting is next month in New Orleans; the sales meeting is at the Amelia Island Plantation—that's in Florida. So, tomorrow it is."

"Tomorrow, thanks."

Adam left the research complex and headed toward the Restaurant Support Operations' General Offices.

* * * *

Raef pushed his chair back from the table—the kids had school activities so it was just the two of them. "It's the way it was done that bugs me—underhanded. I'm supposed to be a friend. Geez. We've worked together for 15 years." Raef looked away, then at the ceiling and back at Jenifer. "You see what I mean, don't you?"

Jenifer began collecting the dishes and placing them on the counter next to the sink. "Adam offered you a job. What level?"

"Five. Jenifer, it's a demotion, remember?"

She came over and sat down at the table. "Is that the best he can do?"

Raef started to reply, then stopped. "I think it's my shot to do something different in an area that can be fun, where I can learn new stuff and re-establish my credentials. I trust Adam—that's why the way he handled today bothers me—but I still trust him. I've known him for 15 years." With a theatrical flourish Raef waved his hand, "Adam Irish—compeer, provider of Saturday morning coffees for fifteen years, friend, and advisor!" Then he sat back. "Yes, he's difficult, but he's predictable. And in Restaurants especially, he's well thought of. He could be a help."

Jenifer went back to the sink, ran the water and started washing the dishes. "I don't know what's best. I really don't. This whole thing is so unfair. I used to believe in WFI. Good people. Moral company. Good products. I was their best fan. Now? Now I just don't trust these people. I simply don't trust them any more—not even a little. Probably never will. I guess you have to do whatever you think is best."

In the morning Raef poked his head into Adam's office. "When do we start?"

"Now. And you get to star in your own screenplay. You have to interview with our key people and convince them of what I already know; that you are the person for the job. Still interested?"

Raef stepped into the room. "Who am I talking to and when does this process start?"

"It starts today if you're ready. You get to chat with your marketing counterparts at the General Office, my peers and then my boss—as soon as I can line them up."

Raef took a step back and leaned against the wall. "I'm game."

Adam motioned for Raef to sit down. "OK. I'll arrange it and get back to you. But before I make the calls, I have three statements and two questions. Stay sharp and remember, it's your job to convince them—there I can't help. When you interview, close the door on Level 6; this is a Level 5 job. Understand?"

"Yeah."

"And finally, have you completed your outside search?"

Raef smiled. "Technically friend boss, that second question is not yours to ask. But I'll answer. I've sent out resumes to the local food companies and I have some opportunities out of state. But my family opposes moves, no matter what. Moving is not going to happen unless all the doors here get closed. So let's meet these people and get me a job."

Adam finished his cigarette and snuffed it out in the tray. "I checked my sources and found the same thing. The job market is terrible; the recession is in full swing. Best to wait it out. I'll make the calls."

During his basic training in the military, Raef had enjoyed various forms of combat training. Matching wits in the interviews with his potential new team was just another form of it and he enjoyed the exchange. In his final interview he met with Clements, the president of the Restaurant Support Operations Division who'd served in that job since its formation. Clements outlined why Raef was the proper choice for the job, suggested the business team's unanimous approval and implied his own endorsement. He closed with, "Could you do one more thing? Meet with one of our collegues later this week—it's an informational interview. Won't take long at all."

Adam reached across the desk. "It's good news, Raef. You're hired. Congratulations!" After a friendly celebrative handshake he continued, "But Clements requests that you to take one more interview later in the week."

Raef raised his eyebrows. "I know. He mentioned it. Someone nervous about the outcome of the first interview?"

Adam shook his head. "No. It's just informational." He turned Raef by the shoulder and they moved toward the door. "We have an agreement. You regain your credibility and show that you are worthy of re-instatement. I get you a hearing. My job is the easy part." Adam, Raef's friend of 15 years, had just become his boss.

The total interview process took two weeks. During the process, before he made the agreement and started work, Raef queried the local job market. He received no responses. In the down job market of 1983, Cargill responded that they had no openings. International Multifoods sent a form letter as did General Mills stating that should he like to apply in six months the market may be better. Pillsbury, the company he had the least interest in, didn't even bother to send a rejection.

From all his interviews over the month-long struggle Raef learned that "everyone goes through ups and downs in a career," that "the early 40's are a man's most dangerous years in the job world," that "people get better through experiences such as these," that he truly would "never miss a paycheck, my friend," that he would "never again take a paycheck for granted," that there was "never a risk that he'd be let go from WFI" (he had too many friends), and that he "truly would land on his feet."

* * * *

Friday afternoon at 4:30 Raef walked up to the receptionist's desk in the executive wing of WFI's headquarters. "Raef Burnham to see Fortune Montag."

"Fortune is expecting you. Corner office on the right. You may go in."

Montag played to win. Handball was his sport of choice. Rarely defeated, he resorted to whatever it took to be sure of a game's outcome. Ability worked the majority of the time. But when intimidation was required, he glared at or even threatened his opponents. He rarely lost.

Aggressive approaches were not limited to sport—he employed similar tactics in business. The result is that WFI entered fields where lesser leaders showed reluctance; ability to manage those businesses led to success. He allowed no failures.

Raef pressed his left ear closed while his feet sank into the deep claret and gray hallway carpeting and he blinked to clear his eyes as they adjusted to the soft light. No sound penetrated this majestic abyss, and though the design included much glass, it drizzled in little light. His ears felt numb, like they'd been covered with sponge. His eyes felt like they were gazing through a fine mist. A single ray of light emanated from the office at the end of the corridor, the one with the door plaque: Fortune Montag, Vice President. Raef stopped before he came to the plaque, adjusted his tie, checked his shoes, and squared his suit coat. He lifted his chin and tapped lightly on the door. "Mr. Montag?"

"Fortune, Raef … we have worked together … Fortune.… Can I get you anything to drink?" He stepped behind his desk and poured two glasses of ice water from the Waterford pitcher on the silver tray and handed one of the glasses to Raef. He motioned for him to be seated at the table in front of the window on the south side of the room; Fortune sat down across from him. The afternoon sun sprayed a golden patina over the corner of the room and softened the room with its glow. Raef raised the crystal to take a sip and the leaden mass in his hands caused him to glance at what he held. *So this is what quality feels like.* And the water stayed cold.

"Raef, I will get right down to business. I have watched your career for some time, ever since you and I had that unfortunate disagreement over the processing system. It ended up that you were right, by the way—we never did make that system pay out. But it was still an idea worth trying. Nonetheless, you got my attention. And I have paid attention ever since."

"That was a long time ago."

Fortune paused with the interruption. "I am pleased for you that you have found a new situation in Restaurant Support Operations. You are an excellent technical person and the corporation needs good technical people. But I suspect that you harbor a desire to return to your former level; Level 6 I believe it was. May we explore why that is unlikely?"

Raef nodded. "Please."

Fortune continued. "First, you had an opportunity—you were ahead of all your peers in promotions and on the list for rapid advancement. Your military background was perfect for the leadership we needed from you. And you excelled in all of your assignments. You were promoted to Level 6. I endorsed your advancement.

"Then you stumbled in your initial assignment. Thank goodness your failing was temporary; you caught on and we were most pleased. Then you refused me in that processing line request stating that we were working on the wrong things—I believe you thought it a fool's venture. If you recall, we are a marketing company and as such, marketing decides what business decisions make sense. You were wrong to resist that direction. I regard your resistance at that time to be ill advised at best, dangerous at worst."

Raef raised his hand slightly. "But you invested three years' development time on it and junked the million dollar system without ever putting a product on the market. A fool's venture would be too strong a statement, but I thought we could spend our time more profitably. That's true."

Fortune continued. "Since that time you have failed in an attempt to launch that Hasty Foods knockoff—your product failed miserably in the first six months and was, quite frankly, an embarrassment to the corporation."

"Fortune, may I interrupt again, please? Yes, we had our differences about the processing line. I'll accept that. But it's not appropriate to pin the failure of that line on me. The products failed because marketing insisted that we match—insisted that we identically match—an inferior product. That was the direction marketing insisted on. Because, as you said, we are a marketing company and marketing decides what business decisions make sense, the product was introduced. That project made no sense and I said so at the time."

"You should have resisted or refused."

Raef shook his head. "You blame me for the processing system—you say I was wrong to challenge you. Here, I did challenge and was overruled. How can you blame me for that?"

"Then you are weak ... that is worse."

Raef leaned forward and started to raise his hand, but took a deep breath, eased back in his chair and remained silent.

Fortune waited. "Allow me to continue. Most recently you seem to have become bored with the entire process. You act independently. You seem, at times, to disdain what is expected of our leaders. We need to be able to count on people in management positions to act according to the corporation's best interests. We no longer have that confidence in you.

"Ours is a meritocracy. Promotion in our corporation is based on performance and requires sponsorship—you act and someone notices. That person then decides that you are leadership material and is willing to guarantee your future performance. You, Raef, have failed to perform and you have lost your sponsorship—we who supported you cannot support you any longer. You will never again enjoy having a champion. You have none now, and you will have none in the future. Do I make myself clear? You will never reach your goal of becoming a director here. You cannot be a success at WorldFoods, Inc."

Fortune leaned forward. "And a final point. You have made religion part of the workplace and that cannot be."

Raef leaned forward. "People come to me and ask advice about their lives. I don't seek them out. I just give them honest answers."

Fortune's lips thinned to a fine line as he focused on Raef. "Not on company time. You are not paid to be a counselor. We have people for that. Such activity is not acceptable."

Raef thought about that for a moment. "I accept that correction. No more on company time. Agreed."

Fortune smiled. "Too late, I am afraid. You are now an example. You had opportunity. You failed to initiate a requested study. You introduced bad products to the market. You used your position to spread your religious views within the corporation. And you have been demoted. Because you are visible, others will see what happens when managers fail to be team players, fail to perform as expected. The corporation gains as much by your staying as by your leaving. Others will fear this happening to them. I requested to see you so I could explain your career options to you directly."

Raef looked away and jerked back toward Fortune. "I never even had a warning. Not one."

Fortune shook his head. "You missed the signs." He waved his hand and shook his head once more. "Let us move to the bottom line. I am told that you aspire to regain the position you have lost. You certainly have the talent to perform at the 6 level and beyond—your psychological rating, IQ, and other test scores suggest that. While it is commendable and even laudable that you hold such aspirations, I must tell you that such hope is unrealistic. It will never happen. There is no road back. No ... road ... back. Do you understand? None.

"In fairness, I thought it proper to inform you regarding what your future looks like. We can use your talent. We have much work to do. But we cannot allow you an advanced position in the corporation, now or in the future. Do you have any further comments?"

Raef's rapid pulse and irregular breathing from the earliest part of the discussion had given way to a steady pulse and even full breaths by the time Fortune finished speaking. Raef never took his eyes off Fortune—never moved his eyes from watching Fortune's eyes, even as Fortune's glances about the room returned to deep glares focused on Raef's soul. Raef never flinched. "So your message is that it's okay to hire this guy, but be sure he understands that there's no hope of a career resurrection. Okay. But neither of us is the final arbiter of the future, is he?

"Fortune, the processing line was a bad idea; I just handled my response to it poorly. The pasta project was a bum rap; you know that. And supporting every action the company takes? I just couldn't—guilty as charged. Thank you for seeing me today."

"You are welcome," Fortune said as he stepped toward his desk. "It is not personal, Raef. We have our ways and they seem to be different from yours."

Raef stopped at the doorway, nodded, waved and left without making any sound.

✲   ✲   ✲   ✲

With all leads exhausted and no other options available on that Saturday, the 14th of May, Raef moved his personal belongings from his private office on the first floor to a vacant desk in a windowless laboratory in the basement of the research center. His star was not just tarnished, it had no luster at all.

This game is over.

BOOK TWO

Chapter 7

WORKING AGAIN

Raef, WFI's newest Level 5 rookie, powered into the parking lot at 7:30 Monday morning and jerked to a stop in his assigned slot. From two slots over Goody shouted, "Some things never change."

"Hey, they leave the sign—I keep the slot. One of these days they'll wake up and I'm a plebeian again. But today, it's nice still to be king."

Goody dropped his voice to a more serious tone as they walked toward the building. "You okay?"

Raef raised his chin and looked at the west side of the research center. "I'm ready—not quite the same thing, but it'll have to do." He looked over at Goody. "And thanks for your thoughts when this all started and over the weeks. It helped to get some distance from this thing. Have to run. New job, you know." He greeted Roger at the desk and turned toward the down stairs that led to his new office.

New office. As he walked into the laboratory that was to be his new home, he faced four windowless walls that captured a work space designed for two people. Two desks faced the wall to his immediate left; the one crowded into the far corner straight ahead was his—the one equipped with a desktop computer and phone and crouched below an overhanging bookcase that held the desk lamp. The chair looked like WWII surplus; the desk too. His new home away from home.

He fired up the computer, checked his phone, arranged some files, books, and project folders, and walked across the laboratory to get a cup of coffee. About 8:10 Adam walked in and said, "Looks good—like you're ready. And just in time. You have a product showing this afternoon at 2:00 for the marketing people—the new line of Breads. Can you handle it?"

"Sure. How many in the line?"

Adam was already heading out the door. He waved over his shoulder and shouted as the door closed, "Just show them."

Raef looked through his shelf library, pulled out the *Product Guide for Restaurant Support Operations* and looked for the Breads specification sheets. When he finally found what he was looking for it actually read, "Breads, Muffins and Quick Breads Specifications". He flipped through the pages and mumbled to himself, "This could be a brief second career. Hang on."

He picked up the large black file and kept his finger in the BMQB page. He walked across the fluorescent-lit basement hallway to the baking laboratory where the other six members of the restaurant research team were busy rolling out dough, inserting pans into ovens, writing in notebooks, and bouncing the banter common to a work crew comfortable working together. Laughter and shouts punctuated the steady din that filled the room—grinding motors, pulsating mixers, whistling convection ovens—and it was only the first hour of the day. Raef stepped to the front of the room. To be heard above the noise he shouted, "Folks. Folks! I have a problem. Adam gave me a 2:00 showing and I don't know squat about what I'm doing. Can I have a little help, please?"

First to move was the bold one, Duggy. "Burnham, just remember, I don't report to you! But don't sweat it. This is part of Adam's charm—happened to all of us. Okay, gang, here we go."

Before Raef could ask where to start, Sandy grabbed four five-pound boxes of Muffin and Quick Bread Mix down from the shelf and set up a 50 pound Hobart mixer with a paddle and bowl and said, "This is what's being shown—we just finished reformulating it."

Sven set two convection ovens to 325ºF, greased a pile of pans and laid out the spatulas.

Duggy came back from putting his morning's project on hold and joined the action. "We have plenty of time, but we have to keep moving. Raef, here's how we have to work. Always weigh up all your ingredients for each mix and arrange them on the work surface. Then do the prep one at a time. Today, since you don't know the line you'll just work alongside whoever is doing the mixing. First the water, then the mix, then the paddles, drop, slow for a minute and high for two minutes. Ready?"

"Boot camp one more time, I think." Raef stepped back to stay out of the way.

"Before lunch you'll be … like riding a bicycle. And it is like boot camp, but there's nothing demeaning about it. Think of it as a crash course: like, 'Do it or you'll crash, of course.' Something like that." Duggy laughed at his own bit of humor, winked toward Sandy and Sven, and with a magician's sure hands moved dry mix to batter to pan to oven and calmed the four foot waves that threatened to capsize Raef's little formulator-in-training boat. While Duggy finished the final mix preparation and cleaned the work counter, Sven and Sandy set the timers, rotated the baking pans, and pulled the finished breads from the oven laying them gently on the cooling rack. Done in shadow, this would be a team of dancers moving in perfect choreography across the stage of a baking laboratory: dancers gliding before and behind each other in full motion guided by unseen signals and slowed only when the action stopped.

Raef leaned back against the countertop and folded his arms across his chest. "What a team! It's been awhile."

Duggy scraped the remnant dough from one of the mixing bowls and laid it in the sink to wash. "Really, it's part of working with restaurants. The back of the house is like this. If what you just saw here doesn't happen there in operations—the real world—the restaurant goes broke. It's part of the culture. And the helping attitude is part of it."

When the last pan of muffins was ready, Duggy slid it across the counter, laid down his hot pads, and washed his hands. "Looks good and it's all yours. Welcome to the new world, Columbus!"

"I think I feel more like one of Cortez's people, and the ships just got burned. Thank you for this morning. I appreciate it." Raef baked backup products for the rest of the morning, prepared place cards to describe the products, and arranged the showing area. Afterward, he committed the specification sheets to memory, scribbled some notes and outlined a meeting agenda. He looked at the clock above the door. 1:15.

At 1:45 Adam entered the lab and called the technical services team over to the bench to review their programs for the new Muffins and Quick Breads. Then he walked over to the work bench where Raef was marking the last of the table tents. "OK. How about a walk-through?"

Raef swallowed hard. "I … I'm doing it?"

Adam shuffled a couple sheets of paper and looked at the products arrayed before him. "What do you have?"

Raef squared his feet, gathered his hands before his belt, looked directly at Adam, and presented the four products. "Our Muffin and Quick Bread product line consists of four products: Cranberry-Orange, Lemon Poppyseed, Banana, and Oat Bran. I'd like to take you through them, one at a time. Cranberry-Orange projects to be our lead product. It contains … and is targeted against Pillsbury, General Mills and Krusteaz, our leading competitors. Lemon Poppyseed contains natural zest of lemon and scored the highest of all the products in focus groups. Banana …"

Adam pushed the agenda sheet away. "Got it. Good start."

"Questions?"

"No. And you can relax. I'll present—unless you want to …"

Raef shook his head.

Adam picked up the agenda and glanced at something half way down the page. "I just wanted to see what you've learned today and get a quick read on your style. You'll do fine and your style works. They should be here any minute. Good job, by the way. Everything looks great."

Raef smiled and half sat down on the stool next to Adam. "Thanks, Coach. Your show. Where do you want me?"

Adam pointed to the seat on the right corner nearby. "At the table. And be ready to answer any questions I miss."

Raef moved to his right. "There'll be lots of those, I'm sure."

At 2:10 voices in the hallway heralded the arrival of Clements—General Manager of the Division, James—National Sales Director, Smiley—Marketing Manager, and Oberman—Product Manager; four of the six people Raef had interviewed in order to get the job two weeks earlier.

Clements—hair perfect, smile in place, voice even, and movements measured—greeted Adam who welcomed him and with a slight motion of his head toward Raef said, "I'd like to introduce the newest member of our team, Raef Burnham."

Clements extended his hand, "Welcome aboard, Raef."

Raef shook Clements' hand. "Thank you, sir."

"Raef put today's showing together."

Clements nodded toward Raef, then looked back at Adam. "What do you have to show us, Adam?"

"I want to present our new four-product line of Muffins and Quick Breads. I think you'll like what you see. They've tested well against the competition and are working well in in-store evaluation."

After an hour of showing, discussing, tasting and comparing, Clements and his team authorized full production. The line was a go.

Adam walked the business team out of the laboratory and down the hall. Raef took a deep breath and exhaled as he closed the door and leaned his head back against the door jamb. The door clicked shut and five white-clad smiling bakers materialized offering silent applause and a litany of encouragements. "Congratulations. It doesn't get any better than that."

Raef smiled, offered a slight bow and dismissed his saviors with a wave of the hand. "I can handle it from here. Thank you." Duggy, Sandy, Akins, Sven and Che broke up into quiet conversations as they melted away into the laboratory. Raef cleared the table, picked up his notes and returned to his desk.

He sat down and opened his notebook to write a summary of the presentation. After writing two pages of notes he closed the book and laid down the pen. A moment later he took a deep breath, closed his eyes and laid his head back against the work counter behind him. For several minutes he didn't move. He barely breathed. Then he opened his eyes, sat upright, grabbed a pen and finished the post-mortem.

* * * *

At 5:30 that afternoon Adam grabbed his Lucky Strikes and walked down to Raef's laboratory. Adam opened the door and pulled out a cigarette as he walked over to the workbench. "Mind if I smoke?"

"No. I used to do a pipe, sometimes cigars, when I was in service—a long time ago. No, I don't mind." Raef sat back in his chair.

Adam pulled out his lighter and put the cigarette in his mouth. "Back home we had a name for these things: fixin's. We had our tobacco and paper and we built a smoke." He flicked the lighter and drew deeply.

"You mean, Arkansas? Like thirty some years ago?"

Adam exhaled. "More like twenty—thirty when I started. But, yes. And I don't think 'fixin's' applies to store-bought Luckys at $15 a carton, but what the heck. Another thing that doesn't fit is why we're stuck here in the basement. I don't like where this team is located any more than I imagine you do. But until the new wing is ready in October, the basement space is the only location available. Just have to hang in there."

Adam held the cigarette and the lighter. "My aunt called today—she's 85 and says she needs 'a visit.' I'll have to take a weekend back home one of these days."

There was another pause. "She rarely makes demands." Adam inhaled again. "Well, how'd it go today?"

Raef searched the length of an awkward pause. "The result was good." He got up from his desk chair and pulled out a stool at the table. "This wasn't easy, man. As much as we've talked about your business over the years ... I know nothing. Nothing. Everything is new. I feel like ..." he raised his hands palms up, "... no natural moves."

"So, you're pretty much on schedule, eh? You'll get there. You just have to get used to the business. This is different from the consumer businesses."

"Well, I'm focusing on one day at a time this week. I was just outlining my 'get-acquainted' schedule when you walked in."

Adam took a final drag on the cigarette. "Do what you were doing, but I want you to put a few things on your May/June schedule. I'm going to take a little time off. I was going to New York for the rest of the week—planned to be back on Monday. But I think Arkansas beckons so I have to change my plans. The National Restaurant Association meets next week in Chicago at McCormick Center and the Institute of Food Technologists convention is in New Orleans in June. I'm attending both and I'd like you to attend both. Put them on your schedule OK? I have to run."

"Work through your secretary?"

"Of course. And why don't you take Jenifer and the kids to New Orleans? We'll cover the meetings; they can do what they do. Your travel, room and car are covered. The rest is yours, of course."

"It's a thought. Thanks."

Adam put out the stub and moved toward the door. "Beginnings are always hard. Don't worry about it, you're doing fine. See you tomorrow."

Adam closed the door and darted up the stairs and down the hallway to his office. *Cancel New York. Line up Arkansas, Chicago, New Orleans. Rats—cancel New York.*

"Barry. Adam. Have to cancel ... a complication." Adam leaned back in his chair and watched a crow float on to the roof just above his window. "I have an elderly aunt who's asked me to visit her. I just think that I'd better head down to Arkansas this weekend ... yep. Then I travel for a couple of weeks and I'll give you a call. Let's plan on something around the 4th ... later. I have a Chicago call on the other line—have to run. Bye."

CHAPTER 8

▼

TRAVEL ASSIGNMENTS

"Can you believe it?" Raef smiled as he finished his eggs Benedict and drained the last drop of coffee. "I've survived three days of the restaurant convention, three evening soirees with our suppliers, and made more than 100 industry contacts. What do you think?"

Breakfast in Chicago's Park Hyatt in the Water Tower District created the beginning of a normal day for Adam at the National Restaurant Association's annual event. Enthusiasm at breakfast did not. Adam signaled a wait person for the check and touched the napkin to the corners of his mouth. Before he could respond Raef moved on to the next thought.

"How far to McCormick Center?"

Adam shook his head. "Nope. That's enough. We'll talk as we go." He laid down two 20's and picked up his briefcase. "Let's see if we can't catch an earlier flight out of Midway. Get a cab."

They walked toward the concierge and pointed to their stored carry-on luggage. Before Raef could say a word, Adam mouthed, "Midway," and the concierge motioned for the bell captain.

As they moved toward the exit, Raef continued. "Three days walking the floors—I'll bet we covered ten miles a day. I met our sales people from this region, got a chance to work the booth with our technical sales people, made up some product, and met a good number of our customers. Not too bad."

They headed toward the cab pulling up to the curb. Adam stopped. "Did you visit any of the competitors' booths? Anything new? New! See anything we should be doing?"

They threw their luggage into the trunk and got into the back seat. "Midway. Well, Pillsbury was featuring frozen doughs—we ought to be in that market. General Mills had a whole new line of mixes, but I don't know if there's any opportunity there. Krusteaz seems to be matching Pills and Mills product for product. Pioneer …"

The cab entered the medieval joust that was the daily sojourn to Midway Airport on Chicago's south side. "How about new ideas? Did you see anything really novel? We need new ideas."

Raef thought a moment. "The French sorbets—they have great flavors. Better than anything I've seen in U.S. products. How do they do that? Can we do sorbets?"

Adam pulled out a cassette recorder and some notes. "Write me a summary of what we saw here with some recommendations for what we should do next. In two weeks it's June, and June is New Orleans and the food technologists. Be sure you're ready. Now, I have to do some work. We'll talk on the other end."

* * * *

Jenifer timed her arrival at the airport to be in front of the door closest to Gate #52 fifteen minutes after Northwest Flight 1412 out of Midway touched down. She pulled up exactly on time expecting to wait. But full striding toward her came Raef equipped with a briefcase at his side, a carry-on dragging behind and all wrapped with a smile. The smile came attached to a nod that led to a kiss and an exchange of drivers and a two-person cavalcade on its way home.

She leaned her head against the window and looked at Raef. "You look good. How'd it go, this first trip under new management?"

He checked the merging traffic leading out of the airport and looked over. "Thank you. Not too bad if you consider that I don't know the products or the people or the town or what's expected of me. I'm not familiar with the meeting or the site. And there's no way to judge the outcome. Actually, 'didn't know' would be more accurate—I did pretty well. I made contacts, prepared product, learned the other side of entertaining. Yeah, it was good. How about you? Thought about New Orleans?"

Life had been a blur for Jenifer since the bomb in April and she hadn't really spent any time thinking about a trip. She turned to look at the road and leaned her head against the headrest.

"I don't know. Mindy's not herself. I think she's concerned that if we're moving she'll have to go through that change of schools thing again. She's … not herself."

Raef slowed the car about five miles per hour. "Is she being difficult? What?"

"Difficult's the wrong word. She challenges things. She gets upset about just about everything. No joy; that's what I'd call it. She's normally a fun kid, but right now she has no joy in her life. And it's making it tough around the house."

"How about Jake?"

Jenifer looked at Raef and raised that left eyebrow about a quarter of an inch. "Jake is being Jake. It's all internalized. If it's bothering him, you can't see it … but it's there."

Raef drove a couple of minutes. The car was quiet. Finally he said, "Take the break. You … we need it. The kids too."

"The kids? Can we afford that?"

Raef turned north on Transway Boulevard and eased into the traffic. "We can't do our usual trip up to the Gunflint—I can't get away for a vacation this year. And I'm covered for the convention: room, meals, travel, car. At one of these events everything's pretty much free. We'll have to work out entertainment, timing, activities—and I might have some business meetings to work around; but that's no big deal. Let's!"

"If there's no hassle with the kids."

"I suppose that'll be an issue!"

* * * *

"What do you mean 'do we'?" Jake and Mindy said in unison. They were trekkers. This was travel.

* * * *

The Institute of Food Technologists Convention in New Orleans brought a smile to all four Burnham's faces. After visiting Jackson Square and riding in a carriage, listening to the jazz performers in Preservation Hall, taking breakfast and dinners at Brennan's and the Court of Two Sisters and K Paul's, and walking the French Quarter for three days, the family had experienced New Orleans and put some distance between them and the near ides of April.

The convention presented itself as Raef's balm of Gilead. The seminar papers, the conversations at suppliers' booths, the luncheons and dinners, the exchanges of business cards all combined to reconnect him with the technical community and return his focus to the future. For Jenifer and the kids, New Orleans offered contrasts and conflicts and beauty and baseness, but always, style. Through the architecture and the food, the music and the costumes, the entertainment and the business, they opened their thinking to consider a world they'd never experienced. And it was fun. For three days they experienced another kingdom—and they loved it.

On Wednesday afternoon Raef finished his work at the convention. When he returned to the room, they all threw on their bathing suits and headed up to the rooftop swimming pool. After splashing around for a half hour and even getting in a few laps they all grabbed some sodas and laid down on lounge chairs to catch a little sun.

From the deep end of the pool Jake called, "Hey, Dad. It's 3:30. What time do we have to be at the *Delta Queen*?"

"Six o'clock. Lots of time."

"And will I be able to join you?" came a voice from behind the row of deck lounges. Walking toward the Burnhams was a trim, well-tanned 40ish man clad in a light blue bikini-brief bathing suit, a Bombay gin martini in hand, towel draped across his right shoulder and enough smile to light up even this sun-decked patio. He closed the distance to the group in ten steps.

Raef waved as soon as he saw him. "Adam. C'mon over. And yes, please do join us this evening. We'll be leaving at 5:30 from the main entrance and walking down Canal Street."

Adam sat down and focused the conversation on Jenifer's piano progress, the decorating of their home, Jake's college plans, Mindy's high school and volleyball, and the fine dining and entertainment all were enjoying in New Orleans. When Adam paused to take a sip from his glass, Jenifer inserted, "How about you? What's going on in your life?"

He smiled. "Glad you asked. I just bought a new house on the south side and I take ownership this fall. It needs a lot of work, but I have friends. Looking forward to it—I'm pretty good at refurbishing, and this is a good challenge." He looked at his watch. "I have to get cleaned up for tonight."

Raef grabbed his towel and stood up. "I'll walk you back. Jenifer and the kids want to swim a little longer."

When they arrived at the elevators Adam pulled Raef aside. He walked over to the window and turned. "I don't know if we'll have a chance to talk tonight but I wanted to let you know that I'm going to New York for a few days before I go back to work—the trip I delayed when you joined the group. Handle things for me 'til I get back, okay?"

"No problem," said Raef. "What's in New York?"

"Nothing special. A friend is having a party and wants me there, so I'm leaving first thing in the morning. I just left a message for Clements so all's covered back at the ranch. I'll be in Monday. Anyway, see you tonight."

At 5:30 the quintet stepped out of the Marriott entrance and headed down Canal Street to the river and the *Delta Queen*. Milling around the *Delta Queen*'s roped off gang plank were 600 fellow conventioneers and friends and families. And standing at the gate, next to the ropes, was Moshe Stavrou, their host for the evening and best known salesperson in the food industry.

"Hey, Mr. Burnham! Can we start now?" Moshe enjoyed a little show. Picking one person out of a crowd for a little friendly jab was standard fare, and Raef and Moshe had worked together for 15 years or more. In fact, Raef had been instrumental in getting Moshe started working with WFI, a relationship that had proved beneficial to both companies.

Raef nodded. Moshe pointed to Jenifer and waved, then stepped aside releasing the Captain to begin boarding the passengers. "Great night for a cruise, isn't it?" As Jake, Adam, Jenifer, and Mindy stepped forward Moshe pulled Raef aside. "How're you doing?"

Raef smiled and nodded, "OK. This little break has helped."

Moshe looked at guests filing by and smiled as he made eye contact with different groups. "Don't forget my comment. You have many friends—you'll never miss a paycheck. Now, let's enjoy the evening."

Raef caught up to his little party a few steps up the walkway and moved with them as they blended in to the mingling crowd. Jake had free run of the boat and disappeared. Jenifer and Mindy chose to explore all the entertainment spots and check out the crowd. Adam excused himself and was gone. And Raef lifted a glass of cabernet from a tray at the end of the counter, found a chair at water level on the far side lower deck, propped his feet on the rail and just listened to the water.

As Raef's mind drifted with the slap-slap of the waves against the side of the boat, a deep voice with a mild French accent broke the aquatic rhythm. "That's a cabernet glass in your hand, and I'd have taken you for a martini man."

"Not for some time, Yves. Not for some time."

Raef started to get up to greet Yves Jarnot, a director of research at WFI and champion of the oppressed, but Yves laid a hand on his shoulder and asked him to stay seated. "Do you mind if I join you? Three days on the floor with all these people—I need a break."

"Yves, always good to see you. Please." Raef motioned to the chair.

After some small talk about the convention, the booths, the new products and ingredients, who was there and who wasn't, Yves moved the conversation. "I understand that you've moved to Adam's group."

"The rumor is true. I'm in Restaurant Support Operations. It's a whole new world—call me Cortez."

Yves loved classical music, the opera and history. "Have you burned the ships?"

"Didn't have to. Someone took care of that for me."

Yves smiled and took a sip of his drink. "Raef, let me offer a few thoughts if you don't mind." He paused and squinted for just a moment; then he continued. "Things happen to people. Just because you got demoted doesn't mean you were the worst Level 6 in the building or that you are a bad person. Other things are in play in this kind of thing. You happened to be in a vulnerable spot and you got moved out. It doesn't mean you're not capable of making a contribution or that you won't do good things again in your career. It means you have to get your feet on the ground and start building again. Am I making sense?"

Raef dropped his feet to the deck and sat up little. "What do you mean 'vulnerable'?"

"We have people who need an opportunity to show what they can do. So we needed to create a position. Your job requires skills, but not the specific skills needed to create new oils or fragrances or some of the other specialties; nor is it so basic that anyone could do it. So, you were vulnerable. And, we need some growth in your area: The new products haven't been successful lately. Or am I wrong?"

Raef laid his glass on the floor next to his chair. "No, that's accurate. But what's next? The career dream is over?"

"Careers are whatever you make them. You have an opportunity where you are. Adam doesn't want to be a department head forever. Don't you have a saying, 'Bloom where you're planted'?"

Raef pressed. "You don't think the lid is on the career?"

"Well, you took a hit and you don't have a champion—a sponsor; but don't let that define the future. Now it's up to you to erase the past. Show them that they made a mistake. You had plenty of friends in the meetings. There was never talk of letting you go. Several people mentioned how you'd been one heckuva development leader before you got promoted, and no one has forgotten that. No, let's see what comes of all of this. Don't get too concerned about what happened—you can't change it anyway. Get past this. That's all I wanted to say. Now I'm going to find the bar and freshen this glass. You okay?"

"Fine and getting better. Thanks, Yves. Can I stop by sometime if I have questions?"

"Anytime. See you."

Raef sat back and let the warm breezes drift over him and the gentle slapping of the waves against the side of the boat calm the white caps that wanted to rise up in his soul. After awhile it was time to walk the boat, find Jenifer and Mindy and begin meeting the guests. Four hours later he was sure he understood why they call New Orleans the Big Easy.

At the airport the next morning Jake threw the luggage onto a cart and caught up with Raef at the Northwest Airlines check-in counter. "Did anyone see Adam last night after we got on the boat? I was all over the place and didn't see him."

Raef thought for a moment. "Adam marches to a different drummer. I'm sure he was having a good time, and I know that he took the early flight to New York. He said he'll be back Monday—I think that means Tuesday at work. Who knows what Tuesday holds."

CHAPTER 9

▼

NEW YORK AND BEYOND

Tuesday morning Raef sat in Adam's office, as still as possible, while the morning ritual ran itself out. It was 8:30 as Adam reached for a cigarette, lit up, took a deep drag and said, "I'm trying to quit. Last year I quit for a week. On the seventh day my entire staff met me when I came in on Friday morning and presented me with a carton and a lighter. I get a little tense … they said the other word is demanding … and some said unlivable."

Raef waited while Adam took another drag. "How was the weekend?"

"Those New York people—they know how to party; yes, they do. And I'm back. What's on your mind?"

"Welcome back, first of all. A few things need some attention. Frozen batters and doughs: are we going to pursue them? And the Italian ice cream concept: any interest? I hear that the ice cream people want to pursue this because they can manufacture it in their cookie operations and utilize their distribution system—and that we aren't going to be involved."

"Good sources?"

Raef nodded. "Quality Control. They had to sign off."

Adam pressed his temples with his fingertips and laid his head back against the chair. "Organize a showing. Invite Clements, Babick, the marketing people and sales."

Raef nodded as he wrote on the pad. "Who's Babick?"

"Quentin Babick. The new division president. He's going to replace Clements next year when Clements retires. Announced last week when we were gone."

Raef watched Adam douse his cigarette in the Sardi's ash tray. "And show them …?"

"… what the world of frozen batters and doughs and top shelf Italian ice cream tastes like. For batters and doughs, we'll pull in final products that we could do as batters and doughs: San Francisco sourdough, some New York, Chicago and local breads (be sure to include the Sofitel's French Bread—let's visit them to see how they do it). Look at our ice cream line—they look like every other product line in the store. We could sure do a better job than that. Show 'em."

Raef punched a period at the end of the notes. "That could just suggest gutless. It doesn't necessarily mean they're ignorant of what's available in Europe."

Adam shook his head. "Does anything tell you they're using a wide angle lens? These people are thinking traditional and U.S. only. What have we got to lose? Let's take the shot. Expand their horizons. Show them the world."

Raef laid his pen down. "We know the world? Maybe it's time to confess that I don't know diddle about European ices."

"Me either. But we're ahead of them. At least we've figured out that people in other places on the planet are doing it better than what we see on the shelf around here. Let's go."

Raef looked at his list. "Batters and doughs I can handle. But ice creams? I think we should bring in a couple of national gourmet brands but focus on the European stuff—the French obviously and some Italian gelato if we can. Remember that little kiosk at the restaurant show?"

Adam peeked at his calendar and placed his finger a couple of lines down. "Two weeks from now?"

Raef thought a second. "We better make that three or even more. We can get the product picked up in Paris and Rome, but clearing customs is a problem. We'll use expediters; it still takes time. And the product has to stay cold the whole time—some risk here. And we have to complete the move from the basement to the new wing."

Adam stood. "Wow. I forgot about the move. Well, three's the maximum time. Set it up. I've got a 9:00." He shook his head. "New York was quite something. I'll see you later."

Raef finished the note on his pad and stepped across the hall to hand it to Alecia, Adam's secretary. She looked up. "What's this? Stage One of the new Raef plan?"

"Nope. Part One of Raef's rules. When you've been given an assignment here's what you do, Ms. Alecia: On the way back to your desk, figure out what you're going to do and the five people you're going to call to get the action going. Then make the calls. That way, when Adam walks into my office after his meeting and says, 'How's it going?' … I demonstrate action and he's pleased because the project is underway. Now if you can handle checking what's on that sheet, we'll both look good."

Alecia read the paper and, crumpling the note said, "I covered him when he was gone—nothing on that sheet makes me look any better," and threw it at Raef who was still standing in the doorway. He caught it. Then she smiled as she turned toward her typewriter, "But give me the sheet back please and I'll take care of this. You never know."

Raef straightened out the sheet and laid it on her desk. "You are a kind person. Thank you."

When Raef got back to his desk he called Bilke in corporate research, the technician who developed the frozen doughs. "Bilke, we'll need to show your product soon. When can we talk?"

Next Raef called purchasing for contacts in international and international sales. In 30 minutes he had products ordered from France and Italy, San Francisco, Chicago, and dozens of stores in the area.

Then he ran back to the office. "Alecia, one more thing. Could you schedule a meeting for July 15th? Twenty people. I'll get you the names. Thanks."

Over the weekend the basement operation morphed to its top floor of the new building rendition. Gone was the separated team grappling with old equipment in the glow of fluorescent basement lights. In its place Raef and the product developers united by the proximity of adjacent cubicles stretched along a bank of windows now thrived in natural light supplemented by high tech lighting that brought the sharpness of their non-glow to the work surface. Just down the open hallway the technical services group maintained visual and auditory surveillance of each other using the same arrangement. Away from the windows and inside from the cubicles the work stations spread throughout the spacious laboratory area: ovens, sinks, racks, work stations, and a conference table in the far corner not too far from Raef's digs. And it was all new.

Raef's cubicle consisted of a doorway that opened to a wall of window, flanked by a desk and files with a computer station on one side and a working desk and file cabinet on the other … all in grey or taupe or whatever the designer declared it to be. The windows overlooked a parking lot and beyond lay the woods with all sorts of wildlife. If he came in early enough he could watch the sun rise over the woods.

Monday, July 11th, Raef called down to shipping. "Have you checked to see when the container will arrive?"

"Good news, Mr. Burnham. In about an hour. Where shall we put it?"

"The freezer in Wing D. I'll work out of there. Thank you." Raef hung up and the phone rang. "Good morning, Alecia … Hepatitis B? That's serious. How's he doing?" Raef stood up and walked around his cubicle with the phone to his ear. "Hospital or home?" He adjusted his glasses at the bridge of his nose and watched another resident crow float to rest on the roof five feet above his second floor office. "When will he be back? … Is 'a few' like two weeks or is it more like six weeks? … OK. Give him our best and ask him to call when he's up to it—we'll limit our phone calls. He needs his rest. Two to four weeks. Wow. And tell him we'll just plan to delay the showing until he returns … Yeah … Thanks." Raef hung up the phone and collapsed into his chair.

Rats! Out of the picture. Major showing. No staff. Suck it up, Ace. This is the NFL. Alright, what do you know and what don't you know? Fill in the voids—you're no rookie. Learn the products. Learn the people. Figure out the objective. Create the message. Get going. Now. You wanted to craft a new career? It starts today. And if Adam were here he couldn't help—not in his condition.

Raef sat down and pulled out a legal pad. At the top he wrote, "Action Steps," and listed 1) review all products, 2) rate individual items, 3) rank potential for the American market, 4) interest probability for marketing, 5) include in showing, yes or no. On a separate sheet under the title, "Showing" he listed agenda, tent cards, timing, people needed, location preparation. After staring at the paper for a moment, he grabbed his lab coat and headed for the wing.

Two weeks later, on Monday the 25th at 5 p.m. Raef closed his briefcase and turned to call Jenifer. "I'll be ready about 5:45 … Club? … See you then." He hung up and turned toward his computer. A raspy voice reached out to him from the doorway. "Got time to give an update?"

Raef swung his head around. Leaning against the cubicle doorway stood a 150 pound sixty-ish man with sunken cheeks, dark circles around his eyes and light brown hair slightly disheveled. He wore Levi's, a wrinkled sweatshirt, and Nike running shoes that had covered a few too many miles and a smile that offered only teeth—no glint in the eyes, no joy in the expression.

"Of cour …"

Chapter 10

OPPORTUNITY KNOCKS

Raef blinked and swung his chair toward the door. "Adam! For you? You gotta be kidding. Anytime. Any time." He stood and started to reach out to help, then lowered his hands to his side. "Let's move over to the conference table. Coffee? Water? Anything?"

Adam shuffled to the table. "Water, please. Just stopped by."

In mechanical slow motion they sat down at the table. Raef looked at his folded hands, then up at Adam. "Should you be here? You don't look … so good."

Adam took a sip of water. "I'm stopping by to dispel the rumors that I'm dead. Okay? This is worse than the worst case of mono. It just knocks the stuffing out of you. No energy." He waved his hand. "Enough. Are you ready for the show?"

"I am, whenever you want." Raef described the products and highlighted the pluses and minuses of each. He outlined the fit of each concept for the American market and estimated the probability that Adam's people could execute a quality offering in the time allowed. "Now let me walk you through the agenda, people and conference room layout." Raef stopped and watched Adam take a deep breath and change his angle at the table. "Sorry, didn't mean to get that detailed."

Adam pushed himself back from the table. "No. Set it up and go without me. I can't help you on the product—you know the products better than anybody. Now, are you ready for some tips on the pitch?"

"Go."

"Pitch to Clements. He's the only voice in the room that makes any difference. Include Babick in the eye sweep as well as the national sales director, but Clements is the one you have to convince, so focus on him. And don't be taken in by 'nice'. He isn't. He's just charming, and that's different. Don't be misled by anything he says. When the meeting is over, thank Clements … then Babick and the rest for coming. You've positioned everything perfectly. They'll enjoy the show. Just don't believe anything that's said about next steps. They won't confide in you. I'll hear from them shortly afterward and I'll pass the word back. Understand?"

Raef brushed a hand across his chin. "My formal introduction to the real world?"

"I said I'd teach you. This is part of the learning curve. Just don't trust what's said in the meeting. This is the game within the game."

Raef leaned into the table. "Got it. Now it's time for me to suggest something: Get some rest." Then he eased back. "Would you like me to drive you home?"

"No. I have just enough gas left in my personal tank to make that trip. Thanks for everything, by the way. How's everyone else doing?"

"Everybody's fine. They'll all want to hear how you're doing."

He turned toward the door. "Tell them I'm progressing and that I can't wait to be back. It's true."

Jenifer parked the car in a vacant stall just outside Raef's office. She threw her gym bag into the back seat, slid over to the passenger side, and looked up at the second story window. Out of the corner of her eye she saw a black Pontiac back up and usher itself out of the parking lot. While she puzzled after the retreating sedan, Raef got behind the wheel. Jenifer pointed toward the exit, "Was that Adam?"

"The man himself."

"And …?"

"I've never seen anyone look that bad and live. He's lost 10-15 pounds, his eyes are sunken and pretty dark, and he's weak and tired. But he sounds great and his thinking is pretty clear. I guess he just needs rest and time, but brother! He's going through something." Raef took off down the curve, entered the cross street and headed toward the club. "He said I should go ahead with the showing. I think we'll set it for Friday. That's the 29th, isn't it? Hey, I need this workout."

*   *   *   *

Clements, Babick and James walked in Friday afternoon at a little after 2 p.m. Clements took the chair directly across from Raef, Babick sat on the chair to Clements's right, and the sales director took the one to Babick's right. The rest of the sales and marketing team scattered themselves around the rectangular table—no one sat on the chair to Clements' left—and Raef's team lined up behind him, like pigeons on a perch, ready to deliver products and arrange the table.

Clements chatted a bit about Adam's recovery, recalled some good times with Adam at the April national sales meeting, and turned toward Raef. "Are you enjoying our division? Getting used to the pace?"

"Yes, I am ... enjoying the division. The pace is something else, but I like it."

"Well, what do you have for us today?"

Raef handed out copies of the agenda. "The objective of this showing is to acquaint all of us with two segments of the frozen market. The information is formatted to help us decide whether to enter this market. Let's begin with the frozen batters and doughs concept: What's on the market and what we could bring to the product mix."

Raef's team brought fresh-baked products to the table, sliced the breads, handed out samples of the French varieties for individuals to break and to judge crust quality, and laid the individual fresh butter plates around the table for easy access. Clements and the rest of the business team sampled and questioned and enjoyed the presentation.

When Clements nodded that the first part of the program was completed, the team passed out charged water to clear the palates, cleared the table of all things baked, and brought out fresh china and silverware.

"Now, let's focus on ices and ice creams." With that Raef led the group through a review of the market: key players, opportunities, state of the competition, and products that might be opportunities for WFI to enter that market and make a significant impact. When the data had been absorbed, the products evaluated, and the discussions completed, the group sat back and waited in silence. Clements cleared his throat and smiled. "Good job. You've certainly given us a lot to think about. Everybody have a good weekend." Then he rose from the table and left with Babick and James in his wake and the rest of the entourage in trail. In fifteen seconds the room was empty.

Duggy walked over and whispered in a low voice, "Great presentation—how'd we do?"

"Too early to tell, Duggy; too early to tell. Let's clean this place up. I need a weekend."

Raef took the weekend off and Monday as well. Adam returned Monday and worked part of the day. Tuesday Raef arrived at 8, dropped his briefcase on a chair just inside the cubicle and walked over to the brewer to grab a cup of coffee—a first cup that had most of the flavor and at least half the caffeine of the pot. As he sat down to review his project file for the day Adam came around the corner, snatched a cup for himself, and motioned for Raef to join him at the conference table.

Raef watched Adam slouch to the table and pull out a stool. "You're back and looking degrees of magnitude better than the last time I saw you. Welcome—we were a little concerned."

"Thank you," Adam said quietly. "For awhile I was a little concerned myself, but the doc says I'm progressing nicely. Isn't that ... nice?"

Raef nodded. "Where do we start?"

"I met with Clements and Babick yesterday and I'm told you did a good job on the presentation. That's good."

Raef straightened. "And ...? Have they made a decision?"

Adam leaned forward. "Yes to your question, but the answer is 'No' to both the batters and doughs and to the ice creams. They liked the products, but they considered the barriers to entry and decided we don't want to take the risk. Sorry."

Raef swallowed and rested his chin on his thumbs while his index fingers formed a tent over his mouth. He lowered his hands. "I don't get it. The products are good. We could produce them on a large scale for sure. They seemed to enjoy the discussion and were quite upbeat. Yeah, some risk presents itself—it's a new area for us. So what's the real problem? Are they afraid it'll cut into their bonuses for a few weeks? What's the deal? They're always looking for new products—these are new. They're looking for quality—these are top shelf. They're competitive. We can meet the cost structure. What!"

Adam held up his hands. "Raef, I'm not up to this. Not today. Maybe not for a few weeks. All you have to do now is understand that the decision has been made, do what you have to do to reach your own equilibrium and move on to the next idea. Today, though, you have to give your notes and the product modifications you've developed to Frozen. The project is going to them."

Raef shook his head. "You're kidding. Frozen? What do they know about marketing in our part of the business? This is a joke. And yes, I'll be a good sport and give them the information. But for the record, this is neither career enhancing nor fun—and I don't find this at all motivating."

Adam slumped forward a little, drew a deep breath and let it out. "You do your job the best you can. Let them do theirs. Remember, we've received a few presidential awards in this division for outstanding performance. You don't get those for nothing. And this all happened before you got here."

Raef raised a hand. "Alright, I'll deal with this. But we'd better start thinking about what's next. I already mapped out our development program for these two lines—we were set for the next year or more. Now it's double clutch time to find a new direction. Any ideas, coach?"

"Just this: Remember, I warned you, 'Don't believe what you hear in the meeting.'"

Just before noon, Goody called and said, "Let's grab a sandwich. My office; say 10 minutes?"

Raef walked into Goody's office and pulled out a chair at the oval table that served as a conference table. Goody had already laid out his sandwich, napkin and coffee and was ready to dive in. "I hear the presentation went well Friday and that the division will make some decisions this week. Heard anything?"

Raef started to open his bag, but paused. "Not directly—but yes. Adam got back yesterday and met with Clements and Babick. These paragons of leadership are not live-on-the-edge risk takers—I repeat, not. They decided the products didn't fit our core strength so we're giving the project, the projects, to Frozen. Can you believe this?"

Raef finished opening the brown bag and began to take a bite of his ham and cheese sandwich when he laid it down and sliced the air with a karate chop, stopping the hack at a 45 degree angle to the table. "Batters and doughs and ice cream lite—what's the risk? It's in line with market trends. Our name lines up with the products. So we don't own trucks—we can work out lease arrangements for distribution. This would be new market territory for us—a real growth zone. What's the big deal? Wimps!"

Goody had just about finished the first half of his sandwich and washed the last bit down with a swallow of coffee before he opened his challenge. "We can all agree on corporate cold feet—happens all the time. What's the real point? What's causing you to fume about one more business decision that headed the same way

9 out of 10 requests go? This isn't unheard of, you know. Why are you making this personal?"

"Because this sucks. I created my own career problem, okay? I took my eye off the ball and got beaned ... demoted. And I want back. Look. If we introduce two new product lines in areas we're not even established in right now, our division establishes a foothold in frozen. This creates a new profit center, makes us highly visible, and says loud and clear, Raef Burnham is capable and worthy of a second chance." Raef paused and took a deep breath. "And they don't have the ... the ... stuff to say, 'Let's do it.' This was my chance. It wasn't same old same old. This was new. New area. New technology for the company. New. Now it's dead and there's no avenue of recourse. Clements has spoken. Big deal ... big ... deal. Man, I'm tired of this 'position is the only wisdom in town' garbage. Geez!"

Goody shook his head and closed his paper bag. "Well, I was hoping for better news, but we go with what we're given, don't we? Now, one more time—get back up on the horse. Adam ready yet?"

Raef pointed across the table. "And that's another thing. I've been in the division, what, two and a half months? I pull this together. Alone, with my group of one half-time person, and get verbal kudos from no less than Clements last Friday. All that work. 'Way to go. Good job.' And the conclusion? No fit? Gimme a break."

Goody pushed his coffee mug to the side. "Let's try it again. Adam ready yet?"

"I think he'll be fine." Raef leaned back in his chair. "He's tough, but you should have seen him last Monday when he stopped by to get an update. He'd been sick for two weeks ... Auschwitz, man. But he's rebounding and I think he'll be up to speed soon. Hepatitis is nothing to fool around with."

Goody looked puzzled. "Hepatitis?"

"Bad stuff."

"Yeah, I saw him today. He said he's weak and tired, but feeling better every day. I think he'll bounce back. But you," Goody pointed a finger, "have to refocus."

Raef started to clean the table, but stopped. "The division? Adam and me? Or just me?"

Goody rubbed the forehead above his left eye. "You. Things happen. You had a shot. You did your best. Your audience received what you presented and they made their decision. It's time to move on. Licking wounds isn't what we do. Move on. And it's actually bigger than that. Reinstatement at your old level isn't just about restoring confidence in your technical ability—that's still intact. The career management people have to know if you're going to play ball ... get in sinc with WFI leadership ... be a person they can count on. Part of that means you have to learn to accept some of the decisions that come our way for who knows what reason. For you more that for most of us, that is a big decision. Do you want to do that? Can you prove to them that you've changed?" He stopped and smiled. "Have you changed?"

Raef took a deep breath, exhaled, crumpled his napkin and laid it on the table. "Goody, you are aptly named. Thanks for your concern. I guess I know my challenge—but this is hard." Raef held his thumb and forefinger up, about a quarter of an inch apart. "I felt that I was this close to resolving my problem—to getting back—and they took the opportunity away from me."

Goody smiled. "What you say is true for half of your problem, but you have a decision to make about the second half. And ... and now you have to find another performance opportunity. Don't worry. You will. How's Jenifer doing with all this?"

Raef looked at the computer in the corner, then at Goody. "I don't talk much about it, actually. I think she's alright. She just feels that the whole thing was a huge unfairness and it bothers her. What can I say? I guess I feel the same way, but I have to deal with the reality—I'm not a '6' anymore—and the other reality ... I want to be a '6' again. She's fine. Thanks."

The two friends shook hands. "Say hello for us."

*   *   *   *

At the Majestic Pines Club southwest of Westphalia two men sat at the bar sipping scotch on the rocks.

"Relax, Mister Clements. Those two projects belong in Frozen and I have reasons to put them over there. Your division will receive one of the trophies for top performance again this year and your bonus will be bigger than last year. But that is guaranteed only if you don't take on any risky projects. Enjoy your largesse. Everybody wins."

"Fortune, you're treating my division like a cash cow. You're not letting us grow, get aggressive. We deliver our 10 percent growth every year ... and you're happy. This is a time for us to act. Restaurants is a big area—across the board it's growing and we could lead the growth. We want to try things."

Fortune took a sip of his Macallan scotch. "I am happy that you still have the fire, sir. But we like it when you deliver. Ka-ching sounds pretty good to us. We count on you to deliver and we want you to keep on doing just that. Phil, you are more reliable than the United States Post Office and we appreciate it. Let me ask you a question. If we awarded you the projects, who would you have assigned the task?"

"Adam, of course."

Fortune waved to a member who walked by the table. "And where would he have delegated it?"

"Burnham."

"Could Burnham have done it alone?"

Clements's face took on a deeper reddish hue. "So what, Fortune? Burnham's small potatoes. He can do the job. We give him some people—sure we promote him and staff him up a little—but we can make this happen and it makes good business sense."

Fortune nodded slowly. "And the message to the research community is that you can mess up and all gets forgiven—do not worry about it. You can be your own person, think for yourself, challenge management, go your own way and we will not mind. What does that say to the managers, the directors, even the vice-presidents? No sir, you know better than that. I do not care how good he is. We will develop those products and we will market them through your sales staff to your customers, but you will not incur project risk, and one of our selected people will receive credit for the development. I know you understand." Fortune took a final sip from his glass as the ice cubes clinked and tumbled. "Shall we join our wives? They are probably ordering the second course."

"After you, Fortune."

Chapter 11

▼

CRAFTING A NEW CAREER

"This doesn't stop what we do," Adam snapped. "You have unfinished work. First, close down the activity on frozen products and stop any other activity you've initiated. Second, meet with Frozen and transfer the project—give them everything we have. Then, meet with me on Friday to plan the next steps. I don't care what happened in your meeting with Clements and Babick—this doesn't stop what we do."

On Friday, Adam and Raef cobbled a list of 10 creative people who could meet with them to help form the new strategy for the division. Raef perused the list. "Adam, are we doing the right thing? These are creative people who can come up with new ideas, but this is a problem solving session you and I can do this without outside help."

"What makes you think so?"

"The issue is simple: We saw an opportunity to set the direction for the division and the concept got taken away. It wasn't a bad idea—Clements and the boys just rejected the idea. Now we need to define a new direction with products that will grow the division at the rate we projected. We can see our need better than outsiders. Even if they are creative, they're still outsiders. And if our effort is unsuccessful, we can still bring them in. Let's take a shot at it."

Adam made a note in his day planner. "All right, Monday morning. Find a conference room and order some coffee. See you then."

Monday morning Raef was the only person in the room when Adam walked to the board and picked up a piece of chalk. "OK. Who's our customer and what's the news?"

"Basics, OK." Raef thought of the primary target for sales. "First, our customers are the operators in restaurants, hotels and institutions—food operations that serve many people every day."

Adam wrote down "operators" and turned around holding the chalk piece like a small antenna. "True to a point. And ultimately it's the person who eats the food away from home. But we actually have a customer before either of those two—our first customer is the distribution system. We sell to the Syscos and Monarchs and Gamble-Robinsons of the world—first."

The two wrote and discussed and wrote and struggled over point after point. They reviewed the division's current operating plan and proposed next steps. They listed WFI's Restaurant Support Operations product line and wrote down their competitive strengths and weaknesses and vulnerabilities. They discussed food trends in the industry—where eating out is going. At 4:30 they put a name at the top of a clean sheet: Opportunities. And near 5 they sat back and looked at the conclusions. "Not bad, Raef. Not bad."

"Adam, why did we do this—I mean us—you and me? Doesn't the division have a marketing plan?"

"Sometimes they need a little help." Then Adam walked to the board and pointed to five locations on the chart for cakes. "Look at this—the priority item we've highlighted. We have a cake line of 18 products—so do each of our competitors. We lead the industry in sales, but if you look at our products and check the formulations you find that they're like individual signatures. Whoever handled cakes over the years put their own little signature on the formula by the ingredients they used—and more than one person did the work. One of these systems is the best. We should adjust the others to capture those qualities—standardize the cake mix offering. Get the quality up and talk about it." Adam stabbed the air with his index finger. "You know how we used to judge whether a cake was good or not good? By how it handled. Operators wanted to be able to pull a cake out of the oven, remove it from the pan in one piece, ice it in about 10 minutes, and move onto the next project. It was all about handling."

Raef shook his head. He always enjoyed the history lessons that crept into Adam's expositions. "Anybody think of tasting it?"

"Sweet. Sort of vanilla-ee. And a little bit moist. That's all it needed. Today, it's different. We have to fix the flavor, present a line appearance, be sure we provide moistness and standardize the line. That's a priority. So with our 3-4-5 customers, food is about taste—sure—and taste includes texture. So we have to create the best tasting, moistest cake in the business; but now it also has to handle well. Then you have a winner."

"Is that all?"

Adam sat down. "Nothing to it. Your work is cut out for you."

Raef looked at the listing. "Now what about your second question? What did you mean, news?"

"We call it new news. The corporation needs new product news all the time, but especially now—anything the sales people can talk about when they go into an operation. Another flavor, an addition to the line—it all helps. But a product that fills a need people didn't know they had, that's real news and it's better."

Raef stood up, slipped one hand into his pocket and pointed to the writing board with the pen in his other hand. "OK, let's take a few minutes and come up with some ideas. Give me an example."

Adam propped himself with his back against the table. "Here's one. Cakes are land-locked. They come in a pan. They're messy. What would make a cake portable?"

"Make it a cupcake?"

"Good start." Adam smiled. "Good. And that concept is our next product line. But it can't be a cupcake; that's too close to the familiar. It's like a cupcake, but with a point of difference. It's lower in sugar and it's twice as big and we'll build it stronger, off the quickbread flavor concept. Ever see those huge muffins at at the coffee shop? I'll bet their sugar-to-flour ratio is just about the same as a cake—and the flour might be just a little bit stronger, more protein. So, that's it. That's our new line. And those are your two new projects. Feel better?"

Raef finished scratching some notes and looked up. "Great ideas. They fit our core business; we can do this. But I'm a little limited in staff. Any help out there?"

"Sure is. Let Akins be your cake guy; you set the direction and let him provide the cake expertise. He's a walking information load when it comes to cake formulation."

"By the way," Raef paused as he lowered his jaw and raised his gaze. "I want to do contour mapping on the cake project—it's a statistical approach. So I'll need a statistician and consumer research; there's lots of experimental design. About 64 bakes just to start on the base system. I've been reading … I think it'll work here."

"Raef, sometimes I think you enjoy overkill. Is that really necessary?"

"You want to optimize moistness, strength, volume, and appearance. And you have a slew of variables—16 in ingredients alone plus bake time, bake temperature, pans, ovens, and the list goes on. This isn't overkill—it's essential if we want to distance ourselves from the competition. And how about the muffins—any help there?"

Adam nodded. "That's basic formulation work, systems and flavors. You already have Che. And how about we assign Sven—he's good at systems, and fast. I'll let Akins and Sven know. You can start making contacts now."

Eight months later the cakes entered the market. That August, marketing shot over the first sales data. Adam read the cover sheet and punched in a number on his phone. "Raef? Adam. Are you sitting down?"

"Just going through my mail. What's up?"

"Numbers are in. One hundred percent product acceptance in accounts. And first round sales increase of 15 percent. Looks like the cake's a hit. Congrats!"

Raef slapped the top of his desk. "Hah. That's one. Now for some good news on the muffins. I'm looking for some excitement there; and if they don't catch on we move the dial and step up to scones. One way or the other, we're going to be in portable food." He kept paging through his mail while he talked. Adam started to respond when Raef interrupted. "Hey Adam, hold on a second. Have you seen this memo from market research? They're going to publish the cake study in the *Harvard Business Review*. It's a case study in the use of designed experimentation. Wow. Interesting."

"Good for them. But I'm more interested that the line sells—and these new lines look like they're going to kick. Anyway, good job on all this. Feels good, doesn't it?"

"I'm just a little competitive, and two-for-two feels great."

The cakes sold in and kept on selling—better and better as the months rolled on. The muffins captured their market and became the product to beat for competition across the nation. Raef's team grew to four people and the team carved out niches for a line of gravy mixes, a line of hot breads, some brownies, and even created a pudding cake for a large national chain. When the team believed it couldn't handle another project, the division bought out a competitor and charged the Restaurant Support Operations development team to integrate the system into WFI's line.

"Adam, Adam, Adam. How are we going to do this? Look at the work load." Raef stood before Adam's desk wearing his work whites—white trousers and white shirt, white socks and white tennis shoes; the uniform of the labs—his clipboard of formula sheets resting on his hip. "We're stretched thin as it is. Rolling a whole product line into our system is … a bridge too far, I think."

"Close the door and have a seat." Adam finished a note and closed the file folder on his desk. "We have to talk about some other developments."

"Adam. I get real nervous when sentences start like that."

Chapter 12

▼

CAN'T MISS AT FISHCO

Adam crushed his cigarette in the tray. "You might have heard that our fish company in Oregon needs a research and development director. I've been working the system and I'm on the short list."

Raef laid his papers on the table beside him and settled back in his chair. "You what? You want to be a salt water guy? Join FishCo? You have to be kidding. No way."

Adam stood up and walked to the window. "I need a change and I love the West Coast. Besides, Brey says I'm a shoe-in. He needs someone inside that organization and he and I are pretty close. I'm just about sure to get it. In fact I think I'd have to … anyway, it's pretty much a sure thing. And, hey, don't worry. I've already talked to Babick about you, that you're ready to take over the division and he's agreed. This is perfect. You've received perfect ratings in each of the last three years. Fives, Man. I don't give perfect performance scores to anybody and you've earned three in a row—and the division likes the results of your work. Everything's selling. People are making money. And we're getting division performance awards every year. I'm in and you're in. That's my response to your concern about taking on the new line. Now, what do you say?"

Raef didn't move but looked straight at Adam and saw nothing. He just sat and looked.

- 74 -

Adam didn't move but slowly allowed a smile to emerge.

Raef blinked and jerked his head ever so slightly. "Wow … a lot has happened since we started this dance. Mindy's in college. Jake is graduating next spring and he's engaged. It looks like we survived the train wreck of '83 and that there is a road back. I'd say this is a surprise, but I'll take one of these anytime. Can I tell Jenifer about any of this?"

"Absolutely. I mean, understand that the final agreement hasn't been put together, but Brey's the research vice-president and he says it's a cinch. Tell her it's not final, but just about. Congratulations to you—you've earned it. Now we have some projects to handle."

Jenifer walked in the door five minutes after Raef got home that evening. "So what's the good news and why did I just pick up steaks?"

Raef took the bag and laid it on the counter. "There is a road back. Adam is taking a job on the West Coast. He's recommended me to Babick as his replacement and Babick has agreed. Is that great, or what?"

Jenifer smiled and put her arms around Raef's waist and gave him a hug. Then she leaned back, her smile dimmed and she frowned just a little.

"What's wrong?"

"Is this in the works or is it a done deal?" She stepped back and picked up an apron. "I don't trust these people."

Raef followed her into the kitchen. "In the works. Adam said Brey told him it's in the bag."

She shook her head. "I don't trust them. We can celebrate the endorsement—Adam went to bat for you and Babick agreed that you are capable and has accepted you. I'll celebrate that; it's a moral victory. But the rest? Not until I see Adam move to the coast and you take his office on the main stem. Sure thing? Never. I don't trust them."

Raef walked over to the drawer and pulled out the cork remover. "My cautious wife. Actually, I'm pretty much there myself. I haven't made any plans to move and I have plenty to do without that distraction. But … this is still exciting."

Two weeks later Adam walked by Raef's cube and signaled him over to the conference area. Adam stood at the windows overlooking the parking area and the nearby woods. He turned toward Raef. "Something doesn't feel right. I don't know. I'm not hearing anything. Something's not right."

At 5:30 that evening Adam came back to the work area and sat down at the table across from Raef, lit a cigarette, and looked up. "I don't know what happened. It's over. No change for me. No promotion for you. No WFI director for FishCo. I don't know what happened. All I know is that the president of FishCo, just before they made the announcement, changed his mind. Changed his mind! He decided that he didn't want an R&D director from WFI. Didn't want to put a WFI person on his staff."

"What did Brey say?"

Adam turned the cigarette in his hand. "What I gave you. He has no answers. And no apologies either. 'In the bag, Adam. You're my man, Adam.' Baloney." Adam took a long draw on the cigarette and stabbed it in the ash tray. "And I'm sorry for putting you through this. I was so sure …"

Raef rose from the table and walked to the window. The marauding crows were laying siege to the parking lot and two came to a rest on the roof line above the window where Raef stood. "I'm disappointed for you. But I'm not surprised for me. Let's call it a day."

Adam stood and began walking toward the hallway. "I think I'll pour a very tall one tonight. See you in the morning."

"Good night, Adam." Raef left his briefcase at work.

After dinner, Jenifer drained the last drop of coffee and placed her cup on the saucer. "Believe nothing of what you hear and only half of what you see; isn't that what my grandmother used to say? I never trust these people. I never will. How can they live like that? I'll never trust these people. That's the life you walked away from? Treating people like that? Good for you. I'd be ashamed if you were one of them."

Raef shook his head. "Well, honey. I didn't walk away from it, remember? They kicked me out of the club and I still want back in. I can do that work. I'd be better at that level than I am at this level. Sorry. I still want back in the game."

Jenifer leaned into the table. "I thought you said you didn't like for them to own you like they did when you were a 6."

Raef wagged a finger. "No, I said I didn't like that they owned any part of me like they did when I was a 6. To me, that's different. Besides, I think I've grown since then—if I were in that job they'd never own any part of me again anyway, no matter what. Goody says that I have to re-think my view on that if I ever want back in."

She smiled. "He said that? Either way, if being a 6 means becoming one of them—forget it. It isn't you. And you know what? They probably know that. What does that suggest?"

Raef took a last sip and pushed the cup away. "It's over—this door is closed. I had a shot. Got an endorsement. Could have been on the road back. Now this tunnel I walk through just got narrower … and longer … and darker. All my goals … I wonder …"

"You okay?"

"I'm going to be."

✳   ✳   ✳   ✳

"Quentin, what did you almost do? I am out of the country for a week and I return to find that my newest division president has agreed to release a quality role player and plans to promote an unqualified person. What were you thinking?"

"Fortune, I'm sure you refer to the FishCo issue. The CEO of FishCo approached Brey. FishCo needs a director of research; Adam desires to work on the West Coast and is well qualified to lead their operation; and Burnham has performed well in his five years with the division. Quality people move up and new situations energize everyone. It appears to be a win/win situation all around, don't you agree?"

Fortune Montag rose from his chair and walked from behind his desk to the windows looking out toward Round Lake. He stood erect and still and silent for two minutes. Slowly he turned toward Quentin Babick. "Quentin. It appears that Clements did not apprise you of certain management rules in place in your division. Perhaps I may provide you with the necessary background—but that is for another day. Today you need only know that Adam stays where he is and Raef Burnham does not get promoted. Am I clear?"

"Fortune, …"

"Quentin, are you a team player? We thought you were. You always seemed to be … I had to call FishCo. I had to explain to their CEO that he had to withdraw his request … take it back … make it so that the request had never been made. Then I had to deal with Brey. Research and Development. I had to … all because … Quentin, this cannot happen again. Adam performs. We need him. Burnham is good insurance for the short term, but he had his opportunity and did not perform. There will not be a second … that is not how we work. Do you understand?"

"Yes, Fortune."

"Thank you for stopping by, Quentin. You have always delivered for the corporation and I know we can count on you to continue to perform as we expect. Keep up the good work. You are having an excellent quarter."

"Thank you, Fortune."

Chapter 13

▼

TRANSITION

Saturday morning the birds were well into their mid-morning feeding when Raef awoke. After a breakfast of fried eggs, bacon, toast and coffee and a quick glance at the paper, he went to the garage, grabbed a rake and attacked the yard.

Five years wasted! Aarrgghh! What does it take to erase failure? Four, almost five years of perfect performance and they still hold back the obvious. Three top ratings in the performance appraisals. Tons of new products on the market—literally. Do they think this stuff just happens? Does anybody care?

Afterward he emptied the garage, hosed it out, culled out some pieces for disposal and put everything away. He walked into the house, washed his hands and toweled off. Jenifer was shopping and the house was still. He poured himself a glass of cold water and stared out the kitchen window.

What do I do? I can't quit.

He took a few sips and poured out the final drops, then laid the glass on the counter. *I have projects but no ownership. I have stability, but no upward potential. I have support but no sponsorship. I can't make anything happen. I can only put pieces in the right places so right things happen. So it's about perception.*

After a minute he turned and grabbed a pad of paper from Jenifer's desk and sat down at the kitchen table. He drew a line across the top and split the page with a vertical stroke. Over the left column he wrote, "Broaden Visibility." Over the right, "Impact." *If I do "A" what happens in "B"?* Midway down the page he wrote, "Grow," and circled it. Then he leaned back in his chair and laced his fingers behind his head. *Hmmmmmmmm.*

Monday morning the spring sun splashed across his desk as Raef lifted the receiver and dialed. "We have to talk."

Raef started talking as Adam came into sight, 50 feet down the corridor. "I spent Saturday thinking about … actually, I spent Saturday puttering around the house and cooling off, just trying to get my feet back under me. Anyway, while I did the grunt work I was thinking about westerns and horses. The thought occurred to me, 'You get thrown, you get right back on the bronc.' I think it's a line from a Louis L'Amour pulp fiction thing I'm reading. 'Get back on the bronc.' We have our work cut out for us."

Adam smiled. "Whoa. Do I get to share anything here?"

"Sorry, Boss. I'm just a little …"

Adam was a third of the way into his sentence, "We have to think bigger," before Raef finished his thought, "… pumped. Go."

Adam started again. "We have to think bigger. We're smart enough. We have lots of experience. We have to accelerate our program. We're small and we're used to moving fast. We have to use those assets to impact how the Center operates. The Center. Not just Restaurant Support Operations. The Center.

"First, the Center should change the way it captures information and keeps it current. The system is broken and needs replacement—you should lead that program. So, start the effort and let me know if you need any support from me.

"Next, the Center has a morale problem and the directors are asking for a team of employees, 5 and below, to suggest issues and solutions. Get on that board and lead it if you can get yourself elected. That's up to you.

"The intern program needs help. I'll get involved in that."

Raef was taking some notes of his own as Adam spoke, but at that point he raised his pen and said, "When you get that in place I'd like to put together a mentoring program for these people when they return to the company. It isn't that any one of us has all the answers, but I hate to see new people get sidelined or even bruised along the way, just because they didn't see some of the rocks in the road. You need a certain kind of vision to survive around here. Getting input from someone who's been there can't hurt. What else?"

Adam reached into his folder and pulled out a piece of paper. "And I have some product ideas. I want us to develop a line of healthy muffins, and I want the product to be as good as the muffins we have on the market today. No typical crumby stuff just because it's healthy. And I want us to win over the company's restaurant business; become the primary supplier. Next, I want to upgrade our cranberry muffin to be the best in the business. And finally, I want to explore high performance work teams as a way for us to operate. What do you think?"

Raef laid down his pen. "I think Napoleon was defeated in Russia largely because he overran his supply lines."

Adam wrinkled his brow. "What?"

"Part of my military training." Raef shook his head. "We can only do so much, boss. We have only so many people and so much time. You outlined a 5-year plan."

"And time was invented so everything doesn't happen at once. Sure. But these … we can do these projects. They make us better and they grow the division. I think we should start today. Now, what do you think?"

Raef stood to leave. "We could get hurt if you overpromise."

* * * *

Raef's family life was poised to change. Raef and Jenifer had enjoyed Jake's basketball career at Calvary and Mindy's volleyball successes at Neill, but both of the kids had grown up. In the spring of 1987 Jake graduated from college, joined a Big Eight accounting firm and that November, married. Mindy left Calvary College the following January, established her own business as a cosmetologist and three years later married. Jenifer re-focused her life to support Raef and keep the family together despite its increasing entropy. And Raef stayed active in their inner-city church.

Chapter 14

▼

CLOUDS ON THE HORIZON

Raef turned Monday's sketchy outline into a compelling screenplay acted out in real life. Daily, from that day in 1987 to the fall of 1992, he and Adam centered workdays on their daily 5 p.m. conference table meeting in the work area next to Raef's cubicle. Every day Adam came back from his office, poured a cup of coffee from the coffee maker on the laboratory bench, pulled out a stool from under the table and sat down. Raef presented the daily progress and together they defined the next day's focus. With Raef's success in changing the product summary system, his solid leadership of the center's leadership study, and his helping to solidify the intern program, Adam's division grew more visible in the center. And the new products caused a stir in the market.

In the first two years Raef's product development team converted the entire product line to remove tropical oils—converted the entire line to soybean/cottonseed oils—and became the primary supplier to WFI's restaurant group. In the third year the team introduced a line of healthy muffins and was in the process of reformulating a good seller, cranberry muffins.

"Why didn't we just convert the whole muffin business to healthy?" Adam asked as he sat down at the table one day in January 1993, lit up and blew smoke toward the ceiling. "Why didn't we?"

Raef exhaled slowly as he straightened the folder on the table in front of him. "That decision was made during the week you were out with your medical thing—the bladder cancer evaluation. The sales director took me aside and asked what I thought of a total replacement of the current line because he thought the new product was as good as or better than the current item. I was pleased he thought the line that good, but …"

Adam tried to erase the scowl but the sharp tone betrayed him. "So, why didn't you go with it? Do the change? It's lots easier to sell one item than to sell two."

Raef shifted on the stool and cleared his throat. "I went the other way with that—different market niches. Two markets to sell two great items. Are we …?"

Adam waved his hand. "Oh, forget it. I don't want to go over all that anyway. How are you going to tackle that cranberry problem?"

"We're going to focus on points of color and increased flavor." Raef squared himself on the stool, leaned forward and pulled a tray of cranberry muffins toward the center of the table. "If we can give the customer more visual stimulation by using more visible cranberries and more flavor to enhance the eating experience, I think we'll nail it."

"Something limiting you?" Adam squirmed in the chair and lit another cigarette.

Raef moved toward the open part of the room, the part with the air flow. "Industry practices, for one. And dollars, I think. The industry doesn't like to mix dried and fresh cranberries—big and small—and changing the can size could be costly. We have to fight this battle on several fronts. I'm on it."

Adam's squirm moved toward agitation. "Alright. Alright. This seems to be moving pretty slow. We'll talk about this again. Anything else?"

Raef thought a moment and looked at Adam. "Yeah. We want to show you some bars. We're concerned about some productivity issues, but we'd like you to see them anyway. And we have another idea—cookies, big cookies. It's a busy season."

Adam stood to leave. "Good. That's it for today. One of these days you have to tell me about why we didn't go with the healthy muffin line—just replace the current line altogether. Have a good night. Oh, one more thing. I'm thinking about converting our group into a high performance work team. What do you think?"

Raef looked hard at Adam. "That's the leaderless, consensus driven concept, right? The team makes the decisions. All votes are equal. A little Japanese influence, perhaps?"

"That's the short version. We have seasoned people here. They all have ideas. I think it would work."

"Well, good management always utilizes all the talents in a group—that's just smart. But I'm not comfortable with this Zen thing. Hey, Duggy's still here. Let's see what he thinks. Duggy, can you join us for a moment?"

Adam laid out his plan and asked, "What do you think?"

"I love it. I like change."

"See, Raef." Adam stood up and moved toward the corridor. "I think it'll work. See you in the morning."

Raef looked at Duggy. "You're a big help."

"What?"

"You kidding? Duggy, what's the point of a work team? Consensus management—composite opinion is better than any one person. Adam's an autocrat. It's part of his charm. He can't relinquish power when it comes to selecting where to go to coffee. How could he possibly make this work in the division? My concern isn't about us; it's about him. We can operate under any number of concepts. He can't. I just don't understand this—why he's doing it. And another thing, I better look for a job because if we shift to this business model, we don't need me. My skills are in leadership and project management. Hey, whatever. The kicker is why he's doing this. I don't get it."

"Change is change, Raef. Don't worry about it. Now, I have to run."

* * * *

Early in February 1993 Raef and Adam sat down at the conference table.

"Raef, the cranberry muffin project—where are we?"

Raef grabbed a 12-page memo from his desk and came back to the table. "We finished analyzing the test last night. We want to go out there and test again. We know we can get the berries into the can, but it'll take some process changes and the plant doesn't want to do that. We think it'll work."

"Make it."

"Pardon me?"

"Make it work."

* * * *

Raef made plans for the team to test on Tuesday, the 16th, in Machias, Maine. Since Valentine's Day fell on Sunday Jenifer decided to invite Jake and his family and Mindy and her new husband over for a beef brisket dinner to lighten the mood. Raef's travel even after all these years was a bummer for Jenifer.

Jenifer set the brisket on slow bake, placed the flowers on the table and rearranged them a half dozen times, selected candles that complemented the ivory linen table cloth, laid out the Lenox china and the Baroque pattern silverware, selected the silver serving pieces and laid them in order on the kitchen counter. Just before everyone arrived Jenifer surveyed the table, adjusted one of the napkins and smiled. The aroma from the baking brisket was beginning to fill the house when the door opened and the house filled with sound.

"Where's Dad?" Jake asked.

"He's traveling this week and he knew you probably would want to play games until late so he decided to take a nap. He'll be down in a little."

An hour later, Raef came down the stairs. "Who could sleep with all this going on? Good to see you." He walked around the room shaking hands and giving hugs and picking up the grandkids. After making the rounds he looked toward the kitchen. "Jenifer, what help do you need?"

Raef sliced the beef. Mindy mashed the potatoes. Jake's wife made the coffee and brought the potatoes and gravy to the table while Jake lit candles and Mindy's husband moved the chairs into place.

After dinner Jenifer served a vanilla bean ice cream, chocolate bars and coffee. Raef declined. "I hope everybody doesn't mind, but I'd rather not play any games tonight. Okay?"

Everybody helped with the dishes, put things away, completed the thanks and hugs and left.

As she closed the door Jenifer looked at Raef. "You alright? You didn't eat much and skipped dessert? That doesn't happen very often."

"No, I'm just off a little. I have a little discomfort down here," as he placed his hands on his abdomen, "And a little pain up here in my left shoulder. I don't know. I don't think it's anything. I'm just off a little."

"The abdomen. Is that pain or just discomfort?"

"Not pain. I don't think I want to run a mile or do sit-ups, but I wouldn't call it pain. The shoulder, that's pain, but it's not a big deal. Three or four on a scale of 10."

"Well, I'm going to read up on what could cause this. I don't think you should be going to Maine."

Raef sat down on the steps. "You know, Sweets, God gave us only one mother for a reason—most of us can handle only so much of that good thing. But thanks for the concern. I'll be fine."

Jenifer called the kids to see that everybody was well—no negative after effects from the food: All was well, so it wasn't the food. Then she checked her copy of *Harrison's Principles of Internal Medicine* and the *Mayo Clinic Family Health Book* as well as two other sources and concluded, "You have appendicitis."

"Thank you, Doctor. Did you ever have this obsession of yours checked? This dream of being a triage diagnostician?"

"I'm not kidding. They even mention the possibility of pain transfer. You don't have to have pain on the right side—it can manifest in several places. You have to be seen."

"Let's see how the evening goes. If I'm not better, I'll go in tomorrow. Everybody happy?"

Monday morning, Raef didn't feel better, but he didn't feel worse.

Jenifer looked at Raef. "You're what?"

"I'm going in to work. Then I'll go see Paul and see what he says. In fact I'll see if he can fit me in this morning. Satisfied?"

"Not really. But … OK."

Raef walked into Adam's office, still wearing his topcoat and carrying his briefcase. "Adam, I can't go to Maine—I'm not feeling well and I'm going in to see a doctor. I think the team can cover the test just fine without me."

Adam reached for the phone. "No they can't. I'm going. I'll let you know what happens out there."

＊　　＊　　＊　　＊

Dr. Paul finished his evaluation and sat on the stool next to the examining table. "Raef, I think your appendix has to come out. It doesn't seem to be an emergency, but we can't delay either. I'm going to schedule it for the morning. For the rest of the day, take it easy."

Raef slid off the examining table, dressed and sat down on the chair. Paul returned minutes later. "Surgery is scheduled for 7 a.m. tomorrow. You're not first, but you're early in the schedule."

"Who does the operation?"

"I like Dr. Silverstein. He's excellent. I've referred many cases to him. I'll stop by later in the morning just to check on you to see how you're doing. You'll be fine. See you tomorrow."

The two men shook hands and Raef walked out the door, down the clinic corridor, and over the walkway to the parking ramp. The sun was high in the cloudless sky as he turned west and headed home.

Shoulder hurts. Side feels … funny. I don't feel like eating and all I've had today is a piece of toast and a half cup of coffee. And I'm tired. Home. I have to go home.

Tuesday morning, Raef woke up several times. The first time was long before what the military called EMNT—early morning nautical twilight—at home, to prepare to go to County Hospital. The second time was 10:37 a.m. according to the clock on the wall at the foot of his fenced-in bed.

Raef looked around and blinked slowly. "What room is this?"

The blue clad attendant scratched a brief note on the clipboard hanging from the foot of the bed and smiled, "This is the recovery room, Mr. Burnham. How do you feel?"

"Did you get the number of the truck?"

"I'll write down, 'fine,' and I'll tell your wife that you're awake."

Moments later Jenifer walked over to the bed, kissed Raef and said, "It was gangrenous; that's not good. The operation took a little while, but everything's clean now. Gangrenous. Can you believe it? Any pain?"

"No pain. Just tired."

Two orderlies walked in and excused themselves. "Mr. Burnham, we're going to move you to your room. Dr. Silverstein will stop in to see you there in about an hour." Then, looking at Jenifer, the shorter of the two men asked, "Would you like to walk along?"

Jenifer nodded and the small procession found its way to the surgical floor, Room 535. The crew adjusted the bed, rearranged Raef's covers, and pulled the tabletop over next to the bed. "That's it for now. One of the nurses is coming to make sure everything is alright, and Dr. Silverstein will visit you on his afternoon rounds. Good luck."

Jenifer waited until the door closed. "I don't think catching a gangrenous appendix just before it bursts is about luck, do you?"

"Honey …"

"I know. Maybe you should rest. I brought my book. Get some sleep."

Dr. Silverstein visited that afternoon. "The surgery went well. It was gangrenous, but it hadn't burst. We got there in time. But you're running a little temperature—not much—so we'll have to keep you until your system catches up. Operations beat us up pretty bad. It takes a little to recover. I'll see you in the morning. Keep the fluids up and do what the nurses tell you."

Jenifer left to shop and get some exercise.

Raef laid back and thought about the test, the test he should be running that Adam was supervising—now. *Rats. I should be there. The plant is fragile about new ideas, but they'd trust us—our credibility is good. But Adam? I should be there. This isn't good. Adam doesn't belong on a plant test. Ever.*

Raef reached over to his platform, thought the better of it, and fell asleep.

The next afternoon Raef began rehab, a walk up and down the hospital corridor. *Where's Adam—what does he think now?*

After a week Dr. Silverstein released Raef and declared him "on the mend." During the first week on home-rest Raef rested and thought. Finally, he pulled out a legal pad and wrote at the top, "How to get back into the game."

He spent the third week walking around the house and working on correspondence from the office. On the fourth week he combined work-study with a program of walking on a track at the club. On the last Friday of his recovery Raef managed to walk 5 miles in 64 minutes. As he picked up his towel to wipe his face and arms, he beamed at Jenifer. "Healed! Good time. No pain. I'm back at work on Monday. Yes!"

That night Jenifer and Raef poured a glass of zinfandel and sat down in the living room. Jenifer looked at the glass as she raised it to her lips and took a sip. "Does it bother you that none of your work team visited you during your stay in the hospital ... or at home? I mean, Adam? Not even Adam?"

Raef ran his finger along the rim of his glass. "No, but it's because I'm not letting it. I didn't like all the visits right away at the hospital from all the people—I was sick. I was tired. That was too much. So I just left it at that. And the Ches came to the house a couple weeks ago—that was beautiful. But the rest? I don't know. But I can't do anything about that anyway, right? So let's not let it bother us."

Jenifer collected the glasses. "Adam disappoints me. Something's ..."

CHAPTER 15

▼

WORK TEAMS

The Ides of March came on a Monday in 1993 and Raef returned to work. After opening up his office, he walked over to the work bench in the middle of the laboratory. "Duggy, the cranberry testing last month; what are your impressions? Was it a success?"

Duggy put down his mixing bowl. "Raefy, I wish you'd been there. I mean, I really wish you'd been there. It was ugly! Adam was impossible. I thought the plant was going to throw us out." He pushed the bowl aside and turned toward Raef. "Words were said. Veins almost popped. It was embarrassing. What can I say? Adam was Adam."

Raef leaned on the counter. "Duggy, let me try this again. Was the test successful?"

"If you mean, did we get the cranberries in the can and can we do it again? Yes. And if you don't mind a body count—yes. But would any of the plant people sponsor us for Soph Hop king or queen? Don't be betting your lunch money. So we got our answer, but we paid a price."

Raef leaned a little closer. "Before I see Adam I need to know, 'Where's the project?'"

Duggy raised his hands. "Real simple? I'll write up the changes so you can convert the process for the next production run. When that happens, you get to handle it. I'm back in technical services where life is tough but people are sane. Who can deal with life in product development? You people are nuts." He wiped his hands and picked up a legal pad. "And oh, your seeing Adam will have to be later, and you better get your notebook. Adam called a staff meeting—it starts in five minutes."

✳   ✳   ✳   ✳

Adam stood in front of the conference room. "First, I'd like to welcome Raef back to a life of backbreaking work and golden productivity. Welcome back, Raef."

The applause made Raef jump. He turned to the group and said, "Thank you all. It's good to be back. Really."

Adam continued. "Now for the business of the day. We're going to incorporate the high performance work team concept into our structure, but because some of us have concerns I asked Darcy to help us out—to facilitate this transition." He lifted his gaze. "Darcy."

Darcy appeared in the back of the room and moved with cat quickness to the front. Her long straight dark hair swept over her shoulders in a lazy fashion. Her clear complexion and sparse makeup accentuated her straight nose, not too full lips and steel blue eyes. At 5'8" and about 140 pounds she could just as well have stepped on set to present Channel 4's 10 p.m. news as taken charge to host this discussion today. Her take-charge bearing was fueled by undergraduate training at UCLA followed by a top five finish in her 1986 Amos Tuck MBA class. Her three years in one of New York's top consulting firms led to her starting her own consulting firm, a group that now four years later listed five instructors.

Darcy placed her hands together at the fingertips tilted forward at her waist, looked at the 14 people seated before her and said, "Hi. I'm Darcy." She finished her 20-minute presentation about HPWTs and turned off the projector. "I need you to clarify three things for me before we get down and dirty. First, what concerns do you have about this program? Second, what's the single biggest obstacle? Third, what do you like about the new direction?"

Kelly spoke before Darcy finished the "n" in direction. "There's no way Adam can empower any work team to function independently. Adam," she looked at Adam,"You're an autocrat. You micro-manage. This is asking the impossible— not of us, you." Kelly looked back at Darcy. "That's my concern."

Duggy looked at Adam. "I've worked for you for what, eight years now? I've seen a little temper … a little volatility? I don't know how you're going to handle this either. I like change. I don't know if you can accept it."

Adam had never hired shy people and the thirteen didn't hold back as they offered point after point about their concerns. After awhile Raef looked around the room and turned to Darcy. "How do you sum up the concerns?"

Darcy went to the easel, picked up her marker and wrote, "#1. Operating style—change too much for director." She turned around and faced the group and said, "Tell me about the second point." A half an hour later she wrote down, "Adam." She took a deep breath and paused. "And point three?"

Darcy no more than asked the question when she had to pick up her marker and begin writing on the easel behind her. After the third page of ideas had been pasted to the wall around the room she stopped writing and asked, "Get the point? You people are not concerned about the change; you're concerned that Adam can't handle it. Adam?"

"I think we need to make the change—need to make it—it's essential. This is an experienced bunch of people. They can self-manage. I'm willing to take the risk. What's the issue?"

"That you'll change your mind after we commit and initiate," Kelly shot back. "Adam, we've been down this road before. You get enthusiastic about something. We buy into it. It dies because somebody had a different view on the thing than what you had. Your track record isn't great, you know."

Adam nodded. "*Touche*, Kelly. But I want to do this. We have to do this."

Darcy walked over to the center of the room. "We've been focused on the problem for about five hours. Process question, Adam. What do you want to do next?"

Adam stared at Darcy and laid down his pen. "I'm willing to go with what the team decides."

Darcy looked around the room. "Team?"

Three hours later the RSO 14 walked out of the conference room with an organization, a plan and a program that outlined how the 14 people—counting Adam—would function as teams.

Walking down the hallway back to the laboratory, Duggy caught up to Raef. "I've got a job, an even better one, out of this. But you; what are you going to do?"

Raef waved his hand. "I'm still wondering about Adam. Why do you think he's doing this? This isn't Adam. And about the other thing, I don't know. My first thought was that I'm out of a job ..." They walked a few steps. "Why's he doing this?"

Duggy laughed. "Well, he's Adam. See you in the morning. Remember, I don't work for you."

"Have you ever noticed? You never did."

In the morning Raef called Adam. "Hey, boss … Your office or are you heading this way? … Okay. Be there in a minute."

Adam smiled as Raef walked in. The two shook hands. "Welcome back. Sorry we couldn't talk yesterday, but I wanted to have that meeting with you in it, and Darcy couldn't work anything but yesterday. You look good. Can I get you anything? Close the door, please."

Raef took his usual chair. "Is there any message in this change for me?"

"We still need leadership. This just gets everyone involved in the process—spreads it around a little. But you do get more involved at the bench. That's for another discussion."

Raef shrugged. "I'm really glad to be back. This was way too long. While I was gone I reviewed all the projects and I see pretty much what we have to do next. Any concern zones on your end?"

Adam nodded. "Yeah, there are. That's what I want to talk to you about. I'm concerned about how you didn't handle that cranberry test."

"Didn't handle! I had what turned out to be emergency surgery. I was in the hospital for a week; been out for a month! Didn't handle? Give me a break."

Adam leaned back in his chair and placed his elbows on the arms of the chair and practiced fingertip taps; then pressed the index fingers to his lips. "Before the test I practically had to force you to set it up. You failed to be proactive. You didn't handle what you should have handled."

Raef relaxed in the chair and crossed his legs. "Well, sir, we have a difference of opinion. And if I missed something just maybe I wasn't up to my game. But I don't think I missed anything. I did set up the test and arranged for the plant to put in place practices they weren't comfortable with. But they agreed to do it. How'd the test go?"

"We put the extra cranberries in the can without too much 'mush and crush,' so I'd call it a success. But it wasn't easy. They were reluctant to change. It was hard."

Raef lifted himself to a more erect position in the chair. "It's always hard when you're doing something the plants aren't used to." He tapped his shoe with his pen and looked up. "My point is that the test was properly lined up—and it resulted in a successful answer. That's my point."

Adam leaned forward and laid his forearms on the desk with his fingers interlocked. "And my point is that you didn't respond to the preparations the way I expect you to. Let's move on."

*   *   *   *

Raef took the spatula from Duggy's hand and laid it on the counter. "Let's go for a walk. I have to vent."

Duggy looked at the clock. "It's a little early for lunch and this is going to look like we're goofing off, Raef—not that I care."

"This is a personnel conference. Legit, okay? Don't worry about it."

"Just remember, I don't work for you."

Raef grabbed Duggy's jacket and threw it to him as they both headed out the door. WFI's research center, perched atop a grassy knoll in the midst of a wood, was surrounded by a perimeter road which doubled as a walking track on off peak hours. Lunch hours sometimes looked like a parade of white-clad clones; today at 10:30 a.m. there were but two. The March sun shown bright in the southern sky and warmed the air to a comfortable 35 degrees. Springtime in Minnesota was the birth of promise.

Raef kicked a rock out of the way as they stepped out on the sidewalk and turned toward Duggy. "Adam thinks I didn't plan the cranberry plant test very well. What do you think?"

Duggy shoved his hands into his pockets. "Forget it. Adam's screwed up. His behavior at the test … he ticked off everybody in the plant; they almost quit working with us, it got so bad. Another thing, he hasn't been in to work before 9 any day since the test. Most of the time it's more like 10. I don't know, but it could be a little too much of the sauce. He doesn't look too good."

The two walked slowly.

Raef watched a few crows outside the circle hop from one cluster of trees to the next, their objective neither declared nor obvious. "For the past six to nine months I've repeated just about everything I tell him in every conversation. I thought it was just a habit, you know like teens do for about four years, but it isn't. He has a problem focusing. Well, our job is execution, not analysis, right? You've worked for him longer than I have, Duggy. What's going on?"

"I don't know. None of us do. But something's wacky. Hey, I've got some stuff in the oven and it's coming out in five minutes. We have to go in."

April and the first couple of weeks in May flew by as the RSO development group and the technical service group learned how to function as high performance work teams. Adam was good to his word and day by day withdrew as a hands-on participant. Micromanagement disappeared. Top-down direction disappeared. Direction disappeared. Adam almost disappeared.

Kelly, Atkins, Duggy, Raef, Sven, and a few others stood around the coffee machine on the 14th. "You know, I think this thing might work—this HPWT thing. He's actually living up to his end."

"I hear there's a conference on Gull Lake this weekend. Wonder what it's about."

"I hate spring management meetings. Always leads to personnel actions."

"Too late. Budget's set. Can't fix anything that's not in the works now."

"Yeah, but you don't know what has been in the works and just not carried out."

Finally, Raef chimed in. "We'll know Monday. Everything else is speculation and it happens every year. Let's wait and see."

*   *   *   *

Monday morning Duggy burst into Raef's cubicle at 8:30 and shouted, "Told you! Conference at the table at 9. Right here. Conference. No subject mentioned. Everybody-be-there-conference. Two bits it's some big change. I love change. Yeah!"

At 9:05 Adam walked in with Babick and Tyler Hoag, RSO's director of personnel. The three men sat at the head of the table. Adam spoke. "On Thursday of last week I was informed that my CT4 count has dropped to 204 and I'm losing count at the rate of 50 units every six months. When it gets to zero you have no immune system left. I'm HIV positive and have been for 10 years; now I've got to begin to focus on my well-being. So, I'll be taking medical retirement as of June 1st and moving to Los Angeles. My last day at work is two weeks from today. Any questions?"

At 10 Quentin Babick stood up. "Adam, you'll be in town for a few weeks while you take care of business, right?" Adam nodded and whisked the corner of his eye with the back of his index finger. Babick continued, "We'll be having a little sendoff between now and then—we'll contact you later this week."

Adam stood and looked around the room. "I'll call you later," addressing each of the team individually with his glance. The team nodded and slipped away.

Raef stood at the corner of the table near the entrance to the conference area. Adam thanked Quentin and Tyler and walked them to the hallway. Then he turned to Raef. "Let's go outside."

They stepped out into the full morning sun and ambled toward a picnic table set next to the trees. Adam eased himself onto the bench and exhaled. "I don't have the energy for a walk today, okay?"

Raef sat on the bench opposite Adam watching him the whole time. "How are you doing, really?"

"Not so well. It takes all I've got just to make it to work. It's all about energy; I have none. And the doctor's concerned that I'm losing count—I don't have much immune activity working for me any more and I have to conserve what I have."

"Why L.A., friends?"

"Los Angeles has a huge community with lots of doctors and state of the art medicine. Good support system for my situation. And I don't have to face the Minnesota winters with the colds and viruses that go along with it. One bug and I don't have the stuff to fight it off."

Raef hesitated. "Is this the first time you've spoken of your lifestyle here at work? Was anyone aware?"

Adam smiled. "First time. I should have come out a long time ago—many of my friends encouraged me to do it, but WFI is a conservative company. Hey, there're more of us around here than you think. One of these days you'll be shocked."

"Adam, I'm still a Bible guy and I don't see any place in scripture that condones the lifestyle; sorry. We've had parts of this discussion over the years. I just don't buy it."

"And Raef, my friend, I have many friends that read the same book you do and they see it differently."

Raef thought a moment, placed his hands flat on the table before him, leaned forward and smiled. "Back in the mid 70s when I got serious with the Lord, it was at a Jesuit retreat center called DeMontreville. The director that week had been to Calcutta and worked with Mother Theresa and her sisters. 'She asked me to teach her sisters to pray. Think of that,' he said. 'Talk about ... brother!' But he did it. He taught the sisters.

"Anyway, he was assigned to be the chaplain to Carville, Louisiana—the leper colony or whatever the term is for the hospital that treats Hansen's disease here in the U.S. In the course of his work at Carville he got to know a man who always wore dark glasses. Daylight or dark, inside or out—dark glasses. The man was cautious, inward, recalcitrant, shy—he was a withdrawn person.

"One day the priest saw him in the hallway and stopped to talk. The man responded with full sentences, looking the priest straight in the eye. As they chatted, the man removed his dark glasses and one of his eyeballs slipped out of the socket, held from falling by a strand of tissue.

"The priest listened to the end of the comment and asked a question as the man reinserted the eyeball and put his dark glasses in place. The man answered the question and said, 'Shall we go down to the center for lunch? I'm buying.

"Telling us this story, the retreat master paused and said, 'We became good friends that day and traveled the country several times since then. Do you know why I was welcomed into his friendship circle? Because he saw that I accepted him even after I saw things about him that he didn't know I could accept.'"

Raef lowered his gaze and stared at the table. He removed his glasses and rubbed his forehead with his hand. "Adam, I'm so sorry. I feel like an ass." He paused and looked at Adam. "In our society today, you're the leper. I knew it half-way through the story and I had to finish. I'm … sorry."

"Not at all, Raef. Not at all. You're right—you also understand. I'm who you say I am—especially now in my condition—in our company—in our society. You understand. Thank you for sharing that story with me." Adam drew a deep breath, raised his chin, and looked toward the building. "I think we have to go in. I have some business to take care of today and I have to pace myself. Sometimes getting up in the morning is almost more than I can handle."

They walked together back into the building and up the stairs to the second floor. At the last step they stopped. Adam held the railing and smiled. "Raef, you're going to do fine. But we should talk later this week. Can you set that up?"

"Done. Friday. See you then. Take care of yourself."

CHAPTER 16

▼

IMPOSSIBLE

Quentin Babick leaned against the wall in his office and watched geese practice takeoffs and landings from the corporate pond that never froze. The phone jarred him out of his reverie. "Yes, Adam ... Has to be one of us, right ... let's see, this is Wednesday ... 11 o'clock ... I'm free. How much time do you need? ... Let's make it 11. I'll block out an hour ... and I'll invite Tyler to join us. See you then." Quentin hung up and dialed Tyler's four digits. "Can you join Adam and me at 11? My office. Adam wants to recommend his replacement ... Good. Oh, and could you stop by now and go over what we're looking for in that job. I just want to review it."

Two minutes later the division's director of personnel walked into Babick's office, shut the door, opened a folder and pulled out a sheet of paper titled *Job Description—R&D Director*. "This pretty well says it all, Quentin. Technical skills—know product development and technical service and be connected in the technical center. Business skills—know the business process and be connected in the corporate and national restaurant community. Personal skills—able to lead and work with people. That's it in a nutshell. This thing isn't complicated and we know who he's going to recommend, so what's the mystery?"

Babick ran his fingers through his hair and locked his hands behind his head. "Yeah, but ..."

Tyler waited. "What? Who do you think is on Adam's list?"

"Short list." Babick scratched his head. "I think he'll pitch Raef Burnham. He rated him 'outstanding' several times and has always pushed his name. When the fish job opened a few years ago … remember all that? I think it's a short list."

"So what's your concern?"

Babick walked over to the window. "We have a new wrinkle. R&D management just entered the game. The center needs places for particular, exceptionally qualified people that need exposure. These people are like NFL top draft choices. Getting one of those now could help us get top people down the road. What if we offered to talk?"

Tyler raised his eyebrows. "To Brey's people?"

"We wouldn't have to accept their recommendation, and we just might gain some points for the future."

Tyler nodded, looked out the window and returned to Babick. "So Adam recommends Raef and you're saying we should still talk to the R&D—hear their thoughts? Who will they try to pawn off on us?"

"Why pawn off?"

Tyler held his thumb and index finger one quarter inch apart. "Because we're small. We're not considered technically strong. They'll want to give us some junior genius who will infuse us with technical strength. Then, when we have the genius trained they'll snatch him or her back and give junior a real opportunity while we're left to retrain another. That's the game. We're about to be a corporate training ground. Still want to play?"

Babick exhaled. "Got any names?"

Tyler shook his head. "All those people are below the radar at this point. Three to five years experience and a couple of promotions into the career. No real book on them yet—they're all stars. I'd just be guessing." He slipped his hand in his pocket, drew a deep breath and let his shoulders settle. He pursed his lips and his eyes focused on something in the far distance. "If this search wanders off in that direction, I'll check around."

"Adam will be here in an hour. See you then."

At 11 Babick's administrative assistant stepped into his office. "Your 11 o'clock is just getting off the elevator."

Babick closed the file and walked to the door. "Adam, nice of you to come. C'mon in. Tyler 's going to join us. Can Connie get you anything?"

At 11:15 Adam concluded his pitch with, "So I'm recommending Kelly as my replacement. She's only been with the company for a year, but she meets the requirements and has tremendous potential. She'll do a great job."

Tyler looked at Babick who sat with his legs crossed, his hands on his lap, staring at Adam. The air held still. Sound stopped. A minute later Babick stood up and walked over to the window, turned around, supported himself half sitting and half standing against the credenza—then planted both hands at his sides to steady the lean. "You're not recommending Raef? You've been high on him for years, pushed him as your successor in the FishCo deal, and now you're not recommending him? We've always assumed he was your second in command, your backup. Why the change?"

"He used to be proactive. Of late, I'm concerned that he's become a little … I don't think he'd push our programs the way he should. Kelly would."

"You gave the guy 5s. He ran the operation when you were sick. The sales force likes him. He delivers. Are you sure of what you're saying?"

Adam closed his folder and put it in his briefcase. "I've thought about this and I've given you my recommendation. That's all I can do." He snapped his briefcase shut.

Babick looked at Tyler and nodded. "Thanks for coming, Adam. This has to be difficult in so many ways. We'll consider your thoughts, but we'll have to talk about it. And we'll see you at the reception next week."

Adam shook hands with both men and walked out toward the elevator.

Babick moved behind his desk and sat down. "Close the door, please. What do you think of that?"

Tyler shook his head twice. "I don't get blind-sided very often, but when I do it reminds me to look both ways before I cross the corporate street. Wow. Something triggered this, but I just don't know. Adam's been pressing to do something good with the cranberry muffin and Raef's been working with the supplier. There's been a little dust in the air over that, but … and Raef had an operation right in the middle of that, but heck, he couldn't help having appendicitis. They have two different operating styles, but this? I don't know."

"Take it a step further. What do we do with the information? The recommendation?"

Tyler put his writing pad on his lap and scratched, "Call R&D-VP," and turned it for Babick to read.

"What'll he say?"

"My guess? He'll say, 'Let me talk to her, but I'd like you to consider my candidate.' Then we'll find out who they're considering for development."

Tyler stood up to leave and lowered his head. "You know what's really sad?" He looked up. "We don't need Raef's skill set if he's not going to be replacing Adam. And if he doesn't replace Adam, his market value drops to zero because every director will wonder why Adam didn't recommend him as his successor. He has no one to sponsor him now, and for sure, no one will even consider sponsoring him after this. Raef's dead. It's going to be hard to place him in the organization."

Babick stood up. "Tyler, if it comes to that, placing Raef is going to be your priority one job. He's given us good work for ten plus years. He may not be director material—and I'm not sure that's an accurate appraisal—but now, who can say? Either way, we owe him placement—so if it comes to placing him, I'm counting on you. Get me some time with Brey."

*   *   *   *

"You just rest easy, Adam … Of course you did the right thing … Raef was good as your number two person, but do you really think he could do all you do? Have your vision? Confront marketing in a strong fashion? Be one we could count on in difficult situations? … Of course not. You made the right decision."

Fortune flicked an imaginary piece of lint from is suit coat and nodded. "You'll have many good years, but you have to take care of yourself now. The corporation appreciates all you have done and our plan will take good care of you."

Fortune hung up the phone and punched a speed dial number. "Brey. I have something for you to consider …"

*   *   *   *

Raef flipped the switch on the overhead projector and the projection screen went dark. Only the cooling fan continued to run. With his back still turned to the now dark screen he gathered his pile of overheads and looked at the marketing and sales group seated around the conference table before him. "That's all, everybody. We start production in June and we're ready. Any questions?"

Comments floated to the front as the business team gathered papers and samples, stuffed random articles in their briefcases, and sprinted toward the door.

"Nice job." "Way to go." "We've got a winner here." Then the door closed and the voice at the end of the room said, "Hearing anything?"

Raef stood straightening the overheads, collecting the cords and wires and pieces of the projector, collapsing the top and arranging his file folder. He looked up to see Duggy leaning against the door jamb, arms folded, smiling. "Anything?"

"Duggy, in situations like this my wife always tells me, 'I just don't trust these people.' This time around we don't even talk about the possibilities. We do our jobs, keep the attitude, and let the chips fall as they may. The division knows my skills. I've performed for ten years. We'll see. I meet with Adam tomorrow about some next steps. Maybe he'll know something. But thanks for your concern."

"Concern! I'm just reminding you I don't report to you … yet. I'll check in with you tomorrow. I'm a little jumpy about the silence. Silence bothers me."

"Change doesn't but silence does? Weird." Raef watched Duggy open the door and leave, and watched the door close slowly behind him.

Thursday Adam called at 9 a.m. "Raef, could you meet with me now?" Raef stood up at his desk when the phone rang and began gathering papers and shoving them into a manila folder marked A—Discussion. "I know we're scheduled for later this afternoon, but I have to out-process and that's going to take some time. Tomorrow's my last day—I'm not coming in on Monday. Can you come now?"

"Sure. Be there in five minutes."

Raef took a final sip of coffee, grabbed the folder and took off for Adam's office. Midway down the hallway he took a deep breath as he slowed his pace and changed his stride to a measured cadence where every footfall suggested purpose. By the time he arrived at Adam's office the voice that greeted Adam was a rich baritone. Gone were any vestiges of tightness or nerves. He walked in, greeted Adam and seated himself across the desk. "How're you feeling, Adam?"

"Good, actually. Thanks for asking. We have to talk about some next steps. I've been busy since last week, thinking and talking to people. What I have to say won't be easy for you to hear, but I'm doing what I think is right. I'm recommending Kelly to replace me. Can you support that?"

Raef swallowed and cleared his throat. "Would you say that again? I'm sure I misunderstood what you said."

"Kelly. I'm recommending Kelly as the next department head for the division. She's too junior to make her a director right away, but I think it's a fit and I've already discussed this with Quentin Babick."

"He supported this? Quentin supported this lunacy?"

"He listened."

"Adam. Why in heavens name are you doing this? You've said for years that I'm your backup. When you almost did the fish job, I was the one who asked if I was really capable of replacing you and you assured me I was more than qualified. Now, when I really am capable, you do this? I don't believe it. I really don't believe it. Why? Have you lost your … Why?"

"Raef, you didn't perform well on this cranberry project and you know how important it is to me. I told you often enough."

"Adam, every project is important to you. They all rank number one priority. If you had 20 projects they'd all be number one. You can't differentiate—it's part of your charm and we understand. We work under those rules every day. And none of us ever give less than our best to any project we work on." Raef stood up and walked behind his chair. "We understand the rules. I've told you before and I'm telling you now, I did't mess up on that project. And any imperfection in my performance … I had a health issue. For crying out loud, you of all people should be able to understand that! Certainly you don't think you've been on top of your game for the past year—past two years? Who's been covering you all this time? C'mon, man. What are you thinking?"

Adam stayed in his chair. He didn't move. "I just don't think I want to saddle you with this job. Dealing with Quentin. With sales. With the system around here. You'd get killed. Nope. I've recommended Kelly and it was the right thing to do. And I expect you'll support the decision when it is announced."

Raef loosened his shirt collar. "What right have you to expect anything? This is betrayal … But what recourse …?"

Adam exhaled and seemed to shrink a little into his chair. "If it's any consolation, I only recommend. Quentin decides. And that could take some time."

Raef picked up his folder and moved toward the door. "Thanks. I'll see you at your reception. Anything else?"

"I made the right decision."

"Wrong." Raef fixed his steady gaze on Adam; neither man blinked. Raef walked out of the office and headed straight to his car. He didn't clear his desk. He didn't turn off his computer. He didn't shut off his light. He didn't tell anyone he was going. He just left.

Clouds that started to form that morning had darkened over the noon hour and now poured their tears as Raef sped along the white-capped lake toward home. Lightning in the distance and its rolling thunder morphed to brilliant streaks that split the sky and instant explosions that shook the car and left a penetrating blackness that was lighter than Raef's mood. *The man is an idiot. Whoever listens to this kind of advice is too stupid to live. I'd be ashamed to be so dim-witted. I'd be ashamed to have a dream ... such an I.Q. AAARRRGGHH!*

Raef pulled into the garage and pushed the button to close the door as he walked into the house. "Jenifer?"

"I saw you coming so I'm making some tea, and I'm trying a new recipe for a banana quickbread—want ... Ohhhhh. You don't look so good; are you okay?"

"Let's have the tea and I'll narrate the latest chapter in this saga we call my 'end of the dream' story."

Raef described the meeting with Adam and moved to the final statement. "I just don't think I want to saddle you with this job," he says. "Dealing with Quentin. With sales. With the system around here. Nope. I've recommended Kelly and it was the right thing to do. And I expect you'll support the decision when it is announced." Raef shook his head. "Does he think it's been any picnic dealing with his idiosyncrasies for ten years? Can you believe it? And he said again later that it was the right thing to do. Incredible. I'm ... at my wits end."

Jenifer stood and reached for the tea. She poured a second cup for Raef and warmed her own cup and placed the pot back on the holder. "I told you. I just don't trust these people. Who knows what the reasons are for the decision. They do what they want. But it's so unfair. I've told you that before and I'll say it again. You work so hard. And I just don't understand. I don't understand at all." Then she thought a little and looked up. "Is that the final word?"

"No. Adam made the recommendation to Quentin, and Quentin usually listens to him. But even if Quentin were leaning toward me, now he'd have to pause and wonder why Adam has quit supporting me after 10 years of solid backing. And it would be known that Adam hadn't recommended me. If I didn't have a champion before, I sure don't have one now. So Quentin would be appointing an R&D leader on his own—he'd be sponsoring me, and he doesn't do that. So he'll lean on Brey for advice, suggestions, and I'm not part of the bunch being groomed for future leadership ... it's over. Rats. But it has to play out. So we wait."

"Maybe you should meet with Babick." Jenifer stood still and shook her head. "I don't know." She picked up the dishes. "Now more than ever, I don't trust these people."

Friday the division gave Adam a farewell reception in the R&D cafteria. A few people stopped by to offer best wishes. Quentin gave his speech. And Adam closed out his career at WFI. He left the building at 4:30 and took Monday off as a vacation day. Adam's days at WFI were history. And Raef was selected to run product development until the division selected Adam's replacement.

✳   ✳   ✳   ✳

During the next two weeks Adam played host to the meeting of two worlds, his work team and his social set, while he readied his goods for sale and the move. The two worlds that had never met—in fact, one of them didn't even know the other existed.

During the next two weeks, Raef and Jenifer joined Adam and his friends for coffee and tea and showings. The team helped mark tables and china and silverware for his moving sale. Work friends and social friends talked and laughed and shared stories of intertwined worlds that had woven a strange tapestry over the semi-silent twenty plus years. Adam closed his days in Westphalia with style and purpose.

Finally, at the end of a long two weeks, a long final day of sales and packing, a hurried dinner, and lots of conversation with Adam's many co-workers and friends, Raef turned toward Adam and said, "Jenifer and I have to leave."

"I know." Adam rose and took Jenifer by the elbow. "Let me walk you to the door."

Raef looked at his slightly stooped friend of twenty-some years. "You all set?"

"Yup. House's sold. Going to ship the car with my stuff—WFI's paying for it. I arranged to be on medical retirement so I'm financially taken care of. And I'm out of here tomorrow."

When they arrived at the door Adam kissed Jenifer on the cheek and shook hands with Raef. Then he paused a moment and stepped forward, gave Raef a hug and sat down on a bench near the door. "And I'm so tired. I need the rest. Thanks for everything—both of you. I appreciate all you've done."

"Will you be coming back for a visit?"

"I think not. Goodbye and be well."

The next day Adam left for L.A. He shed no tears.

Chapter 17

▼

THE REPLACEMENT

"Hoag!"

Five steps and seven seconds later, Tyler stood in the doorway of Quentin Babick's office. "Yes, sir. What's up?"

Babick, standing in the middle of his office pointed to the phone. The veins on his neck bulged. "What's up? What's up is that Brey appreciates so much that we've asked for his input that he's now weighing in on the decision. In fact he's interviewed Kelly and found her pleasant, intelligent, a fine choice to watch for the future and he certainly has no problem with her running technical services for us ... but ... but he's also determined that she's not ready for significant leadership for a few more years. In fact, he's concluded that she needs experience in one of the main line divisions so he's looking into where she'll fit." He paused and drew a deep breath. "And now we're going to lose her also!"

Tyler waited a moment, then another. "What's Brey offered?"

"For now, since she doesn't fit into his immediate grand scheme he said, 'Why don't you keep Kelley for the transition—I don't want you to be understaffed' ... and he's offered us Segath. I thought, 'Who's that, some star floating just under the personnel radar?' So I asked, 'Boy or girl?' And he said, 'Does it matter?'"

Tyler smiled. "What do you know about the candidate's credentials?"

Quentin's voice returned to normal. "The background is okay. Bachelors in Chemical Engineering from Ohio State. Masters in Foodscience from the University of Minnesota. Dropped out of life a few years earlier but seems to have a solid track record within the company since coming here in '88. I think 'not so bad', but I'd like you to nose around and see if there's any bad baggage, okay?"

"When do you need the information?"

"By 2 today. I'm interviewing him then."

"So it's a 'him,' not that anybody cares."

At 3 Quentin buzzed his administrative assistant. "Could you have Hoag come in and meet Segath? Then arrange for our sales, and marketing people to meet with him this afternoon also. Set the schedule. Let's get this done."

At 6 Quentin called a meeting for his key staff. "What do you think? Can this guy do the job? Do we want him or should we press for someone else?"

From across the table, James spoke as he looked around the room. "What happened to Raef Burnham? I thought he was a given. I've let the sales group know my guess on this and encouraged them to work directly with Burnham whenever they had a question. We haven't had any issues in the month we've done this. Why switch?"

Babick looked at his sales director. "Adam didn't recommend him. He recommended ... someone else. I don't know Adam's reasons, but if Adam didn't want to support him, I'm sure in no position to pick him. And Brey has other ideas."

The marketing director pointed to a stack of memos on Quentin's desk. "In your in-basket you'll find about five active projects and our plan for the next year. Burnham and his people are well underway, the early testing looks like we have winners here, and changing leadership in R&D isn't going to make this go better. We have a pretty good track record. Let's not screw it up."

Babick cleared his throat and looked at his HR director. "Tyler, help me out here. We all agree Raef's been doing a good job. Up until Adam failed to recommend him as his replacement, we all assumed Raef was the backup. Now we have clutter and an R&D-VP who actually wants to be involved in filling that job. I'm not in a position—again, not in a position—to appoint Raef under these conditions. So what do we recommend? Of course, Segath was okay, but is that what we want to do?"

Tyler raised an index finger and both eyebrows. "I have a thought. Let's put the entire transition on 'hold' for awhile. Just run with what we have. Raef can run product development and Kelly can supervise technical services. It gives us time to sort this out and get comfortable with the change we recommend. Anything else?"

Quentin looked at the group. "Yeah, one. Raef is gone and I have to tell him. It may not be now, but when this all shakes out, he's going to be somewhere else. Adam didn't recommend him and we don't need two leaders with the same skills doing one job. We owe him solid placement. Tyler, be sure Raef gets a solid position. Get on it."

Tyler scratched some notes and slid a sheet over to Quentin. "No to Segath—tell Brey. Meet with Raef—no future in RSO. Raef still has a job until new position found. Hoag assigned as Raef's coach."

Quentin nodded. "Thank you everybody. Sorry it got so late." Quentin poked his head around the corner to see his assistant still at her desk. "Don't you ever go home?"

"I go when you go. What do you need?"

"Ask Raef Burnham to see me Friday morning; let's say about 10. Thank you. And ... go home."

* * * *

Friday morning Raef arrived ten minutes early for his appointment. He sat down in the visitors' section, picked up the current *Business Week* and opened the magazine to this week's feature article. Tyler walked by and glanced at Raef. "Let's see. The lead article is *Techie Tracks Trends*. Kidding. Just kidding. Here to see Quentin?"

"His call. Are you joining us?"

"No. I have a conference call at 10 o'clock with manufacturing. Catch you later."

Just then the door to Quentin's office opened and his business team filed out. "Raef, glad you could make it. C'mon in and have a seat." Raef stepped inside, laid his briefcase next to the chair and sat down with his back to the door. Quentin closed the door and took the chair opposite, his back to the window.

Raef looked toward the trophy on Quentin's bookcase. "Congratulations on the division's award—our tenth, right? You have to feel good about that."

Quentin smiled. "I do. But I just get to blow the whistle and say 'stop' or 'go.' You people do all the work. I'm happy the company recognizes your success. But I want to talk about some other things." He settled back in his chair. "We all have hated to see Adam go. And we're going to miss him. Raef, you've done an outstanding job all the years you've been with us—and we appreciate that. But now we have to appoint new leadership to replace Adam, and we're going to go outside the division—become part of the bigger picture in research. Until the new leadership is in place, we want you to stay on and direct things just the way you've been doing; you have a job until you find a position that suits you—there's no rush. Tyler will work with you and the organization to see that this all happens in a timely manner. I hope you understand."

Raef fixed his stare on Babick and moved his head from side to side very slowly. "Well, I don't really … understand. I've earned top ratings. We've delivered quality products—on time. My team has supported the plants, marketing and sales perfectly for ten years. Never have we missed a deadline—not once. We're proactive. We bring ideas to the teams all the time. What's the problem? None exists. No, I don't understand—I really don't. This is bogus."

Babick didn't blink. "Adam was your champion. He touted you from your first day in the division as his heir apparent. When he went after that job at FishCo he secured our agreement that you were his replacement if the change was needed. Remember? Now, when it really was time for him to leave, he recommended someone else. And now Brey has asked that our R&D leadership be part of the center's management development cycle—he wants to mainstream our talent pool. Quite frankly, I think there's some merit there. It gives us access to the best and the brightest for the future. But that's my problem for another day. Anyway, Adam left and said we should select someone else. We just don't know who. And we don't know when."

Raef started to rise from the chair, then settled back and took a deep breath. "What …?"

Quentin leaned forward, his elbow on the table and the palm of his hand gestured open. "You've done a wonderful job and we're very pleased. But Adam didn't recommend you and he's the one in the best position to make the recommendation. We have to take that into consideration."

Raef felt his heart leap. "This is a joke, right? Adam's mind left a long time ago—he was very sick! We've been covering for him for six months to a year while he struggled with whatever he struggled with—saying everything twice or three times and then explaining it all over the next day, making the decisions for him and getting his endorsement—and now you have to take his 'failure to recommend' into consideration. Think about it. His immune system … his CT4 count that's supposed to be what, a gazillion is down to 204 and he's losing ground at the rate of 50 units every six months—he'll have no immune system left in two years. What would you feel like? Where would your head be? The guy was hurting and his focus was on other stuff. Geez! What's up with this? You're kidding, right?"

"Raef, I'd actually hoped you'd take this decision better; in a little more professional manner."

"Professional manner? C'mon, Quentin." Raef leaned into the table. "This is my career we're talking about. I get overlooked here and say goodbye to ever playing at a decent level. You're letting Adam in his condition make your decision for you? This is ridiculous."

"But, if I may continue?" Babick raised his hand a few inches off the table top. "Well, here it is. Adam will be replaced by someone not in the division. Filling the position will take some time. In the interim you retain your job while you look for another one … outside the division. Tyler will assist you in your search—starting today. Thank you for helping us out in the transition."

Raef nodded his head once, "I understand," stood, and walked out.

As Raef headed for the elevator he walked past the partially opened door to Tyler Hoag's office. Tyler was just hanging up the phone. "Raef!"

"You called, Master."

"You've talked with Quentin?"

"I understand you're my new handler. Do you mind if I shut the door?" Raef closed the door and turned toward Tyler. "What's with this crap? I'm peeved. This is beyond unfair. I did the job and more. Adam was a basket case and we covered for him forever. And now his words from beyond whatever fog that drove his actions—his words dictate my future. What kind of addled activity is this?"

Tyler closed the folder on his desk and raised a hand. "Raef, settle down. You've forgotten the first rule of big business: The corporation doesn't love you. The corporation's first job is to ensure its own survival. You do good work that benefits us? You get paid and you get to stay. Those are the rules. But the job you want says you have to be a company man—the corporation has to be sure that you will always act in the corporation's best interests. With you, that's not an automatic. You have an independent streak that, to some, is scary. Maybe Adam saw that—maybe someone else did. He may have been concerned for you—that in a month or a year or five years you'd be asked to do some things that he knew you wouldn't agree with. You'd balk, and you'd be gone. Some of us can act without concern in some areas—you can't. Either way, Adam didn't recommend you and no one big enough is going to champion your case to get you reinstated at the "6" level. It's that simple. You wanted to play in the big leagues and this is what they're like. Now do you understand?"

Raef changed position in the chair for the third time. "Tyler, you and I have played a lot of handball over the years and I'll take out my frustrations with you on the court, but this is baloney. I can do the job. Hey, I do the job every day now—been doing it for 10 years. Heck, I've been doing Adam's job for six months; maybe a year, maybe as many as two years. This is wrong."

Tyler waved a hand. "Hold it. The job's only part of the problem and you know it. When you were demoted you had a two-part problem; I'm sure you realized that. You took care of the first part—you re-established your technical credibility. But there's that second part that Adam was concerned about—where you prove to the corporation that they can trust you to always act in its best interests. You haven't done that and you're in a Catch-22. You need a sponsor to prove yourself and you'll not get a sponsor until you prove they can trust you." Tyler folded his hands on his desk and leaned forward. "Now, given that you know what that takes and you're politically saavy enough to know who you could target, why haven't you done that? Or do you even want to? I think you have some soul searching to do."

Raef leaned back in the chair and bit the inside of his lip. Tyler let the words hang in the air … and hang … "Are you ready to move on? That's what we're about, you and I, now. Our task is to get you to the next position—one that uses your skills and provides the best opportunity to reach your goals as you define them. I propose we meet once a week until something freezes over or until you find that new position, whichever happens first. Let's start Monday, your conference table, 8:30. I'll come directly to your office."

Raef shook his head. "Do I have any recourse here?"

Tyler stood up. "In Restaurant Support Operations, it's over and the fat lady has sung. But there are worlds beyond this little division, sir, and we're going to find the opportunity that awaits us. It all starts Monday. By the way, I was wrong about 'it's over.' You have to be the caretaker for R&D until new leadership is assigned. So, suck it up and play nice. I'll see you Monday."

*   *   *   *

That evening over coffee, Raef finished describing the day's events to Jenifer. She listened quietly and finished her cup. "Well, at least I'm not disappointed. Those people did as bad as I thought they would. Again they acted stupid for totally ridiculous reasons. Quentin is nuts. And Tyler—who's side is he on, anyway? How do they keep their jobs with dumb actions like this year after year? This has gone beyond unfair—this is criminal. A gone guy now defines your future?

Where's Adam to defend his actions now? This is 'Ring and Run.' I don't know who's sicker, him or the people who listen to his recommendations. Oh, I'm glad I'm not in the corporate world. Enough." She pushed the cup away. "Where are you with this—right now?"

"I'm surprised, but I'm peaceful. You know, Solomon—in the bible, Solomon?—wrote that if we consider every day as a gift from God and accept what He offers us, we'll live an abundant life. It takes some doing, but in this case … I've done what I can do. The result is very likely not going to be what I thought I wanted, but I'm relaxed."

Jenifer shook her head. "What's next for you?"

"I stay on the job, run product development like I've been doing, and generally oversee R&D until the replacement is declared; that could be awhile. And I look for another position—that could be awhile. In the interim they get eight hours a day out of me and I grow my talents with the rest of my time in anticipation of the future. I oversee, learn new skills, study, network, seek and be open."

"Given how you feel right now, what would you do if you were 55 instead of 52?"

Raef didn't hesitate. "Retire and do something else—I really have little respect for the leadership I see. Tyler's turning out to be all right, and Babick's okay—just owned by the system. I still value freedom as much as I did when I was demoted—they'll still never own me—and I'm starting to see that my perspective is probably limiting my career. But I'm 52 so this kind of speculation isn't very productive, is it?"

"And since you're still part of the youth movement, what're you going to do?"

Raef laid his hand on hers. "Sounds funny, but I'm not the least bit concerned. I'm going to listen to all options and pick the best of the few offers."

Jenifer pulled back her hand. "Why few? You have lots of experience, always deliver products and you have talents in many areas. Why few offers?"

"Age and tradability. The directors know I can do the work and lead teams, but that's not the issue. This is like major league sports: I have no trade value—I just deliver now, so I'm not tradable. But if someone wants the goods delivered now and isn't worried about the future drafts, I'll find a home. Goofy, huh?"

Jenifer stood up. "You mean putting quality products on the market on time isn't value?" She raised her hands and walked toward the counter. "I told you, they're all nuts. I give up. Do what you have to do. I don't understand your world at all. And you have to deal with this idiocy every day?"

"Well, sweetheart, this situation boils down to a simple prayer: Lord, we need help. First, that we do the current job well for the duration. Second, that You open up a good opportunity, but not too soon because I could use the rest."

"I agree with that. When does this new world begin?"

"Monday."

"What happens then?"

"I really don't know."

CHAPTER 18

▼

LIMBO

Tyler was good to his word. For eight months he met Raef every Friday morning at 8:30 to review notes and probe opportunities. In the meantime, Raef kept the product development train on its tracks. The division missed no deadlines. People resolved their own issues. And the division met its numbers, having one of the best financial years ever.

*   *   *   *

Fortune Montag and Quentin Babick met for breakfast the third Wednesday of the month—7:30 in the executive dining room. Today, Fortune shook Babick's hand as he walked up to the table. "Quentin, your division has had an excellent year. Congratulations. We're pleased."

Babick smiled and nodded. The two men ordered.

Fortune looked around the room. "But your development effort is still being led by a level 5 researcher." He watched his guest pour coffee from the carafe on the table. "You have a meeting at the end of the month. You will probably say something to your people about how this good year happened. You may even give some company stock as an award. To whom are you going to give the credit for this excellent year?" He continued to watch as Babick shifted position and took a sip of coffee.

Babick laid his cup down. "Sales, of course—the ones who met and exceeded their quotas. But, once again, we have excellent products. They were developed on time and entered the market exactly on schedule. The development teams performed admirably."

Fortune nodded. "So what are you going to say to your people? ... Certainly someone has held that organization together ... an administrator, perhaps?"

"Alecia Saunders has been superb. She's Adam's secretary—more of an administrative assistant actually ... was Adam's secretary ... assistant. But what happened was more than just administration ..."

"I am sure Alecia deserves recognition for her efforts. And I am sure no one in the division will feel badly about her receiving recognition for all the hard work she has done—especially under the trying circumstances of the past year." Fortune watched as the message sunk in. He watched Babick's eyes until the look suggested that he got it. "Thank you for all you do, Quentin. Always good to meet with you. I am late for another meeting back in my office—you will not mind if I do not stay for breakfast? I must run."

* * * *

On the last Friday in January 1994, Quentin Babick presided over the first monthly division meeting of the new year. After announcing the financial numbers and applauding the division's results for the past year, he handed out individual awards to a third of the marketing staff and half of the sales staff for performance excellence during the previous year. Then he turned toward the product researchers in the room. "For keeping the R&D program on track for seven months, never missing so much as a meeting notice, keeping all the programs on line and every project on schedule, we give our top award to Alecia Saunders, the R&D administrative assistant. What else explains this year's perfect record unless it's that she did her administrative task perfectly? Alecia, c'mon up and receive your 10 shares of WFI stock."

Alecia stood, stepped out into the aisle, and began to walk toward the podium. As she passed Raef sitting on the end of the aisle three rows down, she leaned over and whispered, "We both know that you should be receiving this. Sorry."

Raef reached out and shook Alecia's hand. "It's fine. You've worked hard, done well, deserve recognition. Enjoy."

Duggy, sitting behind Raef, whispered, "Thoughts?"

Raef half turned. "Later."

"And … and we have an announcement," Quentin continued. "As of February 15th a Ph.D. food scientist who used to run a food co-op will be joining us as the manager of research and development replacing Adam Irish. Adam's replacement is one of the leading new people at the research center, has five years of experience in the company, and brings a lot of drive and attitude to our research effort. We'll welcome him at our next monthly meeting."

Raef and Duggy walked to the parking lot. "You asked about my thoughts? If something doesn't break my way soon … oh, forget it. I need to get out of this place."

Raef burst into his office and threw his folder across the room onto the desk. The folder knocked over a dry coffee cup and slid to a halt next to a yellow note that flew off and landed on the floor. He picked up the paper and read the bold stroke verbless message, "Tea? 2 o'clock? My office." And at the bottom, "JM".

At 2 Raef walked through the open door to Director of International's office and peremptorily stated, "Guilty, Jan. So I haven't been keeping you as up to date as I said I would—sue me. Mea culpa, one more time. How're you doing?"

"Ah, forget about all that. I read the papers. Tell me your background. Start with 'Came to WFI in 1967' and walk me through the key points until today. Go. I have 15 minutes."

Raef stepped over to the credenza and poured a cup of fresh tea. "You promised tea, remember? Alright, here we go. I started in mixes …" Raef chronicled his career, punctuating narrative about products and processes with comments on people and places and times. After describing the seven years in the mix area he moved to explaining work on Sprout machines and Collet extruders and roller mills and fryers.

Jan stopped him. "You worked on Collets? Tell me about it."

"I had a crew back at that time, so I was one step removed from the total hands-on-get-sweaty-every day operation. Hey, did you ever work with that snack group in those days? No one could touch the machine when they were in control, but anyone who joined got better just by working with them. Yeah, we did tons of stuff when I was in the snack business. Why?"

Jan pounded the table and let out a laugh. "You want to work with us in International? We're all over Europe. We're expanding into Eastern Europe. And I have some testing in May in Singapore and Bangkok. Let's talk." Jan picked up his phone. "Margie. Please cancel my next meeting. Raef and I will be here awhile."

Raef and Jan discussed life in International, Jan's needs, what the job would require of Raef, and the matchup of Raef's skills with the needs of the division.

Finally Raef took a deep breath and said, "Let me see if I got this right. This is a small division in the company. You'll provide no staff so I'll be required to do everything for myself by myself. I'll be making trips that are never less than 10 days long and can extend to 20 days or more. I get an office in the middle of a lab—wrong. I get to share an office with we don't know who because you gave away the one solitary corner office to a Level 4 just the other day. And I should look on this as my golden opportunity. You're really gilding the lily here, my friend."

Jan nodded. "You got it right. Oh, there's one more thing. I need your answer Monday—I was on my way to talk to another candidate and decided to talk to you instead. Take the weekend. No rush. And if Jenifer has any questions, have her call. Anytime, actually. I don't sleep."

Raef shook hands with Jan. "Monday."

"International!" Tears welled up in Jenifer's eyes. "No. I don't want you out of the country." Jenifer was just putting the finishing touches on a Mediterranean dinner. She laid the chafing dish of sautéed olives and peppers on the counter, sprinkled shredded parmesan cheese over the top and, using a hot pad, placed the dish under the broiler for a finishing touch. "No. We eat international—enjoy travel stories, but live it? Here's how far I go: The cous cous is ready, the pitas are on the table, and the lamb is perfect. That's it. Now, let's enjoy the meal and talk about all this later, OK? International!"

Raef walked behind Jenifer, put his arms around her and kissed her on the neck. "Whatever you say, my dear. But we'll have to take a serious look at the opportunity in hand. And I don't feel like talking about it now either. Let's enjoy."

Out of nowhere Jenifer produced two candles and set them perfectly on the center of the table, two glasses and a basket supporting a reclined Chateau St. Michel Merlot. Then she arrayed the serving dishes and walked over to the sound system where the Berlin symphony began playing Mozart. Raef sat down. "I'm impressed. What's the occasion?"

"I don't know. I just felt like it. Must be the 'tweener' solstice. Does that happen around February 4th?"

They finished the last morsel and laid down their napkins. Jenifer stepped over to the coffee and poured two cups, then uncovered a small plate of baklava and placed it on the counter. Raef broke the silence. "Shall we chat?"

Jenifer paused. "Let's go into the other room." They took their coffees, napkins and the dessert into the living room and sat down on the floor next to the coffee table. She took a sip. "Well?"

Raef paused. "I need your thoughts. This is an opportunity, but some parts … I don't know." He proceeded to explain the job; 30 percent travel and what he thought life with Jan and his team would be like. Along the line he remembered that Jan reports to Mitch Jordan and that Goody Metcalf had recently joined Mitch's division also.

"Really? Hmmm. Anything else? What about your office, staff, things like that?"

"Well, that's quite a change, or at least it will be an adjustment. I have no staff. Whatever I do, I do. And I'll share a small cubicle—International puts two people in one work space. It saves money, and someone's gone a third of the time anyway. Hey, enough for tonight—I don't really feel like doing this in depth, do you? We have the weekend to think about it, but Jan wants an answer Monday. He also said that if we—actually he said if you have questions, he's always up for a call, day or night. And one more thing. They replaced Adam with one of the new Ph.D. food scientists. So my days in the division are numbered, no matter what."

Saturday morning Raef worked in his study. The second floor study looked out over wetlands, but a 30-foot cedar obscured part of the view as the tree provided shade from the winter sun lying 24 degrees to the horizon. Raef started to write, but put down his pen and put his feet up on the adjacent table and sat gazing out the window.

International—what concerns me? Smaller even than Restaurant Support Operations. No staff. No office. Don't know the products. Going to places where I don't know the language, don't know the customs. Don't even know how to run half of the systems I'll be in charge of. Working with people whose skills are way less than in our plants. Traveling alone. Sensitive stomach.

International—what do I like? Adventure. New products. New people. New places. No staff to worry about—no personnel issues. No politics. Help is as near as the phone. I've done tough before—I can do it again. Jan's a good boss. Mitch's an old friend.

International. What the heck. I can make it happen here. Bring it on!

Sunday morning Raef and Jenifer drove around the lake on their way to church. Jenifer reached over and placed her hand on Raef's forearm which was resting on the console between them. "I think you should take the job."

Raef jerked his head to look at Jenifer. "Wh …?" and paused. "So do I, but what're your reasons? I mean, we haven't even talked about it since Friday."

"We've been at peace with indecision, this 'no doors opening' thing, for something like eight months. Friday RSO takes a new direction in its leadership and Jan asks you to do some work where you'd be needed and could get a fresh start. I don't know. But I'm at peace with saying okay, so why not go with it if you think it's the right thing to do?"

"I took a different route but came to the same conclusion. Monday, Jan gets a call. Wow!"

Jenifer laid her head against the window. "Raef, are you still chasing the dream? Can this get you there?"

They pulled into the church parking lot and turned off the ignition. "I've never stopped."

"You're 53. Can you still be promoted?"

Raef picked up his Bible and cracked the door open. "I decided a long time ago that I'll never look at the numbers. I have a goal. They can promote me anytime they want. I'll do the work. I'll get the results. In the end, they have the power and control the outcome—I can't do anything about that side of the equation. So the answer to 'Can I?' is yes, absolutely. If I were 63 instead of 53, they could promote me as an honorary thing. They could do it. It would take a miracle, but they could do it. The real question is 'Will I get promoted?' and International seems to be the only door open for me to test the concept one more time. Let's go in."

Monday morning Raef arrived at Jan's office and it was still dark outside. "It's February 9th. Can I start today even if it's the middle of a pay period?"

"Sounds like a decision—congratulations. There you're redundant and here you're needed. Move your things down to our laboratory whenever you're ready. Welcome aboard. Let's go in and see Mitch."

BOOK THREE

CHAPTER 19
▼

INTERNATIONAL IT IS

Raef dropped a note on Jan's desk. It read, "RB's here." Jan's office and the offices of the other seven directors flanked Brey's command post which anchored the middle of a concave wall a football field long. Floor to ceiling and end to end glass, the wall expressed the architect's concept that the leaders looked out together and, from varying angles, saw the world—together. Raef scanned the acres of snow-covered tundra that stretched to the far woods. After a moment he reminded himself to breathe.

He walked out of Jan's office and navigated the sea of administrative desks that separated him from the International Division's laboratories tucked against the inside courtyard. Inside the laboratory, he surveyed the row of 10 cubicles that housed International's research team. The design accommodated two people in each of the eight interior cubicles—all but one was full. The outer two they set aside for single occupancy, 5s or 6s. *International's technical brain trust.* That's what the organization chart showed. But the single name of one of the 5s hung on an interior cubicle, and the lords of office space had designated that Raef, the only other 5 in the system, would share one of the other inside cubes with a 4. Looking a little closer he noticed that the more spacious end cubes housed a 4 and on the other side, his technician." He glanced again at the bookends. And then again. Work counters that looked like extended kitchen islands filled the rest of the work space—he saw at least six in a quick glance.

Raef moved toward his new office, the one marked with a large "HERE" sign and a large arrow pointing to it. Six steps into the large area he heard a whisper from the blocked off office space straight ahead. "... Took you long enough to get here."

Raef stepped forward and looked around the partial doorway. "Plass. I'm stationed two cubes down from you? They didn't warn me. That's not enough buffer."

Tommy reached out to shake hands. "We're an elite group, Mr. B. We communicate when we want to. Welcome. By the way, we are territorial: I get all trips to Shangri La, so don't get any ideas."

"Shangri La is a fictional place, isn't it?" Raef looked at the family pictures on the desk and the map with colored pins on the wall. "Anyway, I hear you got kicked out of the Philippines for good and now they don't let you go anywhere you can't speak the language or drink the water—it's just what I heard. By the way, where'd the name 'Plass' come from? Something wrong with Tommy?"

"Short for 'plastic.' I came to WFI out of the plastic industry. We used the same equipment and WFI was short operators. It's a good company, so I took the gig. And the people I work with aren't too creative when it comes to naming or they'd probably be in marketing. Speaking of changing businesses, how about you? You ready for this?"

Raef stepped out of the cubicle and leaned against the counter. "Just looking around, I don't know. I'm good at the top; Mitch, Jan and I go way back. Goody's a friend. I've worked with you. But I look at this office arrangement—who's where—and I'm not sure what's happening. Something's loose or just plain out of control. Anyway, I'll get used to it. Now I just need to get my feet on the ground and start doing something."

Jan walked in just in time to hear the last sentence. "I can help there. My office in ten minutes?" Then he turned and left.

Plass waved as he backed into his office. "You have real business and I'm heading for Mexico in the morning. You're going to love this work. See you in two weeks."

Raef took his usual chair at the small table next to the wall of windows. Jan pulled out the other chair after he'd poured tea and placed the cups on the table. "Let me give you the specifics as simply as I can. Between now and May I want you to support the snack operation in Southeast Asia—Singapore and Bangkok. Then I want you to work with our British sales group supporting the snack venture in Holland and China. You can start now. Questions?"

"Nothing but. Do you have any suggestions on my best place to begin?"

Jan pulled out a file. "Here's a list of the products Asia is interested in. Here's the list for Europe. The rest is yours. Let me know when you're ready."

From February until March of the following year Raef led projects in Holland, England, Spain and Italy; and made plans to visit Aleppo, Syria to train staff on Collet operations. He became familiar with London's Gatwick and Heathrow airports and Amsterdam's Schiphol; Northwest and KLM's international lounges; the rental car counters; the rail connections; the hotel practices; and the best restaurants in 20 cities.

Between European visits he traveled to Singapore to discuss manufacturing and distributing snacks for Nang Enterprises and then to Bangkok to train teams. On the first leg of the trip he changed planes at Narita in Tokyo and arrived in Singapore at 1:30 a.m. Sunday. He slept a few hours, then toured the island, visited the zoo, and tried as many of the local foods as he thought safe, and managed a brisk walk through Raffles. On Monday and Tuesday he met the Nang entrepreneurs and roughed out a business arrangement. Wednesday he was on the 8 a.m. flight to Thailand.

For the next two weeks he trained the Global Snacks' staff in Bangkok to manufacture four snacks—everything from cheesy curls to fried sheets. On the 14th day as the final packages of the fourth product were coming off the production line, the owner walked out on the floor to invite Raef to celebrate their new arrangement. The seven-course meal at the owner's club began about 8 o'clock, and only when Raef shook his head, held his stomach and said, "No more, please," did the food stop coming. As dessert was being served the owner looked at his production manager and asked, "Han, are to ready to run the production by yourself?"

Han looked at his plate, then at the owner. "Yes. I am."

The owner watched his production manager for a moment. "Mr. Burnham, I need you to stay another week."

Raef finished the mango he was sampling and laid down his napkin. "Sir, I don't know you well enough to know when you are making a joke and when you are serious. Can you help me?"

"I need you to stay for one more week so that my people are confident to run the equipment. Can you do that?"

"Of course."

124   THE DANGLED ILLUSION

A week later when the plant manager started the production without needing to call Raef, he packed his gear. Twenty-two hours after leaving his hotel in Bangkok he drove up to his driveway in Wesphalia, ready to forget about international travel for awhile.

*   *   *   *

In March 1995 South American Enterprises proposed a joint venture with WFI to sell WFI products through SAE's distribution system by creating a separate corporation. Jan called Raef from a meeting at the main office. "Raef, could you come over here now to discuss products with a team from SAE? They want to talk about restaurant and group feeding."

Raef hung up the phone and headed out the door. Ten minutes later he entered WFI's board conference room and slipped into the chair next to Jan who greeted him with a nod and slid over a pile of handouts. The scrawl at the upper corner of the first page read, "They want to know about foodservice specifics. Can you help us?" Raef picked up the top copies and flipped through the first few pages. He tapped the paper and nodded to his boss.

The SAE leader finished a comment and laid down his paper. Jan offered a slight movement of his left hand and looked at each of the three representatives from SAE. "I'd like to introduce Raef Burnham. Raef's our manager of product development for snack items, but he has eleven years' experience in our Restaurant Support Operations division—he used to develop foodservice products. I think he can answer your questions." Jan then introduced SAE's team—two men and one woman—to Raef, declaring their titles and functions as well as the zone of information they were interested in. "Raef, tell us about Restaurant Support."

Raef made eye contact with each of the SAE people. "Thank you for your interest in working with us. I'd like to frame our discussion by sketching our organization and outlying the product areas. Then we'll discuss the best selling products and I'll tell you about how we make them up—specific steps." He proceeded for about 20 minutes. Afterward he took questions and engaged in lively discussion with each of SAE's representatives. Finally, their chef for South America asked, "Would you consider coming to New Jersey to present these products to my people? I think they'd like to see the products made up and handle them themselves; and I know they'd like to ask you a few questions."

Mitch Jordan, who had taken a seat at the far end of the table while Raef had been engaged in the discussion, looked at the chef. "We'd like to send a team. Absolutely. Raef will handle the product work, consumer and foodservice; and

I'd like to invite our president and his marketing director to join in the meeting. Would that be acceptable to you?"

The chef nodded and looked at Raef. "If you can you be ready in ten days, we'll see you in New Jersey on March 21st. I'll have my assistant make the arrangements."

Ten days later, a limousine picked up Raef and the president of International and his assistant at the Newark airport and drove them along the Hudson to the meeting at SAE's corporate headquarters.

When Raef arrived back at the office the following day, Jan met him at the entrance. "Congratulations, they signed the agreement and the business teams are touching up the wording. They've selected the CEO. We're providing the marketing VP and the quality control leader. The business will locate in Atlanta or Brazilia and research will be handled from here. So, we have to outline a plan and eventually, put together a team. Way to go, man. This is big."

Raef ordered products so he could get familiar with the South American cuisine. He obtained in-country ingredients to evaluate how these performed using WFI's processing conditions and tested products side by side to define differences. Over the next three months he defined the project and made plans for his first trip to Brazil.

*   *   *   *

One day early in May, 1994 Mitch stopped by to visit Raef in his cubicle. No one else was in the lab so Mitch pulled up a chair, placed his feet on a carton of product near the door to the cubicle, and said, "I have a problem …"

Raef lowered his jaw and stared at Mitch. "An intern? You gotta be kidding. I don't like the program—it's babysitting; for the interns it's more about fun than substance. Our intern program is a joke—I don't have time and I don't have a project."

Mitch fiddled with a pencil. "Give him one of those snack problems. Get creative. Help me."

Raef moved his chair closer to his guest. "First, I have no time to babysit—you might have noticed that my staff is out for the century. Second, I'm knee-deep in this South American venture—your SA venture. Third, we have some technical issues in snacks that I need to work on. And finally, our management has forbidden us to work on any project that might work for the intern."

Mitch folded his arms. "Give me an example."

Raef leaned on one arm of the chair and reached out a palm. "How about this? We have a product, a proprietary product that we have made a long time in our own system—never on the outside; it isn't even patented. But if we want to sell it in Africa or China, we'll probably want to manufacture it there. We can't do the big systems that run around the clock and need three shifts a day to produce, so we'd like to develop a small system that could be started up in the morning and closed down at night. This we need to develop, and our leadership doesn't want to spend the time—and, in fact, has told you we can't work on it. Is this a perfect intern project, or what?"

Mitch stood up. "The concept no one wants us to work on. It's yours, but keep it under the radar. We can run it as an intern project, but I don't want to have to defend it down the road. Under the radar, understand?"

Raef assumed his "Brando as Godfather" tone and asked, "Mitch, what are you going to do when this product tests equal to the one we have on the market? And we patent it? You going to keep it under the radar then?" He moved back to his normal speech. "This one's coming home to roost, Mitch. Then what?"

Mitch shook his head. "Hey, just keep the intern busy, teach him something about the business, give him a good experience at WFI, and don't get too involved. Thanks for the help. Meet him and pick him up. My office tomorrow, 10 o'clock.

"Okay, coach. Does this person have a name?"

"Name's Monroe V. Gallay."

"Monroe?"

"My father was a history buff. He liked early 19th century, and 21 years ago was doing some research on the Monroe Doctrine—he favored it, but he wasn't really an isolationist."

Raef looked at the young man seated at the counter just outside his cube. Monroe V. Gallay, Senior, Chemical Engineering, University of Michigan, GPA 3.954. "My guess is 6', 185 pounds, and basketball. That information isn't in your file."

"Well, the size is about right, but the sport is soccer. At Michigan it's a club sport; we don't have a real team. So, a few of us compete with other clubs in the Big Ten. It's fun."

Raef looked at the transcript in his hand and smiled. "I'm impressed by the 3.954. Well, not so much impressed—the grades speak for themselves—as interested. How do you study—the subject is a hobby for me—what do you do?"

Monroe paused, then leaned forward in his chair and looked Raef square in the eye. "I don't go to class. No really. I attend the first class to understand the course requirements; the book, the support materials, the laboratory requirements, the test times and dates, the outside work, and the prof's expectations. Then I study on my own—I never go to classes—and I show up for tests and make sure I get the top grade in the final exam."

Raef leaned forward and raised his hands. "But why the 'don't attend classes' bit?"

Monroe didn't move. "I can't follow the presentations. Usually, they're bad. The prof introduces 17 points in the course of a lecture. On about point 4 or 5 I see there's a leap or error or question that hasn't been addressed and I ponder the gap. By the time I'm back into the game, the prof's on about point 10 and I've missed the material in between. So, rather than play their silly game, I study on my own, take the tests, and move on. Works for me."

The two wove a discussion through courses, grades, skills, sports, social activities at Michigan, intern job requirements, expectations, time demands, the project description, and ended with Monroe's question, "When do I get to do it?"

"Do what?"

"Run the project—on my own. Make some real decisions. Call some shots. Do real stuff."

Raef sat for a moment and stared at Monroe. "July 3rd."

"What? That's like seven weeks."

"Six. That's when I go on vacation. And I always go on vacation, intern or no intern. For the three weeks that I'm gone, you call the shots. Between now and then, learn everything you can about the system we're working on, the people you work with, the political structure in the pilot plant and the way decisions and showings are handled here in the lab. When I leave, I leave no forwarding address, no emergency phone number. The message: don't call—I'm on vacation. When I come back, you'll be within a week of putting together your final presentation and I sure hope you have some answers. By the way, you will have answers. And you want to know what else? I expect a product and a process I can make and market anywhere in the world. You have nine weeks to pull it off. We do. And we're going to have some fun. Now, let me show you to your office and we'll get started."

Raef outlined two weeks worth of experiments. Each experiment took a day to run in the pilot plant. With preparation, a day's run, cleanup, and analysis, they were able to run two tests per week for two weeks; plan the next four weeks together; and after the 12th run Raef announced, "Young man, the rest is yours. I'm out of here. Develop the match and test it in Mexico—I'll see you at the end of the month—market research is waiting for the product."

Three weeks later Raef returned from vacation. He read his e-mails and zipped through the piles of mail on his desk and work table. Then he called Monroe. "I need an update, Star. How about now?"

Monroe bounded into Raef's office two minutes later with, "'Sup?" and then gave Raef the short version of life in the labs during Raef's sojourn into the Northland. After five or ten minutes of conversation Raef held up his hand in a stop motion. "Hey, stop. I've got to hear about the project. Did you do anything since I left? How big is the disaster that's about to engulf me?"

Monroe smiled and struck a pose not unlike that scene of statues in parks honoring conquering war heroes. "I've made you a hero. They're singing songs about you. The thirteenth run—can you believe it, the thirteenth?—was perfect. We took enough product to conduct some focus groups. The groups liked the new snack as well as the old one—American groups—and tasters couldn't tell the difference between the two; at least not at a significant level. So, we made a larger run, produced enough standard product and enough test product to test in Mexico; shipped the product; and we get the results tomorrow. And better yet, you get to be in the meeting. Alongside me, of course. I'm the star. What do you think?"

Raef smiled. "Anybody upset that we're doing this work?"

"I heard our president thought that we'd been told not to work on it, but the international sales guy intervened. He reminded everybody that this was just an intern project that took neither time nor effort from the division's focus, and offered to pay for testing in Mexico just to assess the potential. He even mentioned that you were on vacation during the critical part, so 'how serious could that be?' Not bad, huh?"

"Did you offer to buy him a beer?"

"No opportunity. Been too busy."

Raef started laughing. "Good job. Keep me informed about everything, please. And I'll join you in the meeting tomorrow." Raef looked at the in basket. "I'm in the middle of trying to get some help for the South American venture so I'll be tied up for the day." He looked back at Monroe. "Parity, huh? Parity at 13. P13. This is fun. You know, we could win this little skirmish. Keep going. This could make for an excellent report next week—the intern presentation starring 'The Monroe.' Later."

Raef pulled out the lower drawer on his desk, rested one foot on the drawer, leaned back in his chair and looked out his window. The high tech windows eliminated the glare of the morning sun reflecting off the windows on the other side of the quadrangle courtyard and masked the brilliant blue of the clear summer sky. Bright clouds floated by in single file. Raef leaned over to his computer and punched in 'Cole Elder.' Cole's name, room number and telephone number popped to the screen. Raef dialed the number. "Cole. Raef. Do you have time for a cup at 10? I have some thoughts I'd like to kick around … In the common area … See you there."

At 10:45 Raef laid his cup on the table and exhaled slowly. "Cole, it all boils down to this. I think we have a great opportunity to put together a business in South America. The products are consumer and foodservice. They require design and manufacture in-country. And you're skilled in all aspects of the program. It's perfect. I can do the program and enjoy it, but I need help and you're the man. You can be your own person. I cover the scope and political here. You cover the technical, here and there. It's an open program. You'd love it. And, given my experience with your current program, I can tell you that your future here is better than what you can count on there. Give it a thought and let me know, okay?"

Cole sat and looked at Raef. "Do you like what you do?"

"I love it. This is crazy. My skills are that I lead multiple projects well and I lead teams well—at least that's my opinion. And what am I doing? Individual projects with no people and I'm loving it. What's wrong with that picture? Anyway, gotta run. Let me know."

The next day Raef and Monroe walked into the corporation's small auditorium. As they headed down the right aisle Raef pointed to where they should sit. Monroe looked around the room, then at the presenters in the front. He nudged Raef. "I haven't seen any of those presenters in any of the market research meetings." Raef looked up and made eye contact with the man behind the laptop who smiled and nodded. Raef pulled Monroe down to the seat beside him. "We don't have international market research connections so we hire companies to help us out. Garcia's group is from San Antonio. They help us out from time to time. That's Garcia."

"Thank you for coming," he began. "We have interesting results for you. Let's begin. Our study …"

Garcia presented the results and finished his presentation with, "It worked. The people came—90 percent response rate to our invitations. Current had an 85 percent def/prob; test product was 82 percent."

Monroe leaned over to Raef, "Def/prob? Definitely would buy/probably would buy?"

Raef nodded.

Garcia continued. "And in triangle tests, 55 percent correctly picked the odd sample. The bottom line is pretty sure. Our conclusion: New testers can't tell the difference between the test product and the product that is now on the market. And even if they could, they prefer either one equally. I'd say you have a winner here. Questions?"

Jan had walked in late. "What is the risk of us changing our product to the new process here in the states?"

Garcia laid his pointer on the lectern. "I cannot say. What I can say is this: In new regions where the current product is not known, there is almost zero risk introducing the new product. They cannot tell the difference. What difference they may see, does not matter."

Raef leaned over to Monroe. "Write your presentation. You have a story to tell."

* * * *

Wednesday morning when Raef arrived at his office, he had a visitor, and on his desk a cup of Starbuck's Caffe' Mocha, tall.

"Cole. This is an unexpected pleasure. And thank you for the coffee. I love this stuff. You've given my idea some thought?"

"When do I start?"

Raef pumped a fist into the air. "Hah. I love it when a guy reads a lot of westerns. In time all sentences begin to sound like John Wayne. You've made a decision?"

Cole looked down at his hands then back at Raef. "I weighed the pluses and minuses. I need a new challenge and this is the time to do it. How do we go about making a transition?"

Raef stood up. "Now we do the bureaucracy thing. I don't even know all the steps. Let's go see Jan and maybe even Mitch and work it out. If you could start today it wouldn't be too soon for me. I've just begun receiving ingredients."

* * * *

Monroe spent the week preparing his August 1st final project presentation. This meant a review with Raef on July 28th and a final approval on July 30th. Monroe pulled together his data, organized it into PowerPoint form, and practiced the presentation.

On Monday at 2:30 in the large conference room in director country, Monroe stood at the front of the 50-chair room and presented the snack production replacement intern project to … Raef. For two hours Monroe and Raef discussed, debated, argued, challenged and counter-challenged the data, each other and the conclusions until finally Raef said, "Excellent. You have the content down. Now, when we meet on Wednesday, we'll work on style. Practice that between now and then, okay?"

Monroe shut off the computer. "Hey, why are you doing this to me? We got the data. We got the win. What's with this grilling? This perfection?"

"Here's the deal, Ace. You have one shot to impress some people. I'm assuming someday you might want a job. Maybe one of the places you might be considering is WFI. Friday you have your audience—every one of the directors, many of the department heads, and some key players who might be looking for someone a year from now. This is showtime. You have one opportunity to score big. And one thing I contract for when I accept a mentee—in your case, an intern—is that when you walk out of here you have played your best game. You didn't save anything for another day. And you will walk away proud. If you don't get a job offer, it won't be because you didn't do well or look good. No way. See you Wednesday. I'm meeting with Mitch in the morning. Who knows what that's about?"

Chapter 20

▼

HASTA LUEGO, SOUTH AMERICA

Mitch Jordan, Director of the International Division and now a vice president of WFI, commanded the office once held by the vice president of R&D when Mitch and Raef joined the company. Mitch's desk, a seven by three and a half foot polished mahogany affair, cantilevered into the room like the deck of an aircraft carrier reached into a harbor. And Mitch's high-backed leather chair made even higher by its extended head support blocked out almost half of the 12 foot high book shelf and trophy rack that covered the wall behind the desk. With Mitch at 6'3" and still around 250 pounds he exuded anything but diffidence and with all the plaques and trophies and pictures and books and products scattered around the room on shelves and tables and piles along the floor, the office seemed to—the only word that came to any visitor's mind was—overwhelm.

"Raef, c'mon in and have a seat. Man, it's been a long time. Coffee?"

Raef sat at the round conference table where he usually sat years before when he visited Mitch in other offices. "Coffee, yes. And I'm honored."

Mitch poured a cup from the carafe on the tray next to his conference table. "Because?"

He looked around the room. "I don't get invited to cozy meetings in this sanctuary very often. And you're a busy man."

"Aren't you the suspicious one, but now that you're here...." Mitch smiled and sipped his coffee while he looked over the rim of his glasses beyond the brim of the cup, never for a moment breaking eye contact with Raef. He set his cup on his hand as he settled back on the chair. "We have some business to discuss ... I have a dilemma. Brey has directed me to cough up a player to help Yves Jarnot in a new venture. Personally, I wouldn't budge an inch if it were just to help Brey do anything, but I owe Yves huge—he's a friend—and I want to help him out."

Raef held his gaze. "So what's the dilemma?"

"You're the only person who fits the needs of that group. They need someone with experience formulating bakery products, someone who can work alone, someone comfortable in manufacturing. You're it."

Raef extended the pause. "Again, so what's the dilemma?"

Mitch tossed an off-hand gesture. "I don't want to send you. You're just getting the South American venture going. You've paid your dues around here. I want it to be your choice. I know your goals." He took another sip and laid the cup down on the table. "Let me know Monday."

Raef stood to go. "Let me see if I have this right. You need to provide a body for a new venture. I'm the body. Either I volunteer or you send me, but you'd feel better if it were my idea. And I have until Monday to decide. Is that pretty accurate?"

Mitch stood and started to walk Raef to the door. "When you strip it down, that's pretty close. Can you give it some thought?"

Raef nodded and gave a slight wave as he moved out the door. "See you Monday."

Raef walked down the hallway past Monroe's desk and motioned to him to follow along. When they came to a small conference room along the hallway, they went in and Raef closed the door. "Monroe, Friday you're going to present your project, human resources will give you a pitch for the company, and you'll probably get an offer to join WFI when you graduate. In the interest of full disclosure, let me give you a little inside look at how the game is played—really."

Raef outlined the scenario presented by Mitch moments before and defined the probable outcomes to several scenarios. "When the smoke clears on Monday, I'll probably be heading into new venture land. Why am I telling you this? It's part of life in the big leagues. The corporation has needs and it has assets; we're listed among the assets. Sometimes we get to make choices we don't look to make, but it's part of ... like I said. Now, I have to do some thinking. You ready for your show?"

Monroe stood silent. "How can you just tell me that like it's just an article in the newspaper? You've just learned the snack business all over again. You've been key to setting up the business in South America—you said yourself that you thought this could be a good opportunity, and the business could have a good run. They're closing the door for no reason whatever and asking you to start all over again on something not even defined yet. They're messing with your life, man."

Raef swept a hand across the table. "What I've been trying to teach you for the past nine, ten weeks is that life in the big leagues is about the corporation surviving. If we can craft out a life in that framework, congratulations. But when the other guy has the money, the power and defined needs, we take on more pawn character than we might like. The trick is to survive as an individual. Maintain your own ethics. Meet your needs and carve out a good future in the process.

"Beyond that, I always hope to have some fun doing it and help some people along the way. That's the dream. I'm sharing with you so that when the questions come at the end of the week, you can answer seeing the big picture. If you decide to come aboard, it's with eyes wide open. Bottom line? Heads up. I still enjoy my work. I enjoy new challenges. I have dreams that may or may not be realized. Hey, I'll be 55 in the fall and there's some magic to that number. And I'm not worried about the answer to my question—not in the slightest. Change is always interesting. So, don't you be worried on my behalf. Okay? I actually enjoy new challenges and I still get up every morning, excited to come to work. I even like this company—it's still one of the best. Now, make that presentation great and make us both look good. I have to consider some scenarios."

Monroe looked at his watch. "We're going to review the program one more time, right?"

"Monroe, you're ready. Just polish it a bit. No more reviews. I'll see you Friday for sure."

The big hand on Friday's clock seemed to move like the second hand on a normal day. At 1:30 Monroe presented his intern study, "Project Newby: Congitos in Mexico," to a packed room at the research center. Scattered around the room, placards in Spanish announced the new product and offered free samples to anyone interested. Half the audience was under 25, and most of those had one or two more years of college to go—the interns were a loyal lot who cheered one another on in their presentations. The remainder of the room was filled with directors, department heads, project leaders, and a few of Monroe's new friends from around the company.

Monroe concluded the presentation with, "… and the market research results were conclusive. The test product is equal to the product on the market—and it's not differentiable in new markets. The conclusion: We can introduce in new markets using the new process if further testing supports these data. Are there any questions?"

Several directors asked brain teasing questions. A few interns threw some soft pitches. And the early afternoon finale ended right on time with a round of applause for the latest *wunderkind*.

Raef, sitting in the front row, stood and thanked everybody for coming; then turned and shook hands with Monroe. "Excellent job. Well done. HR wants to see you at 2:30. I'll catch you before you go today. Now you have some people to meet. Enjoy."

Monroe received his offer, submitted his report and stopped by Raef's office before heading out that afternoon. "Hey, I got an offer."

"Do you like it?"

He leaned against the door jamb. "I do, but I'm going to think about it a little bit. I have time. And I want to see what happens to you."

Raef waved a hand as though he were brushing away a fly. "Don't let that worry you. I'll be fine. Enjoy your year. And if we see you back here next summer, good for both of us. If you choose to go another way, that too will be a good decision. You'll know what to do. I wish you all the best, young man. Keep in touch."

Monday morning Raef walked into Mitch's office and shut the door. "I've thought about it, Mitch, and here's the deal. I'll take the job and get you off the hook. But I have a concern. WFI has a bad habit; they ask people to go out on a limb for a new venture, then they cut the venture off and those who volunteered? They leave them out in the cold. I want no part of that garbage. So, I'll volunteer and make this easy for you, but I want a round trip ticket, in writing: Burnham helps us out on this venture, makes it work, and gets to return to International when it's done—or not. It's his call. Do we have an agreement?"

Mitch nodded. "I'll take care of it. Thank you."

Cole Elder stood up and turned toward the window of his cube, away from Raef. He ran his hand through his hair and spun around to face his friend and venture compatriot. "You're going where? In one week … you're going where?"

Raef sat in the chair next to Cole's desk. "Project Reynolds. It's a concept that one of the new marketing vice presidents is taking on personally. He wants a senior product developer assigned 100 percent to his project—no other responsibilities. No staff. Just bench operations. We're starting from scratch and we want to be national in a year. Mitch has to provide a person ... his term was 'cough up a body.' I was selected. I volunteer or I get sent. Either way, Mitch provides."

Cole sat down. "How do you feel about that? I mean, how much of this crap are you going to put up with?"

Raef rested his head on his hand. "I'm a little bummed. South America sounded great and I thought it could be my ticket back into the bigs. I've just finished my Pimsleur Spanish tapes—actually did a lunch with some of the Latin people around here last Thursday. We spoke nothing but Spanish for about a half hour. Man, I was spent; that's hard work. But it was a terrific experience and I'm getting better every day. Now I'm working on vocabulary and special focus on verbs.

"The second part, though, is that I love new concepts and this was beginning to take shape. Actually, I think this was a unique career opportunity for both of us, not to mention the fun we could have had doing it. We could have ridden these rails to a pretty good outcome. Not being able to do what we discussed is a let down. More important, how about you?"

Cole leaned forward from his chair, elbows on the desk, and rested his chin in the "V" left over after his wrists propped against each other. "I feel like I look, I think. Deflated, a little peeved, maybe even slightly betrayed. I'm kind of a glass-half-empty guy anyway. But way back of it all, I'm still a little excited and it still feels like I made the right decision. I have to think about this a little, but I don't think I'll complain to Mitch about the switch. I think I'll just saddle up old paint and head into the skirmish. The challenge sounded good to me when you pitched it and the intrigue still fascinates me. I'd rather have tackled this new world through our partnership, but I'm going to go ahead. What the heck, I needed a change anyway. This is just a little bigger than I'd planned. Yeah, I'm going to be ... better."

Raef ran fingers along his forehead. "Well, I still feel bad about how this is playing out, but some of this stuff is just out of our control. We have the rest of the week. Let's evaluate all the ingredients, select the most important development projects for you to focus on, and I'll get out of the way of the master."

"Then what?"

"Don't know. We'll see Monday."

✱ ✱ ✱ ✱

Jonathan Brey and Fortune Montag stepped out of the corporate limousine and walked into WFI's corporate hangar. The driver grabbed two briefcases and two travel bags and ushered them to the Citation VII standing alone in the middle of the hanger. "Have a good trip, gentlemen. See you tomorrow night."

The two men boarded the aircraft, buckled in and greeted the captains as the aircraft fired up and began to move down the tarmac.

"Jonathan, how'd you staff the new venture on your end?"

"I followed your lead. I selected Yves Jarnot to support your guy and instructed him to get a top developer out of Mitch's area."

"Excellent. You understand why I asked for this?"

Jonathan looked out the window as the Citation began to roll down the runway. "My guess? The South American venture will be successful. The leader of the R&D team will move to become a department head or director. And you want to pick who that is … or isn't."

Fortune looked at Jonathan. "Burnham did a good job setting the program up. He probably would develop good products—and on time. Elder can handle the products and presents no side issues. But … you understand."

Brey nodded. "Burnham's perfect for what Yves needs. I'm just surprised you don't want to use him in a bigger capacity. He's capable."

"There are other issues. Old ones." Fortune sat silent, gazing out the window for several minutes. He looked down and pointed. "Look at that, Jonathan. I never get tired of the view from 40,000 feet. Look at that. You can see the curve of the earth. It's incredible. I never get tired of the view."

Jonathan smiled and shook his head. "Fortune, how do you maintain your enthusiasm? You fly 100,000 miles a year keeping track of all of our operations. How do you do it?"

"I like what I do. Do you like what you do, Jonathan?"

"Very much."

CHAPTER 21

▼

ALOHA PROJECT REYNOLDS

"Yves, I don't know how you always manage to attract the best talent," Raef announced as he entered his new boss's office, the office that shared a wall with Brey, the head of R&D.

"And that would be you? Why not? Come in, please." Yves Jarnot was WFI's chief director and Raef's new boss. Twenty years ago the R&D-VP who was Yves's friend and Cornell University classmate, had introduced terms like "vice president" and "my number two" into a recruiting discussion and spirited Yves away from a promising career at ConAgra. WFI never actually promised anything but a job, but Yves took the position anyway—and ran with it. That VP was long gone and Yves was still thriving, but not as the vice-president in charge.

In his first five years at WFI he managed to create three business platforms that had grown to be significant profit centers for the corporation. The corporation promoted two of his direct reports to director in the next two years and, in the process, noted his people development talents—this career progression became a trend over the next 15 years. Now, at the 20-year mark of his career, every director at the center had served an apprenticeship with Yves; without that mark on the resume, no one advanced to director. And Yves held their markers.

Yves's office shouted corporate America, but it whispered culture. Cezanne prints hung on the wall just behind Yves's head and in the locked bookcase below stood first edition copies of Victor Hugo's *Les Miserables* and *Les Travailleurs de la mer* side by side with Gustave Flaubert's *Madame Bovary, Salammbo,* and *Trois Contes*—all in French. English was his second language, and he had mastered it, almost at the diplomatic level—almost.

Raef's scan of the room jerked to a halt at the first of the books.

Yves looked from Raef to the bookcase and back to Raef. "So you like my taste in literature, and maybe in art and you are wondering about whether I have a soul; what is my taste in music. Let me puzzle you no further. I marvel that Ravel became so popular and I despise *Bolero;* you will not hear it in my office, on my car radio, nor in my home. And I love the opera—French, Italian, German—it makes not to me a difference; I love it. And as for liking to be surrounded by talent, you are right. Please, be seated."

"Why opera?"

"The passion. The clarity. The artistic demands on the performers. That is what I listen to in my car. Sometimes I get so impassioned I forget about the speed, so I use a fuzz buster in town. But why? Part of growing up in Paris, I guess."

Raef took the visitor's chair directly opposite Yves's desk. Yves opened a folder and took out two decks of papers; he handed one to Raef and laid the other on the desk before him. "We have some business to discuss. Before I begin about the project, do you have anything you want me to know?"

"I do, Yves. You and I go back a long time. When I was demoted you gave me good advice that has stood me well for twelve years—remember our discussion on the *Delta Queen*?"

Yves nodded. "I do."

"I appreciate all you did for me then. But I want you to know that my goals today are the same as they were back when we spoke in New Orleans: I work to be reinstated at the '6' level. I earned the shot in Restaurants. And I was on the road to doing it in International. Now I take this challenge with the same goal in mind—just so you know. I've changed over the years, but my goals haven't and my motivation hasn't."

Yves pressed his left temple. "I accept that and I appreciate your forthrightness. But I can guarantee you nothing. Adam did you no favors when he selected someone else as his successor; that has caused all the directors to wonder why. Why—if you were so good as he often said you were—why did he select someone else? No one will champion your cause. But that is not what we are here to do. We have a job. Let me tell you what it is."

Raef raised a finger. "Excuse me. Would you?"

"Would I what?"

"Champion my cause. Recommend me for reinstatement to a '6'?"

"We haven't worked together. We'll see." Yves motioned to the paper. "Let's talk about the job."

Raef picked up his copy. "OK. I understand the sponsorship game and I don't come in here ignorant of the challenges. I'm just saying that my goals haven't changed. When we put this product on the market—whatever the project is—I know you'll support me. That's all. Now, let's hear the details."

Yves raised his eyebrows. "Still the fire, so late in the game?"

Raef smiled. "You've still got it and you have me by a few years."

Yves lowered his chin, but his eyes stayed on Raef. "Not that many. May we proceed?"

For the next hour Yves described the project, its timetable and Raef's role. Raef challenged, requested amplification of ideas, suggested changes in developmental direction, and smiled at Yves's summary. "Any questions?"

Raef looked at his notes. "I've asked most of them as you shared your information. But you said that we're going to put five items on the market in one year. If we don't even know what technology we'll need to develop, I think we need a team of about four people; another level 5 person and some technicians."

Yves pointed an index finger at Raef. "I anticipated your needs: You have four people now. There's ..." and listed each person and their credentials.

Raef wrote down the names as Yves spoke. When he finished, Raef tapped the list of names and shook his head. "Well, I admit, that's four more than Mitch said there'd be, but look at the staff. I know these people. One is pathetic—but she'd done some fine work for P. Dank Reedy on the dessert project two years ago so she thinks the person can do no wrong and has sponsored her. One is a part time person; and in this case that means uncommitted. One is just plain unqualified. And the one star in the group works only Fridays. No, we need some help; real help. I'll get started, but see if you can't do something about all this."

Yves closed the deck and placed it back in his folder. "No problem. I always try to upgrade my staff when I can. Now we have work to do. And you said you would like to have your office back in the work area rather than where you are now?"

"Yes. It's better for me to be where the action is. Can you arrange for the move?"

"Tomorrow. I have already called."

Over the next twelve months Yves was true to his word and Raef was true to his word.

Raef scoured the reference shelves and the archives for WFI projects surrounding freshness. He interviewed the corporate division staff trying to find breaking news on how to prevent staling in baked products. He initiated studies, designed experiments and established synergisms. His team worked on formulas for ten concepts that might lend themselves to a new form of packaging and a new delivery system.

Yves found a former consultant who was stuck at level 4 and needed an opportunity to show off her skills. By the end of the first year she had proved her talent even to the most skeptical, and convinced Yves that she was a level 5 performer. And he brought in good technicians and procured equipment to make processing evaluation easier.

By the fall of 1996 Yves presented the project to Lawton, the vice-president in charge of the new business efforts. Minutes after the discussion Yves walked into the lab. "Raef, I have good news. We are going to test Project Reynolds in four cities in early November: Columbus, Charlotte, Kansas City, and Minneapolis. What do you think?"

"The test product will be our duct tape equivalent, but I think we can mock up items that will get us consumer answers. You handled that well, Yves. Let's go."

Raef stepped toward the door, but Yves held up his hand. "I have another piece of news. I have been asked to lead the corporate effort to study nutritional uses of soy. The idea has been one of my favorites for a long time and I have finally gathered enough support. I start there on Monday. Project Reynolds will move into a division that has people to assign to the effort, money to test and grow, and manufacturing support to take it to the next level."

"Which division?"

"P. Dank Reedy's. Portable Foods. We meet with her this afternoon. Chin up. You wanted an opportunity to take this national; now is your chance. You are the expert. You know the products, the process, the market, the people—everything. This is your chance."

Raef stepped back into the room and closed the door. "Yves, she's an academic—never got dirty when she was at the bench. Had her technicians do all the grunt work. She's connected nowhere. The book is she's bright, but clueless—zero people skills—and nobody trusts her."

Yves pursed his lips and hung his head for a moment. "You're wrong about the 'not connected' part. Fortune Montag is her sponsor, so if you do well with her, she could be your ticket to a '6'. The time window for you is closing. Think about it. This may not be all bad. You have my vote. Now you get the chance to get her vote. Possible?"

Raef leaned against the door. "When's the meeting?"

Yves turned to pick up his phone. "3 o'clock. Her office."

"Yves, I miss you already."

* * * *

Three weeks later P. Dank Reedy stood with her administrative assistant, Myron, finishing the rearrangement of her remodeled office. Her new design called for new wall textures, new colors, new furniture, new draperies, new design in combinations not seen in the center—or any office deco creation session either. Her four- by eight-foot redwood desk reached into the room like it was grasping for more power. Her high backed leather chair sat with its back to the windows, disdaining the all-glass wall and the landscape architecht's dream of a manicured lawn it overlooked. The chair faced the door. Across the desk from 40 inches away, two redwood chairs highlighted in teal sat two hand widths apart squared to the desk. On the left and right walls, Myron helped place several modern paintings. P. Dank busied herself arranging the photos of Golda Maier and Gloria Steinem and a young Betty Friedan just to her left to face the room.

P. Dank thanked Myron for his help and closed the door. Standing with her back against the closed door she laid her head back against it and closed her eyes. After a moment a slight smile tugged at the corners of her mouth. She opened her eyes, then the door. "Myron. Raef returns today. Please see that I get an update on the tests as soon as he gets in. Thank you."

About a half hour later, P. Dank looked up from her desk to see Raef walk to the open door and stop. Raef was dressed in khakis with a casual shirt and walking shoes. The casual business attire movement added to the relaxed attitude the corporation fostered. P. Dank brushed her suit coat when she spotted her guest. She smiled, stood and walked around the desk to shake hands. "Raef, please come in. I'm so anxious to hear about the groups. Myron, two cups of coffee please."

The two walked back into the room. At 5'9" she was almost his height, but with her 2 and a half inch heels, they both noticed the difference. P. Dank motioned Raef to take a chair in front of the desk. He searched the room while he sat down and his new boss walked back to her position behind the desk. "I'm anxious to hear. How did we do?"

Raef looked around. "Nice office." He scanned a bit further. "Interesting art." Then he gave the topline—we did well. He presented the positives—the products are the right products for the line. He mentioned the concerns—we need to increase moistness and make the products easier to handle. And he suggested next steps—we can do this and be ready to test in six weeks.

Myron walked in with the coffee and P. Dank sat silent for a little. "Good. Now let's talk about next steps for you. Yves told me of your aspirations. I can't do anything for you at this time. If, however … if you manage to take this project national, I can move you to level 6 with full support of the center. That's what I have in mind."

Raef pursed his lips and swallowed. "That's a worthy goal for both of us."

* * * *

For the next year Raef and the team tested and developed and tested and finalized the entire product line for the portable foods market. After the third set of groups the product line received the highest ratings of any new ideas on the corporation's list. "We're ready, gang. Let's go."

"National test market? Not just plain national? You said 'test market'?" Raef shook his head. "Why? These are solid numbers—the best in the test. This thing is gold. Our goal has always been to introduce nationally. Why test market?"

Lawton spoke in a quiet voice. "The numbers are soft. We need a 65 on the def/prob scale and we only got a 62."

Raef shook his head. "What we need is a good indication that our product will do well. The difference between a 65 and a 62 is meaningless. C'mon, Jared. This is our best shot for this year. Let's go."

Lawton nodded. "That's why we're selecting this project instead of any of the other three to test market. You ought to be pleased."

Raef lowered his jaw slightly and looked at Lawton. "I am. I just want a better shot."

"So do we, Raef. And if this is as good as we think, we'll get it after we read the test market."

Raef looked at the timetable. "Six months from the start of the test market?"

Lawton nodded. "Approximately. So we'd better get started. Your estimate says it'll take until Christmas to prepare the production site."

From the last week in August until January 8th with only Christmas week off the team staffed the production startup in Indiana. For 18 weeks they left Westphalia on Sunday evening and returned Friday evening, having spent the 120 hours between running a baking/freezing operation in a little town in the country for 24 hours a day. But on January 8th the product was shipped to the test cities and the national test market began.

Raef took a week off for vacation and returned to work on a Tuesday in the middle of January. As he sat down to his desk Laurie, the Super 4, pulled up a chair at his table and said, "So, have you heard about the promotions?"

Raef settled back in his chair, not bothering to open his briefcase. "No, tell me."

"Well, I'm now a Level 5—isn't that special?"

"Alright!" The two exchanged high fives. "Congratulations to you—about time. You should have been hired in at that level. Way to go."

"And ... the rest of the team got raised a notch."

Raef waited for the rest of the sentence.

She paused. "That's all I know. Gloria and Carla and Don. And me, of course."

Raef looked out the window. "It sounds like I have to talk to P. Dank. Let's talk later."

Raef called Myron. "Does P. Dank have a moment this morning? ... 10 o'clock is fine. I need 15 minutes."

At 10 P. Dank Reedy hung up the phone as Myron stepped in the door. "Raef Burnham to see you." She stood. "Raef, welcome back. Good job in Indiana. Congratulations. Nice vacation?"

"Thank you. We did well."

P. Dank sat down and motioned for Raef to do the same. She watched him change position. "But?"

"I'm waiting for what's next."

P. Dank glanced at her calendar, then at her watch. "Boy, this has been tough. I've been able to promote everybody in the team. They're, you know, at levels where there's room to move so we were able to do something for everybody. I think everybody's pretty happy and I was glad to do it. Made me feel good."

Raef sat up in the chair, eased forward and locked in eye to eye. "Am I missing something here?"

The director eased back into her chair and slid the chair back away from the desk. "Your case, you mean." She changed the angle of her chair. "That's more difficult. I tried to get you to a level 6 but there was no support." She leaned forward in her chair. "Here's what I did: I got you a 3 percent raise. HR said no, but I thought, 'What's the purpose of being a director if I can't make some calls on my own,' so I went ahead and authorized it anyway—forget the protocol. Congratulations on your second raise this year. Good job."

Raef didn't move. "Fine. Thank you. But didn't we have a little understanding about why I took this job and what I'm working for? When we spoke last summer, you understood that."

P. Dank played with the ring on her right hand and looked at the pictures to her left. "I tried, Raef. Really, I did. No support. Nobody would get behind moving you to a '6.' The project didn't go national. Not enough weight."

Raef leaned back in his chair as he laced his fingers behind his head and looked out the window behind P. Dank. He dropped his hands and stood up. "Okay. I want to exercise my option—today. I'm off the project. What's next?"

"What do you mean, 'What's next?' We have a national test market to support and you're on it."

"No … no, I'm not. My contract says, 'Until the project terminates or goes national.' You declared that national test market is some kind of line in the sand … finish line when you promoted the rest of the team. This is your version of national, but it's not enough to benefit me—so I want out. Now, if you please."

P. Dank sat straight up and swept a gesture toward Raef starting with, "Hold …," as her hand caught the cup on her desk and spilled the contents over the surface and landed the cup on the floor six feet from the desk against the wall. "AARRGGHH! Myron!"

Myron came in with a box of tissues and wiped off the desk, patted the floor, and apologized and apologized and apologized to P. Dank … to Raef … to the floor.… Raef stepped over to the wall and picked up the cup and handed it to Myron. Myron tried on a smile that didn't quite fit, bowed once then twice, and left the room.

P. Dank resumed her position behind the desk and brushed her hairline with her left hand. "Where … where do you want to go? Lawton is very protective of those who stepped up to help him. You get to name it. Back to International? New Ventures? Name it."

"I want to think about it a little. I'll get back to you. Thanks for the raise."

* * * *

After dinner, Jenifer and Raef piled the dishes in the kitchen, poured a small glass of liqueur and moved to the living room. Raef set his glass down on the coffee table, sat down on the floor and leaned back against the sofa. "Darlin', what do you think I should do? She's an idiot. I can't believe anything she says. I don't trust her. Nobody does. I'm through with Project Reynolds and I can opt out of Portable Foods. Thoughts?"

A sip of Grand Marnier on a cold January night in Minnesota can create a very romantic setting and this was, actually. Raef and Jenifer sat on the floor in their living room with the draperies open and watched snow cover the cul-de-sac. Calming. Calm. After a long silence Jenifer said quietly, "You're 57. You chase a dream. You can't force promotion. If it comes it'll be because they want to honor you. You want to work about eight more years. The work ought to be something you enjoy. Do you want to go back to International?"

He shook his head. "The last six months—that's enough travel—for me, for you, for awhile. I don't think it's the best thing unless it's the only opportunity presented. And Cole is doing fine."

"From what you said, you get to pick."

Raef took a sip. "Here, I'm the skeptic. They're not too good at keeping their word."

"Does that include Lawton?"

He smiled. "No, actually. He's been outstanding, but we'll see. I'm the once-burnt-twice-shy kind of guy."

"Then I think you should wait and see what happens next."

* * * *

Fortune Montag leaned forward and slid the divider aside. "Driver, Dr. Reedy will be returning to the General Offices after you drop me at the hangar. Will you take her back, please?" He closed the divider and looked at P. Dank. "Holding Project Reynolds to a national test helps us gauge the market and buys us time. Now, what did you offer your people?"

P. Dank Reedy brushed back a stray strand of hair on the right side of her face, then laid her hands on her lap and smiled. "I was able to promote four and give Burnham a raise."

Fortune paged through some papers in the folder laid out before him. He turned to P. Dank. "Everybody happy?"

"Delighted—the four ... yes. But Burnham, no. He resigned from the project and is considering his reassignment. I don't know how all that will work out. I don't know if I handled it the best ..."

"We have plans for you, P. Dank. Do not get involved with his next steps; they are not your concern. I want him to stay in Portable Foods and I do not want him back in International."

P. Dank uncrossed her legs and turned toward Fortune. "How do I do that? He has options."

Fortune closed his briefcase and opened his door as the limousine came to a stop at the WFI hangar. "Let Chap talk to him. Chap Daggett has been selected to replace you when we move you up in a couple weeks. Without our getting involved he will make Raef an offer that is attractive to Raef and worthwhile to Portable Foods; I am sure of it. You can begin to get ready for your next assignment." He stepped out onto the tarmac.

"Thank you, Fortune. I'll let you know."

He turned toward the plane and waved as he walked. "That will not be necessary."

Chapter 22

ONE MORE TIME AND A HALF

The next morning and early afternoon Raef and remnants of the Project Reynolds team gathered at the Menaga Hills Golf Club to immortalize the startup and further swell WFI's archives. They compiled the project report. The national test market status provided the project a forward lean that felt like success. That success coupled with the recent lifts to individual careers created a near festive mood for the (some called it) post mortem. Raef thought the latter term—apt.

He waved farewell to the team, gathered his papers, tossed the three-year episode onto a pile of broken dreams cornered somewhere in the back of his mind and drove back to the office. He plopped himself in front of his computer and hit "send and receive" while he reached for his phone. Before he could punch the first digit, a voice from the doorway said, "I've asked Chap Daggett to speak with you. He'll be calling in a few minutes." Raef cradled the phone and glanced at the doorway, then snapped back to stare at the speaker. "Thanks, P. Dank, but why …" Just then the phone rang.

"That'll be Chap." And she was gone.

"Barden Park isn't too far from the center." Chap fired up his Ford 250 Extended Cab and pulled out of the parking lot. He looked over at Raef. "Let's grab a Starbucks and take a stroll over there. It's a beautiful day and we have to talk."

Chap was known for his casual meetings. As they walked along the twisted path Chap shared his musing. "What do you think would happen if a guy, after 31 years with the company, got to do whatever he wanted and was good at? Do you think that's an experiment worth trying?" Chap laughed at Raef's concerned look. "You're a natural for the job."

Chap Daggett was a legend. The rumor mill placed him as a CIA trainee while in college. Academic major: Russian. But along the way he seems to have switched to Chemical Engineering and moved to foods when he graduated in 1975. A Nebraska farm kid, he still worked his 6-foot, 210 pound frame hard enough on the weights to suggest he could still do a full day's field work.

"Chap, what are we talking about?"

He continued. "You have experience in every product and process we have. You've been in all of our plants. You have a network rookies would die for. Hey, I cut you loose and you're free to do the job the way you want to. What could be better?"

Raef finished his coffee and threw the cup into the receptacle. "Hold on a second, okay? What are you talking about and why are we talking? You're in agriculture. You work for Brey ... How does P. Dank get to ask you to talk to me about anything? Why ...? I'm listening, but I don't get it."

Chap pushed both hands deep in his pockets, stopped and leaned toward Raef. "Excuse me? Is there a question here that might require an answer? Perhaps by me?" Dressed in khakis, a casual shirt, white socks and earth shoes, he was a display of substance over style. Known around the labs as the first person to master the capabilities of his MacIntosh years before WFI had converted all systems to Windows, some wondered if he really had wandered very far from his original major. In his career at WFI he had worked as a plant engineer, figured out the limits of large systems as a researcher, introduced new approaches to systems development, and reorganized pilot operations for the corporation. While introducing all this change, Chap alienated some people but reached the level of director despite his contrarian approaches. Not everyone loved him, but everyone respected him.

"Let's boil this down. I've been assigned to Portable Foods; I report to P. Dank Reedy. I think productivity is the next big opportunity and I need someone to pilot the program—you're my choice. Does that pretty much answer everything?"

"Sure, about the job. But why with Reedy? You're a director. She's a director."

Chap turned and started walking again. "I'm junior. She's being groomed and is about to be moved up, so I'm learning the division. It's about the worst kept secret in the building, but no one dares ask about what's going on." Chap flipped his hand as if to discard an invisible object into the air, raised his eye brows and tilted his head questioning the ways of the unknown. "But I'd rather talk about you."

He enjoyed his reputation for placing talented people in zones of opportunity and benefiting from the results. But Raef, a 57-year-old on a quest, presented an enigma. "Why do you still chase that rainbow, Raef? You've had a great career. You enjoy an outstanding reputation. You've done well." He stopped. "Then why?"

"A long time ago the corporation screwed up. I've forgiven them for being stupid, but I'm willing to give them another opportunity make amends. Twice they could've allowed me to reach my goals here at the center—to be a success: They failed to act—both times. I think … I believe even that WFI can still learn to …" Raef put a foot on a rock alongside the trail and leaned forward bracing himself with one hand on his knee. "Do you want to tell me that my skills don't match up to … you fill in the blanks. We have a lot of dead wood at the '6' level around here—one of them works for you now, right down the hall. Heck, we have dead wood at the director level. It's part of corporate life. With the exception of a few of our best and brightest—and you can count those on your left hand—I'd take on the rest of the 5s or 6s, one-on-one, any day even having been out of the game for 15 years. Nope. My eyes are still on the prize. As long as I'm here, they have the opportunity to recognize their error and reward performance—publicly. I'm still waiting."

Chap walked a few steps, his head bobbing in an extended nod. In a few steps he came to rest and sat down on a park table. "Let's move to the bottom line. I'll be in charge of Portable Foods in a little while. What about my offer—to run my productivity program?"

Raef sat on the bench and leaned back against the table top. He removed his glasses and rubbed his eyes. Then put the glasses back in place and adjusted them. "I'm in. What do I need to know before I start?"

Chap slid down to the bench. "The rules are simple. Productivity is the next big arena. Every product—we can formulate it better. Every package—we can make it better. Every process—we can perform better. Nothing is sacred. But we don't compromise quality. And here's the kicker: Every project must deliver $1 million savings per year or it's not worth your attention. In a little while I'll get you a top engineer and a technician. Anything else? If not, I'd suggest you get started."

"What about reporting? What do you need to know and how often do you need to know it?"

Chap got up and headed back toward the car. "That's your call. If you think I need to be updated, tell me what I need to know. But I don't want paper. And don't spend a lot of time wordsmithing the information. I need information, that's all. Got it? And if I feel out of the loop, I'm not bashful. Oh, does that mean that you've decided not to go back to International?"

Raef leaned his back against the rear panel of the truck. "Not going back is tough, but Cole copes well and he's absolved me of my leaving him out on a limb. More than that, I don't want that much travel and I do want freedom. And I like your concept of productivity so I'll see you by the end of the week. Got room?"

When they arrived back at the research center Chap dropped Raef off at the entrance. "I have to run over to the office, but one more thing … about the rainbow? You might consider redefining what you mean by success—your definition might be a little narrow."

Raef started to say "What?" but left it at, "… see you later."

When Raef got to his desk he called the information specialist, purchasing, operations and packaging. When he finished with his requests of packaging he called the Portable Foods' director of marketing. "Lanny. Raef. Could we meet later this afternoon to discuss where the division would be in five years? I'd like to talk about some specifics." Then he called the library and closed with, "See you in five."

As he passed Chap's office on the way to the library, Chap waved him in. "Man, it took you less than an hour in your new job to ruffle the division feathers—that's a new record. I held the old one and I'm no piker." He stood up, pointed at the phone and laughed. "That was our marketing director. He asked me why someone from a test market project not even assigned to his projects is asking to meet with him to talk about where he's taking the division in the next five years."

"What'd you tell him?"

Chap, in an exaggerated motion, adjusted the tie he wasn't wearing. "Profitability is back in style—and that he'd like you."

Raef raised his hands and stepped toward the door. "That ought to be a fun meeting. Why don't you send him my picture so he can warm up to the idea that we're really friends, he and I. Gotta r … Hold on." He stepped back toward Chap's desk. "Why the suspicion? Same team, right? We make products and processes better amd save money for everybody—that's huge to these people. No job losses. And we're Public Enemy Number 1? Why?"

Chap planted a stockinged foot on his desk and leaned forward. "It's the system. The system exists to perpetuate itself. Like it is today. No ripples. Second, you are butting up against career paths. These people have figured out how to get to the next level if nothing changes—now you're in the way, changing things. Third, the world is full of stodgy thinking even if the minds have been molded in the best schools—and not just stodgy; mind locked thinking. Finally, the words you've given me about all levels of the corporation; these people live scared lives. They own good jobs and it's not easy to go get another job that is equal to or better than what they have now—at least, not without a lot of work. Oh, they talk a good line about their mobility and marketability—don't believe it. They're scared. That thinking, cuffed together with humans' change-averseness and we have our problem.

"You are a threat. Raef Burnham and his henchmen equates to Ghengis Khan and his warriors—here to destroy our way of life. Remember, hyperbole's my thing, but you do represent a threat. That's why I wanted someone with your background to run this operation. You know the products. You have credibility all over the place. And your skin has been thickened daily for years—you're ready for this challenge."

Raef smiled. "Keep talking like that and your days may be numbered. Have you considered that you have something at stake yourself?"

Chap shrugged. "I have, but this is the right thing to do, so let's do it."

"Does our team have anything going for us politically, like system support?"

Chap rolled out an org chart and tapped the top box in the Portable Foods Division segment. "Only the top guy. The president of our division thinks this is the best idea we've had in years and can't wait to see your results. He needs the bucks and it's tough to generate an additional $1 million bottom line for the division this year by increasing sales. Our stuff goes right to the bottom line. So, yeah, you're sponsored. Does that help?"

Raef pointed to the name in the box at the top of the chart. "I'll practice dropping Dov Ogden's name in my conversations. This helps. And this," pointing to the productivity file on Chap's desk, "this … is the right thing."

Raef launched the studies, met with people, outlined zones for deeper investigation and set project priorities. The first week in April, two months after he had started reporting to Chap, his new boss walked into his office. Raef feigned a wide-eyed, open-mouth shock look. "Pardon me, sir, but may I see your ID? I'm unaccustomed to strangers walking into my secured office and making themselves comfortable."

Chap looked up and pursed his lips. "I told you I didn't need to know everything you are doing. You've been around. You know what needs to be done and I'm sure you're doing it. No, I just want you to know you get John, my best and brightest, and I want you to challenge him. No grunt work-discipline-character-enhancing stuff; no I-used-to-be-an-Army-captain-and-I'm-still-tough stuff; just technical challenges that will keep him up nights. It'll take a couple of weeks, but get ready for him. Oh, that reminds me ..." Chap had stood to leave and sat back down again. "I want you to continue with the mentor group, and could you get some presentations ready for the technical conference in the fall?"

Raef nodded. "I'm doing the mentoring—on the steering committee. And we're working on a paper about plant testing and another about our work in productivity."

Chap stood again. "Good. And I'm finding you a technician. She's one of the best workers in the building and I think she'll be available about the time John is available. So, by June 1st you should be on your way. I hope you have something for them to work on by then."

Raef opened the folder on his desk. "I have. Could I bring you up to date now?"

"Can't. No time. I have to run."

On June 1st two events occurred simultaneously. Fortune Montag appointed P. Dank Reedy to lead WFI's new Soy Applications Division and Chap, the Director of Portable Foods created Raef's new productivity team.

By September 1st the new team completed pilot plant testing of the first three productivity projects and John took Wave I (Project Low Hanging Fruit) to the plants for preliminary testing—initial stages. Over the winter of 1998 and spring of 1999 John changed the manufacturing processes and the division began to save the money.

In May Raef began the evaluation of Wave II (Project Squeeze) concepts. All were top sellers, so they encountered exponential resistance to their efforts even thought the first wave of changes had been successful. Despite the resistance, Raef's group moved to pilot test two more $1 million cost saving projects during the summer of 1999.

In early August, when Raef returned from his annual sojourn on the Gunflint Trail, he picked up a phone message from Chap: "See me when you get back." Raef's stomach flipped. He hung up the phone and took a deep breath. Two minutes later he stepped into Chap's office and closed the door. "I don't have much of a record with this kind of message, so ... I think I have to go to California pretty quick."

"What does that mean? On what?"

"I don't know. But I'll think of a reason. I really don't feel like surprises today. So ... What?"

CHAPTER 23

PROJECT FLEET—THE RISE AND FALL

"*Project Fleet.* Interesting name. Start ship date is what?"

Chap looked up. "Christmas."

"Which year?"

Chap sat there.

"You gotta be kidding—it's August!" Raef walked over to the wall and leaned his back against it. "Four months? You're kidding, right? Well, how many people are you giving me to create this miracle?"

Chap sat there.

"No. C'mon. Hey, give me a feel for this thing. How …? What's the business—the point of the venture? To see if there's money in the Internet? Duh!" Raef leaned against the wall and shook his head.

Chap looked at Raef, lowered his head slightly and kept his gaze focused eye-to-eye with Raef. "No, we want to see if we can conduct a profitable business in food on the Internet in a manner that fits our ways of doing business … see if we can conduct a profitable business doing it our way."

"Four months? Someone's nuts. How many people are you going to give me, six?"

"None. You're in this alone. That's the beauty of this thing. Think about it." Chap smiled and rubbed his hands together. "Listen, with your experience it won't take long. You'll figure out the manufacturing while you're doing the formulating. Heck, you'll probably get done by …" Chap flipped his calendar, "October."

Raef moved back to the table and sat down. He shook his head. "Not with the focus groups, market research tests, and the do-overs that marketing'll require. This is a two year operation. Maybe you can get it chopped to a year. But four months? Not on your Aunt Tilley's whatever. Not possible. And I'm the optimist."

Chap smiled. "No, that's what I mean by 'the beauty.' Do you know how Web sites work? First, they're always under repair, so we put the site together in a couple of weeks. We let people find it and try to order—it'll give us a read on what they really want. In the meantime you do the formulating.

"Then, when you think you're ready, we start taking orders and shipping. No testing. No focus groups—hey, if after 30 years in the food business you don't know what a good dessert is, we'll never know. No market research. Just put it together and go—fix it on the fly. By the way, the product selection meeting is this afternoon over at the main office. At 2 o'clock. Pick good targets. It'll make your job easier. Oh, I'm assuming you're accepting the assignment. When we're through with this you'll be leading the Internet task force for the company. Do you think there's a promotion in that?"

WFI's Consumer Kitchen sat on the ground floor of the main office building, near the west entrance, just off a small parking lot. The 150-foot carpeted showroom swept north from the reception area and hugged the west wall. The west wall was floor to ceiling glass and opened to a full view of oaks, maples, and ash decorating a Waldenesque pond. The pond's 20 shades of green with some sky and water blue poured in and cast its hue on the roomful of tables set for show.

Down the middle of the room ran the dividing wall between the show area and the preparation zone. Behind that wall a team of eight home economists and food scientists prepared the 150 samples for presentation. Thirty minutes before the guests arrived, project managers placed the table tent markers on the three- by eight-foot covered tables. Fifteen minutes before the guests arrived, the kitchen team played traffic control and guided the plates and trays and pans of products to their assigned landing areas.

At exactly 11 o'clock Raef and the kitchen team stepped back to review the layout. At 11:05 the support group walked in. And at precisely 11:10 the marketing and market research contingent dashed into the room panting apologies for being late: "Fortune needed an update for the board meeting review over in the wing." One of the support team leaned over to Raef and whispered, "Important stuff that." He smiled.

But *Project Fleet* was on its way with an objective understood by all—to sell good products on the Internet and prove that this is a business. It was a monument to clarity.

WFI's consumer specialists who interacted with the buying public every day, selected the samples shown and chose the benchmarks—the products everyone agreed were the best representatives of quality. Several homemade recipes were selected as ideals, recipes that used only fresh ingredients and were handed down, grandmother to grandchild to kitchen rep, through the years. The rest were "Mrs. Fields"—brownies, bars, muffins, cookies. Debbie Fields had created quite a name for herself in the fresh baked goods arena, opened mall shops all over the place, and expanded into a mail order operation—Internet business, actually. Her name said "quality," and her customers agreed.

The team divided the samples into categories, selected the categories that would work best as finger foods, and eliminated all but the beignets, scones, brownies, and cookies.

Raef picked up the final offering and adjusted his belt. Keeping to any designated weight was just about impossible in this line of work, but he kept up the fight. He wiped the corners of his mouth and reached for a glass of water. "I have a few thoughts on technical challenges."

"And some of these categories—they aren't us," declared the marketing contingent.

Packaging and distribution and graphics offered similar declarations.

"Who starts?"

"Product."

Half an hour later the team had eliminated the beignets and the scones, defined the five products in the line, agreed to the targets, and launched the project.

"Want to see the products in four weeks?" Raef shouted as people began moving toward the door. Everyone nodded, waved, and vanished. *Project Fleet* was on its way. But *Project Fleet* had no people—almost none. It had no hierarchy, and …

The next four weeks felt like the *swoosh* in comic action movement. Raef had gone to work early the day after Labor Day, which meant oh-dark-thirty in the morning and, for the rest of the month, come home any time after 7 p.m.—dusk or beyond. But by October 1st his product line was ready for show.

After the review Chap closed the meeting room door and turned around smiling. "Five products in four weeks? How many iterations—by product, how many formulations?"

Raef sat down on the stool next to the products. "If there were serial numbers for each formula, those before you would be 001, 001, 003, 002, and 001A. Scale up to pilot plant will take some more work. But we're on the way."

Chap looked at the timetable. "Good work. How'd you make your choices?"

"You mean my market research? Hallway testing like, 'Which do you prefer, A or B?' They all beat their benchmark and these are great! Better than anything on the market. Better than some fresh bakeries."

Chap scratched his right eye brow. "I mean the real thing. Market research. Do you have consumer test results yet?"

Raef shook his head. "There won't be any. No time. These are good. They'll meet consumer expectations, and the competition can't touch us. If we have issues we'll fix the formulas on the fly—we can turn this around in days. Besides, I have plant tests next week."

Chap furrowed his brow. "Where?"

Raef poked Chap in the shoulder. "I gave them two choices when this project began: a production location here in town or my garage if they couldn't find anyone who'd work with us. It's not that complicated. We don't have to go nuts on the road and we don't have time for the travel!"

Chap, long used to these black and white answers from Raef, smiled and raised both eyebrows, "So, where?"

"We're going to produce in The Corner Bakery, a nice little shop—not so little actually—across the river and just north of the freeway. It's about forty minutes and we can handle that."

He listened to Raef's answer and looked puzzled. "And you're testing when?"

"Next week. All week. Monday, Tuesday, Wednesday, Thursday and Friday. It'll be a tough week, but we have to evaluate the product, adjust, check out the packaging for each product, and try out the Internet system. Once approved, we're good to go. If we hit glitches we'll be scrambling."

Raef reached into a bag and pulled out a handful of products and laid them on Chap's desk. "Production starts December 1st. Hey, these are for you. We can do this, you know. Large scale."

Chap held his stomach. "Ho, Ho, Ho. Ready by Christmas. Well, let me know how you're doing … at least, once in awhile. Somebody might ask … It's possible."

Raef spent September getting his products ready, October testing them at The Corner Bakery a half hour away, November finalizing the formulas, and early December setting the plant specifications for the products.

*   *   *   *

Jay sat at his desk just off the baking floor at The Corner Bakery. His office crowded itself between the entrance that looked out onto the parking lot adjacent to the freeway's frontage road and the employee cafeteria. It was Friday afternoon. Normally, Fridays were a winding-down, cleaning up process as the plant prepared for the slower weekend business. But today, the rest of the plant was beginning to crank up to make up for the interruption caused by Raef's tests. Jay looked through the glass wall out onto the production floor and let out a sigh. "Whew. Now, *that* was a week. Tell me about your results."

Raef took off his safety helmet and hairnet, wiped his forehead with his hand, and laid his notebook alongside the chair. "I think we're home. Our team met, reviewed the results, took lots of samples back to our place, and concluded we can write it up."

Jay squinted at the term. "And 'write it up' is good?"

Raef smiled. "Write it up. Yeah, jargon. We have to create a document that outlines everything about a product. The report includes the reason for being, a product description, the formulas, the process, production parameters, the whole deal. With that document anyone, presumably at least, could go out and produce this product. Impressive, huh? We guard those items closely. You'll have a copy of what we prepare."

Jay reached for his file and held up a piece of paper. "We do it on one sheet."

"What?"

"Convey production information." He handed the sheet to Raef. "We do all that you are speaking of on one sheet; one sheet per product. Coffee?" Jay poured two cups as he watched Raef page through some notes. "Do you think this will fly?"

Raef put his notes down. *"Project Fleet?* Man, I hope so. But I'm just a little afraid we're putting you through a lot of hoops and wasting a ton of your time. You know, setting up the whole computer operation, integrating it into our billing system—that's a huge investment on your part."

Jay waved a hand. "Don't feel sorry for us. You told us two things up front: Most of these projects fail—so be warned; and people like us always come out better for having worked with you. I'm willing to go with that. Not to mention, look at all you've taught me—it's free learning I'm getting. You guys have thousands of hits a day on your Web site and want to run a business alongside that. I get to watch from inside to see if it works. It doesn't get any better than that."

Raef folded his papers and stuffed them into his briefcase. "You guys amaze me. Did you ever read Kiyosaki's *Rich Dad Poor Dad*? He talks about entrepreneurs compared to folks that rely on corporations for their security. Our kind of people think that your world is risky, betting your future on your own decisions. But he says that the risk is in the corporation where the individual can be gone in a moment."

"Risk is real in our world," Jay said as he leaned forward with one elbow on his knee. "But the part I like is that I'm the one who gets to control it, at least to a degree. And risking getting involved with your company is controlled: The downside is quantifiable. The upside is huge. And I get to learn for free. I think that is a wise involvement—for both of us, actually."

Raef squinted. "Jay, are you going into the Internet baking business?"

Jay changed expression. "It depends. Ask me next year. I'll know a lot more then."

Raef nodded and grabbed his things. "I'll bet you will."

Jay laughed. "If I don't, it'll be for good reasons."

Raef started toward the door. "Let's plan on a startup around the seventh of December. Between now and then, I'll be in touch."

"Mr. Burnham, it was a good week."

*   *   *   *

"That's fine, but how are sales?" By mid-December the production team had conducted two complete runs, packaged the products, and shipped them all over the country. Good data showed that freshness and quality arrived with every shipment and customers were pleased. But a lot of the data were in-house orders where company sales people were checking out the system or buying product for corporate meetings. In some cases it was marketing asking friends to order. Nothing was real yet. Raef sharpened the point of his question. "How are the real sales? Is any real person interested in our product?"

"Not so hot. But we have no advertising dollars, and it's early."

* * * *

On February 10, 2000 Raef received word that Adam Irish had died in Los Angeles. It was a sad phone call, but he had been expecting the call for just about seven years. They'd spoken by phone over the years—definitely at Christmas—and the conversation was always warm and friendly. But they never got together after that day in 1993.

Requiescat in pace.

* * * *

Project Fleet sales and deliveries rose in February, but they tapered off in March. The team waited for the April charts with the calmness of expectant parents.

Late in March Raef drove over to have lunch with Jay. "*Project Fleet* isn't going to make it, Jay. Surprised?"

Jay put down his piece of pizza. "No. A little disappointed—I thought you … we could pull it off. But, no. I see the orders—the lack of orders. It's too bad."

Raef wiped his hands. "Yes it is. But we held our "Fish or Cut Bait" meeting yesterday and the outcome wasn't wonderful. We're going to push some things, and we'd like you to continue to work with us for two or three more months. We'll try not to get in your way, but we'd like to explore some ideas. You willing?"

"Of course. I can always fit your runs in. What's next for you?"

Raef pushed himself away from the table. "I'm presenting three technical papers to our research staff in May and two processing papers—and we're publishing two patents. It's going to be a busy summer. And I still have the productivity work going."

After another cup of coffee Jay looked at Raef and paused. "Was there more to this project for you than just selling a few more desserts?"

"Why do you ask?"

Jay opened a hand and presented a slightly quizzical expression. "You have a little more passion for the idea than I'd expect from a man in this stage of his career. Oh, I like focus. I look for it. But with you, it's something else. Owners have that passion, regardless of age. Lawyers, sometimes. Some writers I know.

But I don't see it among the hired guns—managers—people who work for companies. Unless they're at the top. Hey, what do I know? Just asking."

"Good insights, Jay. I'll have to think about that. But the short answer is 'Yes'."

Raef drove west into a March sunset. *What IS next for you, Raef? Fleet's over—kiss it goodbye. What's next? The career game is over. That's a fact—so? Reset my sights. But man, those were good products!*

*   *   *   *

At the last team meeting in April one of the shipping people asked, "How do we look?"

The MBA in charge of the program laid down the report in her hands. "What are you seeing?"

"Not so good. We started out in December pretty good. January was growing well and February too. But March tapered off and April has tanked. We don't quite get it."

The MBA continued. "The shipping reflects our activity; we're testing the system. But what you see in shipping doesn't reflect real sales—until these last six weeks. The last 45 days hand us real sales. It means that our programs aren't gaining traction and we have little left to try."

Around the table individual conversations broke out and the room filled with the mumble of chaos.

"One at a time please. One at a time."

Raef, from the center of the table opposite the marketing director, looked around the table then fixed on the director. "What's the problem? Product quality tests well—those results are outstanding. What do you think it is?"

The director settled to a declarative monotone offering in a matter-of-fact voice, "No money. We have no money to spend on promotion. There's no message whatever reaching our undefined target audience. No one knows we're out there and we have no way to attract their attention—it's as simple as that. We have to see if any of our concepts catch on. And we still have four weeks."

This game is over.

On May 1st Raef and Jenifer's fourth grandchild was born, Raef was invited to attend the June R&D management weekend on Gull Lake, and he continued with Wave III of productivity projects, teaching in production school, preparing for the fall technical conference, writing the first of his two new patents, and making plans for two weeks on the Gunflint.

The June *Project Fleet* meeting was over in ten minutes, but the conversation and analysis by the team lasted an hour.

The director concluded the business portion of the meeting with, "… and I thank you all for a great effort; it just didn't work out. Thanks again, everybody. Enjoy the rolls and coffee and stick around as long as you'd like."

Raef sat down next to the director. "What do you think the real problem was?"

He answered with a tone of care. "The corporation just doesn't believe there's money to be had on the Internet for our kind of business. They were unwilling to fund the operation. Our rules of engagement were that we could spend on development, but not on promotion. It was the kiss of death."

Raef responded to the finality. "It got you answers. Were they real?"

The director nodded. "I think they were. Hey, we had a good product. We outlined good production, packaging and delivery. But left to normal market forces, there was no pull out there. No repeat purchases. Too costly. No push. Time to walk away."

* * * *

The Gull Lake management conference blended focus and fun. The research center's management team invited three level 5s to join in the discussions; each of the 5s had worked for WFI more than 25 years, endured mid-career setbacks, and continued to function at a high level since the level adjustment. The 30 attendees boarded a bus at the center on Monday morning, traveled the 2 ½ hours to Gull Lake, grabbed a light walking lunch, and broke into golfing foursomes for the afternoon. The schedule called for morning meetings on Tuesday with afternoon golf and an evening discussion session. And Wednesday was scheduled to begin with a wrap-up session in the morning and close with a bus ride back to the center.

Tuesday after the evening discussions Raef walked out onto the deck and watched the sun set on Gull Lake. Quiet blanketed the shoreline. Once in awhile the call of a loon pierced the cool night air, but the only other sounds were the clunking of aluminum boats as the staff prepared for tomorrow's fishing excursions.

"Raef, you look fit."

Raef turned. "As do you, Fortune. As do you." The two men shook hands.

Fortune turned to watch the setting sun. "I wanted you here for two reasons, Raef. First, you have insights from the working level and you are not bashful about sharing. Second, I wonder how your career is progressing."

"Well, I contributed what I had to the conference …"

"Thank you for that. You did not disappoint."

Raef turned to face Fortune. "The second is a more complex issue."

Fortune turned his back to the lake and leaned against the rail. "I do not think so. Have you been successful?"

Raef turned his back against the rail and slipped his hands into his pockets. "Is that the question? I thought you'd ask, 'Was there a road back?'"

Fortune thought a moment. "Those are the same questions, are they not?"

Raef leaned on one elbow and looked directly at Fortune. "I used to think so. Now, I'm not so sure."

"Explain please."

Raef placed both elbows on the rail and stared into what was left of the sunset. "I made some errors and admitted my failure. But you didn't warn me about my need to correct a behavior. I refocused. I set new goals for myself, goals with two components—the parts I can control and the parts I can't. I control how hard I work and whether we reach our objective—in that regard, I've not failed even once in 17 years. Not since April 1983. Whether you reward me by putting me in areas of greater responsibility—situations that match up with my abilities, my demonstrated abilities—is out of my control. Yes, I still seek advancement—recognition, actually—in your hierarchy. But your decision to withhold that advancement doesn't constitute career failure—not from my perspective. The issue is complex."

Fortune stood erect. "There is no road back. That was the statement. That is the fact. Failure to regain one's former level is failure. Anything else is semantics."

"Fortune," Raef shook his head. "You have position power in this discussion. But one day it would be fun to take these two perspectives before a neutral audience and see what we conclude about the meaning of success—I'd enjoy the debate. Success … failure. Is the issue position? Influence? … Or does something else play a role? That would be fun."

Fortune lowered his voice. "Raef, you would not win even there." He paused and looked toward the center. "It has been nice talking with you. Now I must get back to the rest of my guests. I am sure we will talk again."

Fortune concluded the Wednesday wrap-up session and the attendees boarded the bus for the ride back to Westphalia. Raef slid into a window seat and laid his head back as the bus eased to cruising speed and the early rumble reached up to its familiar drone. *Success … failure … does something else play a role? Hmmmm.*

BOOK FOUR

Chapter 24

▼

INEVITABLE

Nighttime challenged Raef with a dream.

He sat straight up in bed at 1:45 that morning and stumbled to his office in the next room to get a piece of paper. With the words of Bobby Darin's *A Song of Freedom* still playing in his mind, he scribbled five stanzas, then the sixth, and laid them on his desk to review in the morning. *I haven't heard that song in fifteen years—then this. Freedom! How does a person spend thirty-some years in a large corporation if his life focus is freedom?*

Then he pulled out a notebook, picked up the pen and dashed off a heading:

"NOTES ON A DREAM."

As I awoke at 1:45 this morning the words to "A Song of Freedom" were on my mind. Why?

From my first day at the research labs on 1/16/67 until the morning of Friday, 4/15/83, I would have done (almost) whatever it took to be a success—have title, been a Director/VP—and I expected it to happen.

At 9:00 a.m. on 4/15/1983 they tampered with that dream. It ended. Reconstruction of a life began and still continues.

Some have termed this my defining moment. Maybe it was. But the result of that tampering is that I am FOREVER FREE! From the deepest recesses of my being I declare DON'T TREAD ON ME; and I resolved then as I do now, YOU WILL NEVER OWN ME AGAIN—EVER!

So, for the eighteen plus years since, I have been fiercely independent—and I love it. Thank you. I appreciate the results. So I sing Darin's simple song of freedom.

Raef closed the notebook, slipped it back into the desk drawer, and went back to bed. Jenifer reached over and touched his shoulder as he lay down, "Everything alright?"

"Everything's fine, darlin'—everything's just fine. Go back to sleep."

*   *   *   *

Raef swung a left-hand turn, pulled up to the Sandstone Road Starbuck's, parked the car and sprinted to the double door entry. "Mocha Grande, please. Extra cream. Running a little late today. Have you seen Clyde?" He looked around. The last Saturday of the month was his self-designated "writer's coffee" where Raef met his sometime coach and all-time writing encourager. They'd met at the Swim and Fitness Club seven years ago, found mutual areas of interest and in the last year began monthly coffees to discuss the art and craft of writing. Clyde, a practicing psychologist and former U.S.Army Reserve Colonel, was usually on time—today he was 15 minutes late.

"No, but you guys never miss, do you? That'll be $3.56."

The coffee shop scattered 15 tables in a half-moon array around the ordering counter. A set-apart table in the northwest corner promised quiet for whoever claimed it. Today the homesteader was Raef. On the east wall laptops clicked while writers, entrepreneurs and a few students tapped on the keys, paused, looked up and around, squinted at the screens and tapped the keys once more in interrupted staccato bursts.

Raef laid his file folder on the table and sat down partially facing the street. He reached into the folder, brought out Jack Bickham's *Scene and Structure*, and opened to his marker. In the years when Raef was learning to control pressure in his life he had learned to always bring a book or other work to an appointment. That way, if anyone was late, time was never wasted and temper stayed its rise.

He started to read when he looked up to see Clyde mouth to the counter, "The usual," as he turned toward the table. "You wouldn't believe it. I was sitting in the barber's chair 10 minutes ago when I remembered what today was. Sorry."

Clyde's *Warbirds in Flower* was in final rewrite, so the conversation started there. Coffee appeared. "Table service—only for you guys. Hope you're having a good day and let us know if you need anything." After a brief summary Clyde wrapped up his thoughts and said, "Enough of that. Where are you with work? Have you decided to call it a day yet?"

Raef took a sip. "You kidding? I have five years left in my non-contract. Actually, I've thought a little about retiring at 62 but haven't given the subject a lot of thought." He held up the Bickham book. "No, I'm just working on my hobby—preparing for my next career when I can try my hand at what you do."

Clyde pulled out a pouch of natural sugar from the pile on the table. "What's today's topic?"

"A dream." Raef waited for a reaction, then moved on. "Mine. Last night. It was Bobby Darin's song about freedom—part of his last work." Raef described the specifics and stopped. Then he started laughing. "What am I doing, telling a psychologist about a dream? Well, tell me your thoughts … and don't send me a bill!"

Clyde smiled, tore the sugar pouch and poured it into his coffee. "It was inevitable."

Raef squeezed his eyes half shut. "What was?"

Clyde stirred the cup. "The outcome in your career—well, what happened in '83. If you really put the premium on freedom that you described in the dream … your being put down a notch—was inevitable. Your attitude, independence, would brand you 'not a team player,' and down you go. It could have happened in the first couple of years or in the last few, but it was inevitable."

Raef shook his head. "What about skill?"

Clyde wagged a finger. "The issue wasn't whether you had skills; it was whether you had the right skills. The corporation needed to know it could trust you to always do the right thing—what they needed in the way they needed it. They realized they couldn't rely on you and both of you still know that was the case. You thought it a virtue to be that 'moral'—they didn't." He leaned forward. "Didn't it ever strike you that you felt free and aggressive at a Level 5, but that you felt constrained, even imprisoned, at Level 6? You told me about all that stuff." He sipped his coffee. "What do you think of Level 6s and above?"

Raef shot back. "They're lackeys. And I don't trust their motives."

"All of them?"

"No. Some are pretty good people."

Clyde set his coffee aside and leaned forward. "So, they're not all amoral—puppets?"

Raef leaned forward against the table. "No. But I know that at the 6 level WFI owned some part of me they had no right to; at 5, they didn't."

"And you've concluded that since that was true for you, it must be true for all?" Clyde got up and poured a second cup. "Here's my point. You could have found a road back. You're savvy enough to have figured out that all you needed was a sponsor and you're flexible enough to have made the adjustment—if you really wanted to. But you didn't seek one out. Why? My answer—because you didn't want to make that adjustment. You didn't want to do it. They knew it and you knew it—really. Inevitable." He left his words hang in the air. "Some people can give in some areas and not be the less for it. You couldn't—or at least you didn't think you could."

Raef emptied his cup and placed his napkin inside. "Part of me wants to cry right now, Clyde. I'm not kidding. Damn! I came to WFI in 1967 when the world was upside down with Viet Nam and everyone marching in the streets. I came as a Captain, U.S.Army to a company looking for the next leaders. Man, perfect. Right skills. Right place. Right time.

"Over time I got pretty good at making products, took a ton of business courses and learned the business cycle, and pioneered lots of new practices in research. In 1976 I was the second youngest department head they'd ever created, and I'd only been with the company a little over nine years. It doesn't sound like much in the fast track world today, but the greatest generation was in charge then and they were hard to convince. They believed in time in grade. They wanted everyone who advanced to spend a certain amount of time in each level, on specific jobs. Fast track then meant you got those jobs."

Clyde nodded. "Like the military. What happened when you finally got promoted?"

Raef edged forward in the chair. "We had no mentoring program then, and when I started a new job, I was terrible. I'm … no natural moves. Eventually, I figured out the system, but to me maintaining a business was a charade—like role playing or following dance steps painted on the floor. Boring.

"I understood leadership and I loved pushing the limits, living on the technical edge—but play acting? Forget it. And I didn't like being owned—expected to act in a particular way and say certain things when it came to ideas."

Raef leaned back in his chair and raised his hands. "Whoa, listen to me. Anyway, it's too bad. I feel like I never got to play my best game; like I never got to do what I'm best at—leading groups to do needed work. Maybe that's because the entry fee for that race is more than my fragile account could handle. Freedom … I don't know. Does this limit my career outcome to failure?"

Clyde was looking at his hands, just listening. "What do you think, Raef?"

Raef smiled. "Ah, the psychologist re-appears. That's good. Anyway, no, I don't think so. We did some good work over the career and I'm still giving WFI a good day's work for a day's pay. Now they have the opportunity to do the right thing—you know, like in the Oscars where they allow 'Lifetime Achievement Awards'? They can give me a Level 6 title in that spirit. Anyway, that's the latest version of 'Raef's goal.'"

Clyde laid down his cup. "Actually, I think that goal has been in place for some time. But you're really not expecting anything, right?"

The two sat silent for a minute. The last of the morning crowd straggled out and the luncheon line began to get longer. Clyde laid his glasses on the table. "What's next?"

"My crash project just ended. Jenifer and I are heading for vacation in a couple of weeks. Then we'll see."

"Next month then?"

"Right here."

They walked toward their cars. As Clyde opened his door he leaned on the roof and shouted to Raef, "Keep your head down."

Raef cupped a hand to his ear to cut off some of the traffic noise. "Pardon me?"

"Watch yourself. It's not over … you know … until it's over."

Chapter 25

▼

Approaching Countdown—The Purchase

Raef and Jenifer drove north the first week in July meandering through the back country, stopping now and then for coffee in the small towns along the way. After a walk along the breakwaters at Grand Marais, some shopping and a cup of cappuccino they headed 25 miles inland on the Gunflint Trail to East Pine Lodge nestled one mile off the trail on East Pine Lake. Beyond the lodge and back in the woods was Cabin 3, their home for two whole weeks of solid quiet and relaxation. They unpacked the car and stashed everything in the cabin. A half hour later Raef settled back on the porch chair, propped his feet up on the rail and heaved a deep sigh. "How many years have we been coming north?"

"I don't know. Sometime in the mid seventies," Jenifer answered to a hummingbird perched in mid-air just outside the kitchen window. She looked toward the trees. "I just love the shadows up here, especially later in the day. And can you hear that 'Oh Canada-Canada-Canada' bird singing? Very welcoming. Nice."

For the next 12 days the two vacationers read and walked and lazed around and watched the Northern lights until 2 a.m. and got up between nine and ten every morning and walked the back roads and trails and lay out on the dock and cruised the lake in a rented boat and photographed moose and just enjoyed the land of no televisions, no radios, no telephones, no newspapers—peacefully.

Saturday of the second week Raef leaned back in the hand hewn maple porch chair and sipped the morning's first cup of steaming coffee as he gazed at the far shoreline stretching toward the morning sun rising over East Pine. "Last day of vacation, Sweets! We're going to have to run up to the lodge and pay the bill sometime this afternoon." He paused and took another sip. "And we were going to talk about a retirement date so we can do some planning. You know? 62 or 65—the planner … Ah, that's too heavy for today. But one of these days …"

Jenifer, wrapped in a ball at the round bar table that served as a breakfast nook at the west end of the screened-in porch, warmed her hands around the steaming mug of coffee. She glanced at Raef then stared at the streaming vapor rising from the cup. "It's hard to believe that we've been here two weeks, isn't it? I could get used to no phones, no TV, no newspaper." Then using both hands she brought the mug to her lips, took a sip, and laid the cup back on the table. "No, two weeks is enough. Don't you think?"

"Yup. But I love pulling back. Now, it's time to face reality and pay the bill. I'll see you in a few minutes."

Raef startled a chipmunk as he began his walk down the stony trail, through the parking lot filled with cars half packed for tomorrow's journey home, and up the board and stone steps to the lodge.

"Here's the bill, Mr. Burnham. And will you be signing up for next year?"

"Cabin 3, one more time—yes. You know, we've had that cabin at this time every year since you built it."

Dave scratched a receipt and marked his book for next year. "And we appreciate your business. By the way, did you see this morning's headline?"

"No. I make it a point not to check the news when I'm up here. Why?"

He pulled a paper off the rack and handed it to Raef. "Your company just bought a competitor. Good news?"

"Better to buy than be bought. Let me see that." Raef scanned the article. "Wow! Well, good news? We'll see. Anyway, take care. We're out of here in the morning. How much for the paper?"

Dave waved. "Take it … Next year."

Raef tripped on the doorsill as he pushed open the solid pine door, caught his balance, squinted toward the mid-morning sun and stepped out into the crisp, fresh air.

"Did they have it right?"

"What?"

Jenifer zeroed in on Raef. "The bill. Did they have it right?"

"Family finances—our game of intrigue." Raef nodded. "Same number as you."

"Is there a problem? Hey, I'm over here." Jenifer waved her hands. "Is there a problem?" She cupped her hands around her mouth. "Earth to Raef!"

"WFI bought Global Nature International. Man …" He shook his head and looked up. "Hey, either way, we have one day of vacation left. Good for a hike?"

* * * *

Mondays after vacation Raef usually used to get back into the flow of the city. When the alarm went off at 7 and he showered and got cleaned up, Jenifer rolled over and squinted at her clock. "You're going in? Have you forgotten what happened the last time you didn't create a little distance between relaxation and WFI?"

Raef walked over and kissed her. "Sorry. I've been awake for awhile—I have to see for myself what's going on with this purchase. I'll call you later if I learn anything."

Jenifer rolled over and pulled up the covers. "I just enjoy lunch out … but I think your head would be behind your desk and you wouldn't enjoy … sure … bye."

Raef flashed his badge at the north corridor guard and headed straight for his office. As he opened the stairway door Plass shot through heading for the meeting rooms. "Plass, you've had quite a busy time while I was on vacation."

Plass, three steps down the hallway, stopped and turned. "What were your first thoughts?"

"That it buys us markets, but I don't know about the blend of the two cultures. What do you think?"

Plass smiled. "Opportunities and challenges. Gotta go. Welcome back!"

Raef headed toward his office. "Now that's an understatement!" Raef opened his office door—the phone was ringing. *7:35 a.m. I'm supposed to still be on vacation!*

"Raef Burnham … right away, Chap. Your office or mine?" Before he could notice that Chap was no longer on the line, Chap walked in carrying a handful of memos and closed the door.

Chap leaned on the desk. "What would you say if packages were offered?"

Chapter 26

▼

TRY THIS ON FOR SIZE

Raef set his briefcase on the floor near the door and stopped to savor the aroma of beef stew that filled the house. Jenifer called from the kitchen, "I'm trying a new recipe—James Beard's. Hope you like it."

"Couldn't wait, I see."

Jenifer, standing at the counter, finished slicing the Havarti. "I thought some cheese might go well tonight. And I found a nice Chardonnay—it doesn't go with beef, they say, but I felt like it." She laid the cheese in domino fashion around the center of the tray. "What are you going to tell him? Chap."

Raef finished pouring two glasses and handed one to Jenifer as they sat alongside the coffee table. He raised his glass to eye level as he looked at Jenifer. "Cheers. Welcome back to the world." They clinked glasses, took a sip and set the glasses on the table. "I don't know. Like we talked about up north—I thought we'd go another 2 to 5 years, didn't you? If that's the case, I don't need to tell anybody anything. Chap is just planning. He's asking just in case the question comes up." Raef paused a moment, then sat back.

Jenifer looked out the window. "The house is paid off and the kids are doing fine on their own. We don't have enough savings to quit working, do we? I always figured you'd work until 65—or at least 62. I don't know."

They chatted for awhile. Finally Raef put down his glass. "Let's enjoy a great dinner, a quiet evening, and tomorrow I'll make some calls. We have plenty of time. He doesn't need an immediate answer."

Tuesday morning Raef made an appointment with Ivan Swenson at Main Street Financial.

Wednesday morning a gray sky hung low over Arrow Lake as Raef and Jenifer wound their way along the shore. Winds whipped up choppy waves and bent shoreline trees toward town, and the unseasonable 70 degree temperatures threatened to dip into the 60's before they stepped out into the fresh air again. Raef turned south onto Wesphalia's major thoroughfare, glanced toward the Main Street Financial Building and swung the black 2000 Buick Regal over toward the curb. "Do you believe this? A parking place in front of the building. That never happens!"

Jenifer paused as she stepped out of the car and ran her eyes along the first floor windows, first to the left, then to the right. Main Street Financial occupied the first floor of the three story red granite building on the corner. She raised her eyes to the second level and rested at the corner peak. Red granite highlighted by taupe lands and grooves opened to large windows set back from an overhang to preclude the need for blinds in the street side offices. She looked at Raef. "All balanced and classical. Nice."

"I think it's supposed to whisper, 'wealth'."

Jenifer lowered her voice. "Well, it does."

Inside, the designed tile floor stretched the full twenty steps from the entry to the extensive mahogany desk at the far end. From behind the desk a receptionist held court over the foyer—the stone, the plants and any person who dared to challenge the space. As Raef and Jenifer crossed the unmarked ten foot approach limit she declared her challenge: "Do you have an appointment?"

"We do," Raef smiled. "We do. We're here to meet with Ivan Swenson. Is he in?"

"May I say who's calling?"

"The Burnhams."

"I'll call him."

Raef and Jenifer looked at each other, then glanced around the room—and considered the granite benches. Before they could decide to sit, Ivan walked through the door and began the handshake as he broke into the room. "I'm Ivan

Swenson and you, of course, are the Burnhams. Welcome. Could I get you some coffee?"

"I'm Raef. This is Jenifer. And yes, black, for me, please."

"And black for me, too," Jenifer added. "May I ask, is this granite Italian?"

Ivan pointed to the outside pieces that could be seen through a side window. "*Rosa Beta* is the name for some of the Italian used on the exterior; but some is from the Walmarge Granite Company somewhere upstate. And some of the interior decorative pieces are marble actually, *Opera Fantastico, Noisette Fleuri* from Italy also. So, yes, to your question. Now, if you'll follow me, my office is right over here."

The trio walked from the atrium through a short corridor about halfway through the building along the Fifth Avenue side where the sun would be, but not today. The round table to the left was filled with 3-ring folders. The desk mimicked a triangle kitchen with counter space on the left, front, and right. In the far right corner was a large screen computer running a Wall Street ticker updating stocks continually, endlessly. On the far table rested more 3-ring binders. And on the left was the business desk.

Ivan offered Jenifer the chair on the far side of the table and Raef the one with his back to the door. He moved toward the chair next to the designated desk portion of the room, laid a pad on the table, and motioned his assistant to come in with the coffee. "Now, what can I do for you?"

Raef laid out the story of WFI purchasing a competitor and their need to develop a specific financial plan that would allow them to establish personal timing targets.

Ivan asked about current income, 401K's, stock options, savings, home ownership, expected inheritances, and debt.

Next, Raef and Jenifer filled out separate personality forms to establish their risk tolerance. In less than twenty minutes they established their financial compatibility: they were risk averse, individually and corporately, when it came to money. Then Ivan ran myriad computer programs projecting probabilities and risks based on the estimates provided in the conversation and suggested he could work up something specific for retirement now and for retirement at 62 and at 65. He'd get back to them in a week.

Raef looked at Jenifer. "Done." Then turned to Ivan. "A week it is."

Ivan closed his folder and moved toward the door. "I think you're going to be pleased with what I'll have for you."

When they were on the sidewalk, Raef stopped and looked out over the lake. "What do you think?"

Jenifer slipped her arm through his. "This is a big step. Are we doing the right thing?"

"Doing? So far, we're just asking questions."

* * * *

Over the weekend, Raef drove upstate to spend a little time with his 91-year-old father and 88-year-old mother.

"Hey, fella. How about a cup of coffee?"

"You're on, Dad. How's Mom today?"

"Fine. She's resting. She rests a lot these days."

Raef whisked the comment away with a wave of the hand. "Well, I'll see her before I leave, but I wanted to chat with you ... about retirement."

"Retirement? You? How old are you—60?"

Speaking with a nonagenarian about quitting work at 60—I have to be nuts. "I will be in a few weeks. But the question is real. WFI just bought ... a company, the transition won't be fun, and I'm considering closing down my program, retiring—I just need your thoughts."

His dad poured coffee. "First of all, don't be too anxious to quit. If the family genes hold for you, you have a career ahead of you in retirement that is almost as long as the one you just spent at WFI. So think about that before you make your move."

Raef laughed. "Always the optimist. And the flip side is that each of us has today. We just don't know if we have tomorrow. I'll have to balance those two thoughts. But I like your perspective. Here's a question though: How much money do you need to retire? Some financial people say the income should be at least 80 percent of what it is while you're working. Some say more. What do you say?"

His dad shook his head. "That's baloney. I mean, unless you and Jenifer want to travel the world four times a year ... travel is expensive—it's the unknown. But if you want to live like you've lived, it doesn't take that much."

Raef leaned back and sipped the coffee. "I've run the numbers and it seems like 50-60 percent covers the needs ... Yeah, the numbers look okay. But I keep hearing the experts."

"Your mother and I've been able to get buy on my teacher's retirement for a long time ... I wouldn't worry about it. More coffee? Oh, and I made some cake!"

"You?"

His dad held up an apron. "Me? I'm becoming a regular Betty Crocker. Want some?"

After some more coffee, some cake, a walk to the garden and a chat on the porch, Raef and his dad shook hands. "Thank you. I needed your perspective. I'm not going to see Mom today—I'll call her later."

His dad shook his head. "Yeah, probably best we don't wake her. Greet everybody for us. Come when you can."

"Next Saturday. We'll do the lawn, trim the hedge, and take care of some of the tomatoes. See you then. Oh, and I'll call tomorrow."

* * * *

On Tuesday Jenifer called Raef at 11:15. "We've got mail—a packet from Ivan."

"Did you open it?"

"Are you kidding?"

"Afraid it says we can do it? Or afraid it says we can't?"

"Yes. And lunch is a cheese and veggie sandwich … with a little soup."

"Perfect. See you in fifteen minutes."

* * * *

Raef opened the 11" x 14" manila envelope, pulled out the pile of stapled documents, and laid them on the table. "Any guesses?"

"Would you just read the thing, please? Just read it." Jenifer's tone was an exaggerated tense, but the smile and glint in her eyes said something else. "What does it say?"

Raef assumed his Dustin Hoffman *Wag The Dog* tone of voice. "Well, first it says that if we can invest everything we have at 10 percent interest forever without risk, we're fine. But if we can't, maybe we're not fine."

Jenifer stood up and reached for a towel. "Enough. Enough. What does it say? Can we do anything ever? At 65? At 62? I'm not kidding."

Raef leafed through the five or six documents and placed the palm of his right hand on his neck and shoulder and stretched his neck against the pressure. "I'm going to have to take a little time with this. These are two piles: 62 and 65. Interest rates on savings of 6 percent, 8 percent and 10 percent. Caveats. Then a comparison page: what we will need at retirement versus what our estimates project we will have. Then the longevity charts—look at that; they quit at 95. Dad would be honked. I have some studying to do."

Jenifer put on her pleading look. "Doesn't he give a summary recommendation or something?"

Raef shook his head. "No. My guess? In a year it won't make much difference whether we keep working or call it a day. I'll look at it tonight. So far, so good. Now, I have a meeting. Have to run. See you about 6."

Jenifer smiled and sat down in front of the pile of papers. As Raef walked toward the door she raised her voice: "I really hate reading this stuff, but I'll go through it this afternoon. We can talk about it tonight?"

Raef nodded and smiled as he began to close the door. "Tonight."

* * * *

Two weeks later Raef and Jenifer wrapped up their meeting with Ivan Swenson. "So, it's within our capabilities whenever we decide?"

Ivan nodded. "Yes, it is. But I think you're going to want a little more income than you're projecting. Think about it."

As they walked to the car Raef put his arm around Jenifer's waist, drew her close and kissed her lightly. "Done. We'll figure out the timing as we go along. How about lunch? Donnelli's?"

* * * *

October and November raced by with project activities, travel, family birthday celebrations, and Thanksgiving.

On December 3rd Chap walked into Raef's office, pulled out a chair behind the small meeting table and, as he lowered his 220 pound frame into it, peered over the top of his reading glasses. "What would you say if packages were offered?"

"I think we've had this conversation before."

Chap didn't flinch. "But I never received an answer."

Raef took a deep breath as he lowered his chin and opened his eyes just a little bit wider. He watched his boss settle deeper in his chair, rest his left forearm on the table, squeeze down the corners of his eyes to the beginning of a squint, and purse his lips ever so slightly. "How long do you think it will take to close this deal, SEC and all?"

Chap shrugged. "Oh, it'll take three months minimum; six months most likely." He smiled and gathered his papers. "Forget the imminency. Talk it over in your house and get back to me tomorrow. Not urgent. Just time sensitive.

And, oh. I've recommended you for the Benchmarks Task Force. They're looking at some best practices in other businesses. I thought you'd be a good fit. Help 'em out, Okay?"

※   ※   ※   ※

The next morning, Raef walked into Chap's office. "If they offer a package, I'll take it."

Chap picked up a note on his desk. "What if they don't?"

BOOK FIVE

Chapter 27

PREPARING FOR FINALS

Raef enjoyed the sunshine and the cold December air as it burst in through the half-inch opening on the passenger-side window. On days like this, the two-mile drive to the main office always lifted his spirits. Once inside he walked the carpeted, mahogany-lined corridor of the new wing to the corner office with the sign alongside the door:

Lehi Weaver
Corporate Director—Employee Services

He stepped into the glass-walled office and squinted into the morning sun now just under the ceiling bars in the southeast corner. "Thanks for seeing me."

Lehi's office location, furniture, and art work declared the occupant's level, but so did every office in the building. It was WFI's way. At the director level all furniture was wood; and at the corporate director level even the wood type was specific. Anything unique about the arrangement originated with the occupant or the occupant's designer, but in Lehi's case no designer was needed.

The six-foot credenza on the far wall was laden with family pictures and trophies from myriad corporate sports activities. In the mix Lehi's six kids expressed delight in the challenges of sport and the rewards of art and music. The prominent center focus, larger and better framed than the rest, held twenty-five people sitting on the porch of a cabin. Near the center were two couples in their sixties. Behind them were several couples who looked a little like Lehi. And all around these adults stood, sat, and knelt fifteen kids besides the six shown in the individual shots. Raef looked at the array, then at Lehi. "I feel like I'm part of the audience or that maybe I've just been adopted into the family. That's a fine crowd."

Lehi nodded and smiled, then motioned for him to take a chair in front of the desk as he himself sat down on the chair just a couple of feet away. "Thank you. They're good people; we have a lot of fun. Well, your call didn't sound urgent, but you sounded like you had something on your mind. How can I help?"

Raef crossed his legs and laid his hands on his lap. "Will there be packages?"

"Doing some thinking, are we?" Lehi settled back in his chair, smiled and adjusted himself in the chair. "So much for small talk, I guess. That's terrific." He paused for a moment. "Just terrific."

Raef crossed his ankles and moved them under his chair. He leaned forward resting his forearms on the arms of the chair and adjusted his position. "I'm just thinking, you know?" Then he leaned back once more, both feet on the floor.

Lehi moved his head from side to side as he spoke. "No problem. No problem. I just enjoy the directness. But to your question, no. No, there won't be any packages. We purchased a competitor. We will need all the experience we can muster to make this transition work. And it will take some time to get the deal done. No packages. Make your plans."

Raef sat there a moment, rubbed his left temple and looked directly at Lehi. "I don't know if this information helps or hurts, but it gives me a base to work from and that's all I needed. I asked for just a few minutes: I'll take no more of your time. No packages?"

Lehi shook his head.

"Thank you." They shook hands, and Raef headed back to his office.

✳   ✳   ✳   ✳

At 4 o'clock Raef met with Kip Lane, the vice-president and director of productivity who oversaw the division. "Packages?"

"Absolutely not."

Raef tapped his pencil on his notepad. "Well, I'm beginning to make some plans and I have to know what I can count on for income. It would help."

"I'm sorry, Raef. There will be no packages. Period."

Raef thanked him and left.

CHAPTER 28

THE TRANSITION II

The Benchmarks Task Force charged into January 2001 with plans to understand how four companies from activities outside of WFI's areas of interest could teach WFI better business practices.

"Why are we doing this?" The representative from Quality Control looked around the room waiting for an answer. "We're a food company. I've worked here 25 years and know the system pretty well. Sure, we have to do things better, but going to a window manufacturing company to learn new business practices? C'mon. What are we going to learn there?"

Ted Stiles, the 29-year-old superstar head of Field Operations walked over to the table near the window and poured himself a cup of coffee. "Raef, you want to handle that one?"

Raef shooed away the question. "It's all yours, Professor."

Stiles walked over to the table and sat down. "We want to see how people in other business worlds see problems and organize to solve them. And, we need to find out what results they get when they're through and how they measure progress. Plus, this Iowa group is big on Japanese-style manufacturing approaches. They've studied with Toyota and adapted many of their practices—manufacturing articles about their success appear all the time. We have to visit these people."

"What about the other three?" Lorna Green asked. "I know about the container company and their unique product niche. But the movie production company and the radio station? I don't get how they're going to help us."

Ted looked around the room. "Lorna, let's take your career as an example. You graduated from the U.S.Naval Academy at Annapolis in when?"

"1990."

"Perfect. You served six years aboard a destroyer, smelling the diesel fuel and leading sailors. Then you left the military and joined WFI. You spent four years in a plant and now you're here—Operations, right?"

Lorna nodded.

Ted looked up. "All different worlds. What did Annapolis training and the plants have to do with what we're doing today?"

"They shaped my perspective. It's all problem solving—the problems get different is all."

Ted looked back at Quality Control. "All different ways to see and solve problems—that's my point. We need fresh approaches and we start next week on our first team visit. Everyone can make it?"

Lots of nods preceded sharing of concerns, but quickly the eagerness to see how others do their work drove the rest of the conversation that closed the meeting on an expectant note. When the conversational din dropped a few decibels, Ted raised his voice slightly. "People? We'll see everybody at the corporate hangar at 7 a.m., Monday. Have a good week."

For the next two months the team departed every other week to visit a different industry and benchmarked procedures that could be brought into WFI. During the intervening weeks Raef's productivity team crafted two other cost savings concepts that changed a cash cow's makeup procedure enough that marketing demanded the team conduct focus groups. The groups required that Raef and the team travel to Charlotte, St. Louis, Columbus, and finally Minneapolis to test the idea.

At the end of March the market research company who had conducted the tests presented their findings. When the test leader ended his comments on his last PowerPoint chart, Chap looked at Raef. "What does all that mean to you?"

"Great idea. Huge savings. But the people identify the total product with the way they've been making it over the years. If we change the method—even if we make it easier to prepare and save steps—they will regard it as a reduction in value and quit buying. Successful operation, patient died. We have to drop it."

Chap smiled and turned to rise from his chair. He looked first at Raef; then scanned the roomful of researchers. "You asked a good question. We didn't waste a lot of time on the quest. The customer has spoken. Let's move on. Good work everybody. Too bad we couldn't implement it—we could use the dollars this year."

※　　※　　※　　※

"You're comfortable with the decision?"

Jenifer nodded. "You know I'm never certain, but ... yes."

※　　※　　※　　※

Chap sat with his shoes off looking out over acres of ... he saw nothing. Mondays in April always made him contemplate new: new seasons, new products, new ways of looking at things, new. And actually, his view stretched over acres of lawn and ponds and trees just beginning to bloom—but Chap saw little of it. "The SEC just ruled on the acquisition. We keep most of the purchase, but we don't get all the pieces we wanted. And there's a brand name dispute brewing. My guess is that they'll close this deal in the fall. What do you think?"

Chap spoke as much to himself as to his guest, but he looked across his desk at Raef, legs crossed, elbows resting on the arms of the chair, hands comfortably intertwined on his lap. "Actually, I'm here about another matter. I'm going to retire at the end of September."

Chap held his gaze steady, but leaned forward with his elbows on his desk. Then he sat back. "Have you picked a date?"

"Whatever the last working day of the month is—I think it's the 28th. Can you handle the next steps or is there something else I have to do?"

Chap slapped his hands together. "Not unexpected, I must say. Write me a note. Be specific about the date. And include a statement that you'd like to be included if packages are offered. Beyond that, you don't have to do anything for now. What made you decide?"

"It's time. Jenifer and I talked. I think this merging of the companies will begin in about October. Then we'll go through the two year transition which I think is going to be pretty ugly. And another thing, Lehi and Kip assure me there'll be no packages. So, it's time."

Chap lowered his head. "You believe them?"

Raef smiled. "I've made the decision knowing that's the speech their handlers expect of them … I'm making the decision for my own reasons."

"Yeah. Okay. I'll make some calls. Stop by later. Maybe I'll have something. Good choice, by the way."

The meeting over, Chap reached for the phone and hit speed dial. Raef got up and as he closed the door Chap said, "Lehi, this is Chap. I want to stop down and chat about some personnel moves."

※   ※   ※   ※

"Raef, Chap. The ball is rolling. Your final day is September 28th and your official retirement day is October 1st. Gentlemen, start your engines!"

※   ※   ※   ※

Lame ducks lead interesting lives. During May and June Raef presented papers at the technical sessions, completed his term on the mentoring steering committee and closed out his projects in productivity. He took most of July off for vacation and used August to work out transitions.

Chapter 29

PREPARATIONS

Closing out the projects proved simpler than Raef anticipated. By the end of the summer John owned the productivity work, Raef's mentees had positioned themselves for their next moves, and Raef was ready to plan the closing.

Monroe, Raef's first intern, had joined WFI, finished two years starting up operations in China and moved back to Westphalia just in time to announce his plan to leave WFI—he'd been accepted at an international business school in Spain. Another former intern was presenting her snack project to her business team and had just submitted applications to business schools in the states—Harvard, MIT, and Stanford among them—and was waiting for acceptance letters. And John, now head of the productivity project, was considering graduate school as a Ph.D. candidate in Chemical Engineering.

✳   ✳   ✳   ✳

Dov Ogden opened his monthly meeting with the announcements that certain people were leaving the division and certain others had just joined. In the military the process was called Aloha—hello or goodbye, depending on the situation. After the expected listings Dov paused and looked at Raef for an instant. Raef caught the look and shook his head slowly. Dov proceeded to list the agenda for the morning without acknowledging this as Raef's last meeting before his retirement. "And when we're through with the business portion of the morning, we want you to experience some of our new products. They'll be served at the tables in the back of the room. Now let's move on to The Big Picture."

Dov, in his late thirties, dark hair, clear eyes, 6'2", athletic and charismatic, was typical of WFI's division presidents. After he received his MBA at Wharton, he joined WFI and worked in the corporate planning area for three years, then marketing in three divisions and finally as president of Raef's division. Any of the other presidents would show the same pedigree: MBA from one of five schools, top 10 in their class, demonstrated broad vision and tours of duty in several marketing divisions within the company. Dov and Raef had worked together during Dov's first division assignment and created a bond that endured.

As the meeting moved along Raef's thoughts drifted toward some of their early discussions. Dov worked from the front of the room to impress his team how difficult it is to change the direction of a division as large as Portable Foods. He likened it to turning an aircraft carrier around and underlined the enormity of the task with, "It takes six miles to turn a ship that large to go in the opposite direction. Six miles. Think of it." Raef was enjoying the story and remembering the Web site picture Lt. Jon Jelski had sent him of the U.S.S John Stennis turning into the wind. All the while Dov continued his story listing the challenges the division faced. In three short sentences he swung the discussion to a halt. "We know why we aren't achieving our objectives." He looked at Raef knowing the veteran had the answer. "Mr. Burnham, why is that?"

Raef, following the story and interjecting his self-talk, had moved past his interpretation of the concept—*We're working on the wrong things; it's obvious*—and was waiting for what came next. Then he realized Dov had asked a question. *AARRGGHH! He's looking at me. What did he just say?* He tried to scan his interior instant replay but found that he had wandered off Dov's river of thought and was paddling on a minor tributary—and the boss was waiting for an answer. *Wrong things, Boss. But I don't know the question and I'm afraid to ask.* Raef smiled and shrugged his shoulders. "Dov … I'm sorry. My mind is enjoying turning the aircraft carrier into the wind and right now I'm focusing on the U.S.S. John Stennis. I have the picture on my screen saver—I really do. My fault!"

A chuckle rippled across the room. "No problem," Dov continued. "I get a little long in my stories sometimes." He looked back at his audience. "The point I'm making, people, is that we're working on the wrong things—the wrong things. We have to shoot higher, reach farther. We have to push ourselves. That's what I was getting to."

* * * *

Raef walked in, dropped his briefcase to the floor and pushed it into the corner with his foot, then closed the door. Jenifer called from the kitchen, "That's timing. I'm cooking rice and it'll be ready in about fifteen minutes."

"Let's chat a little before dinner," he said as he grabbed the railing and helped himself up the stairs. "Would that work?"

"Everything okay?"

"Yeah … No, not really. Do you … oh, let's just sit down." Raef went into the kitchen, poured himself a glass of water and grabbed some crackers and cheese. He walked back into the living room and settled into the easy chair. He laid his head back.

Jenifer walked in wiping her hands on a towel. "Ohhh. What's not okay?"

Raef laid his head on his hand. "Do you remember, just before the bottom fell out of this career in '83, when I sat down with Fortune and a few people in marketing and said, 'We're working on the wrong stuff? Well, it happened again—the situation—today. I had a chance to say it again … this time as an actual insight … and I couldn't. I couldn't even say it out loud!" He shared the Dov Ogden events and shook his head. "How long … do we have to keep confronting our same demons? I felt paralyzed. Afraid. Geez!"

Jenifer eased back on the sofa, then laid the towel on her lap and leaned slightly toward Raef. "Well, you're the only one in the room who even knows that connection exists, so that's not a problem. So, what's next?"

"I think it's time to close out the career. It sure feels right. But this stuff today? That was … disheartening." Raef sat quiet for a minute or two. "Let's pick another subject. Do you think anyone will show up at the parties?"

Jenifer picked the towel off her lap and stood. "If it's October, there's Halloween. And if it's November or December, there's the holidays. But September? What else does anyone have to do on a Friday night in September? They'll show … I think. Ready for dinner?"

"What's on?"

"Zone chicken with rice. And I picked up a movie for later."

"So we're into timing, are we? Sounds good."

✳   ✳   ✳   ✳

Fortune approached the glass-walled corner office. Lehi Weaver caught the motion, looked up and leapt from behind his desk crossing the distance to the door in a matter of steps. "Fortune. Please come in." Small beads of moisture formed just above Lehi's upper lip and the slight glisten on his forehead graduated to a glimmer. The professional casual speech wizard fell through some hidden drain beneath the brain and words tumbled over each other to burst forth and explode from high in his throat. "Please, come in. What can I do for you? Could I get you anything? Were you on my calendar? Did I miss something?" Then, with a deep breath and a motion toward the chair in front of his desk. "Please."

Fortune glanced around the room. "Thank you, Lehi." He nodded to his left, "Please close the door," and remained standing.

Lehi closed the door and walked toward his desk, then stopped and turned—his feet moved like they had trouble finding a home. He looked at the chairs around the conference table, then at his desk, then his chair, then at Fortune. Finally he took a deep breath, let his hands fall naturally to his sides, and looked at his visitor and let out a sigh. "How can I help you, sir?"

Fortune ran a hand along the edge of Lehi's desk and walked toward the window. "Do I understand that you are planning a retirement celebration for Raef Burnham?"

Lehi squared his shoulders, nodded and smiled. "Yes, sir. Late in the month."

Fortune stopped, turned and stepped toward Lehi. Eyeball to eyeball from less than a hand-breadth away Fortune stage whispered, "This cannot be. Cancel it."

"It's …" Lehi's voice cracked and he cleared his throat. He moved a half step back. "It's … it's already arranged." Then he swallowed and stepped to the side of his desk, adjusted his shoulders and stretched his neck to loosen his shirt collar; then he countered with, "Plus … plus it is standard practice … standard practice … Employees with more than 30 years' service are entitled to a party."

Fortune stripped the warmth from his response. "This is unthinkable and you know better."

Lehi stepped toward the window and waved a hand as he gave a slight tilt of the head and raised his eyebrows, "Actually, two parties."

Fortune laid a hand on the corner of the desk. "What … are … you … saying?"

Lehi turned and raised two fingers as he took a half-step toward Fortune. "Raef is having two parties. On Wednesday, the 26th, we have scheduled the center's open house. On Friday, he celebrates off campus with the guests of his choice. Two parties."

"Make … them … small."

Lehi ran a hand through his hair. "That's not so easy. Open houses vary, but my guess is that this will draw probably 200 guests. And Raef has invited 140 to his little celebration downtown—I'd expect about 120 to show."

Fortune opened the palm of his hands. "Do you have any idea what you are doing? You are glorifying a lackluster career. The man failed as a department head, had a vagabond career in who knows how many divisions and now you are celebrating—celebrating—that kind of career? What kind of message does this send to the research community?"

Lehi raised his eyebrows and tilted his head. "Something about a second chance?" He leaned forward and placed a hand on the desk. "True, he was demoted; but that was before my time. But a failure? Hardly. Have you looked at his record over the past 17 years? He's done good work. He's effective."

Fortune moved toward the door. "I want to talk to him."

"That should be easy." Lehi cleard his throat. "I mean, you're on his invitation list." He moved to open the door for his guest. "You should receive yours tomorrow."

"The open house—no objection. That says nothing. But the private party? No. Tell Burnham I want to speak to him. He will cancel the private party. We won't have to."

Lehi dropped his head and asked in a low voice. "How can he contact you?"

"I am out of the country between now and the 26th, but I will visit his open house. We will meet afterward. Make the arrangements."

Chapter 30

▼

PARTY TIME

"The Open House—when does it start?" The center's receptionist had to answer that question about 100 times that Wednesday morning and early afternoon. "Two o'clock with a little program afterwards." Wednesday, the 26th, was "Honor the RB" day for the Portable Foods Division and it left room for little other activity.

That afternoon Raef walked down to the cafeteria and stopped at the door. The banner over the far wall shouted, "Good Luck, Raef," in multi-color and graffiti script—a gift from the graphics department. Twenty tables set up with white table cloths and table tent decorations laid out landing spots for over 160 guests. Reaching across the room from left to right the dessert table called out to the guests to sample the goodies piled end to end in artful display—a respite in their trek through the celebration. Attendants stationed themselves along the buffet route testing their ability to help guests find their way, then scurried back to the kitchen to get the food ready. Today this was no longer the cafeteria—it was party town.

Dennis and Plass walked over to Raef, looked at each other and smiled. "Man, I hope somebody shows up. This could really be embarrassing!"

Raef raised his hands in defense. "Hey, I'm nervous enough about that. Are you guys ready for a photo or two? I mean, not many, but at least a few? My wife's going to be here—I think she'd like that. And I think at least one of my kids." He looked over his left shoulder, then his right. "Who knows? I don't know if anyone can get away...."

"Relax," Plass pounded a fist into his open hand. "Got you covered."

Dennis turned and swept a hand across the room. "This'll be filled in a half hour. After awhile we're moving the party upstairs for some fun—we've prepared a little schtick. And nothing's off limits—still, right?"

"I trust you two. I don't know why I'm saying this, but have at it."

Dennis and Plass turned to leave. "See you in church, partner. Oh, Lehi was looking for you."

Raef looked over to see Lehi Weaver wave as he crossed the middle of the room. "Raef, Fortune Montag wants to see you after everything this afternoon. He's just now landing and will catch you after the roast upstairs."

Raef looked at his watch—1:45. On the far side of the room Chap repositioned two tables and pointed to various places as he chatted with the foodservice manager in charge of the reception. Foodservice workers, used to scurrying, walked even faster with each minute but the room changed less and less with each adjustment.

Behind Raef a voice called, "Do we have the right place?" He turned to see Mindy bouncing year-old Courtney on her hip as they charged down the hallway, closing fast; Jenifer and Jake trailed by a few steps.

Raef took Courtney for the moment and greeted the family with hugs all around. "In the words of my father, 'I thought we were going to have to start without you.' This is some setup, isn't it? I hope someone shows."

Jake looked around. "I see Mr. Dennis and Mr. Plass have been hard at work. Nice." Then, looking back at Raef, "The rest of my gang will join us tonight at the Twin Oaks—everybody sends congrats." Then, looking over Raef's shoulder Jake extended a hand, "Mr. Chap, it's good to see you again."

"Good to see you, Jake. Hi, everybody." Chap looked at Jake, then Mindy. "Can I steal your dad and mom for a bit?"

Chap touched Raef's elbow and began moving toward the center of the room. "I need you and Jenifer to move to where the receiving line will be. People are beginning to arrive."

"A line?" Raef rubbed his palms.

Chap offered Raef a questioning look. "We set tables for 150 plus for this first part. Can you believe it?"

"When I see it, Chap. I'll believe it when I see it."

And then they came. An hour later new faces were still arriving and the line extended around the corner into the main room and beyond that, into the hallway. Those who passed through took desserts and a drink and joined friends at the tables. After awhile some stood, but only to join another table. No one left.

Willy Pearl was the first person to walk through the line. Willy, the first person to report to Raef when he joined the company in 1967, was today the longest tenured African-American employee at the Center. "Still no 'hads' in your history, Mr. Burnham?" Willy asked with just enough rhythm and tone to hint at his years growing up in Atlanta a long time ago.

Jenifer stepped up, "'Hads?' What are 'hads'?"

Raef stepped back. "Willy, you explain it."

Willy rested a hand on Raef's shoulder for a moment and smiled. "When the Captain here first came to WFI he didn't know any black people. Some of us brought him around and we told him about the people we always meet who say, 'I had a black friend,' and we'd say, 'What happened, did he die?' Those are the 'hads.'" Then, looking at Raef, "Well?"

"Willy, I have no 'hads' and I'll have no 'hads' in the future. Thanks for everything. Let's do some golf."

"In the spring, Captain. In the spring. I'm headin' for India next week. Be there for a few months."

Jenifer looked at Raef as Willy walked away, "I don't think I ever heard that before. Cute."

And the line kept coming … and coming … and the tables filled up. Mindy found people she knew and Courtney didn't—that led to an eventful afternoon for both. Jake shook hands with engineers and slapped a few backs with the service crew he'd worked with during his college summers on the outside maintenance staff.

At 3:15 Chap closed it down. "That's it, Raef." He turned to the crowd. "Folks, we have to move the party upstairs. Dennis and Plass have put a little something together—it should be fun. Anyone who hasn't finished talking, please stay and have dessert and coffee and join us upstairs when you can. See you upstairs."

*   *   *   *

In any other building the room would have been a mezzanine, but WFI had enclosed the brick expanse and created a conference room. The party organizers dimmed the lighting toward the back of the room and brightened the front with photo projections to be explained later. Dennis honchoed the roast from behind a lectern in the right front corner of the room and a camera crew captured every snippet of communication from a perch on the left.

No sooner had Raef and the family sat down than Chap presented the order of march and held out the microphone to Dov Ogden who walked to the center of the stage and began the program. "I've been with the company twelve years—ten of them in marketing. On my first marketing assignment I had the good fortune to work with Mr. Burnham. On our first meeting he drew me aside and said, 'Could I tell you how to be successful in your business? Always listen to your product development people—they know the product.' It was good advice and it has stood me well these 10 years. But he's losing it, you know. It's time for a change. Here's what I mean. The other day we had a meeting and I asked him a question near the end of a little talk I was giving. His response was, 'What? I wasn't listening. I was thinking about something you said earlier.' He'd checked out, people. Checked out. It's time. Yes, it's time."

Then Ogden shared stories covering Raef's 35 year career—well, actually his last 17 years. He began with, "We have no file—I checked—of Raef's work from 1967 until 1983. No one has any idea what he did back then. But since 1983, the record has been outstanding. Let me recount some of the contributions … and for all this, we are grateful." Dov walked across the stage and planted his feet directly in front of Raef and Jenifer. "You have done well, my friend. I will miss you. The company will miss you. Best of luck." Dov nodded with a slight bow, smiled, handed the microphone back to Chap and sat down.

Chap watched Dov walk to his chair. "I can't top that, but we have a few who are going to try." The stories continued with other speakers and finally Dennis's roast—everybody came to see the Dennis performance. It was always a classic.

One of Dennis's stories involved Raef's habit of sharpening pencils when someone stopped by for a visit. The practice rankled Dennis. So, one night while he was working the night shift in the pilot plant, he took Raef's Boston Vacuum Mount pencil sharpener and reduced the crank length by half and placed it back in its original position. One week later he stopped by for a visit. Raef, reportedly, laid out the pencils and began the sharpening. Except the crank required so much force it lifted the sharpener off its moorings. As Dennis told the story, slight trickles of sweat began to move down Raef's brow as he continued to try to accomplish the task. Dennis found he had to leave the room before exasperation engulfed Raef and uncontrollable laughter overcame Dennis. According to rumor, Raef realized he'd been had … but it took a few days. In another tale Dennis's adjusted Raef's chair "a half click a day" so that his feet eventually almost didn't touch the floor." He only realized it when Jenifer heard the story at a Christmas party and shared what was happening.

After twenty minutes of stories, cartoons, film clips, and near personal attack, Dennis closed the entertainment and handed the microphone back to Chap.

"Well, that's it, folks. It's been a good career." Then, he turned toward Raef. "We've been blessed to have you as a co-worker, mentor, and friend. Good luck to you and Jenifer." Then looking over the audience he cleared his throat. "There's food downstairs, everybody. Be sure to stop by."

Chap walked over to Raef and Jenifer. "We'll see you Friday night. This was nice, wasn't it?" Before Raef could answer he added, "Fortune is back and would like to visit with you."

Raef wrapped up the conversations, accepted well wishes from many friends and co-workers and arranged for Jake and Mindy to take Jenifer home.

"Anything serious?" Jenifer asked when she heard about the change in plans.

"Naah. This game is over and Fortune hasn't been that big of an issue. I'll be home in a half hour. Okay?"

Jenifer left to find Mindy and Courtney. Jake stepped over and shook hands and gave Raef a hug. "This was good. Congratulations. I understand you're meeting with Fortune. Be strong. See you at the house."

As Jake turned to leave, Fortune's administrative assistant approached Raef. "Mr. Montag is waiting for you in the director's conference room."

Fortune stood across the conference table from where Raef entered. "Fortune. It's nice to see you. May I assume that this is not a social visit?"

"Raef, sit down, please." Fortune sat down and Raef took the chair across from him. "Congratulations on a fine party. It appears that you were well thought of."

"People were kind. We have an open house of some sort for everyone who leaves R&D. Nothing heroic. But this," he touched his right temple, "… was … fine."

Fortune leaned back in his chair and laid his right arm on the table. "I agree. Now, how about letting this be your farewell—your entry into retirement?"

The pause hung in the air. Raef sat silent while he lowered his chin and stared directly into Fortune's eyes. Finally he broke the silence. "Why?"

"Do you not think that 120 people and a gala event is … inappropriate? Raef, you are a realist. Look at your career. I think we can agree that you have been anything but successful. Y …"

Raef landed his second foot on the floor at the same moment his forearms skidded to a stop on the table and his whole body leaned over the wooden plain that separated the two men—the complete action took one second. "Pardon me?" The plosive exploded into Fortune's sentence.

Fortune didn't move but stacked his words in a verbal shoe and slipped them like a blackjack dealer dealing cards onto the conversation table at a metered pace in monotone—no inflection. "Yours has not been a successful career. You never reached your stated objective. Following demotion you never even regained your position much less the level above that. Yours is a textbook example of failure. Why should we hold you up as something to emulate?"

Raef leaned back and rested his wrists on the edge of the table. "Fortune, you and I both know that all of us try things and some things fail. The difference is that the buck stops in R&D. We own our mistakes—it seems, forever. You bury yours. You pin it on some low level tech nerd, blame the outcomes in some unpublished report seen only by your archive-keeper or, if the blame is believable enough, on the developer—and you march on unscathed. Then you get touted as the great initiator—the marketing genius who generates ideas, who starts things. Hooray."

Fortune motioned with his resting hand. "Are you speaking of something specific?"

Raef paused again, then nodded. "In '82 or '83 we crossed swords over that technology you wanted to champion because someone read in some food science magazine or HBR or WSJ that it was going to be the next great thing. I challenged you because it didn't meet our criteria. Later, you tried it and it failed, and you still smart from your failure some 20 years later—and you're pretty sure I'm the only one who has it documented."

Fortune flicked an imaginary piece of dust off the table. "Do you actually think that I even remember that fiasco? It was long ago and it was inconsequential. We, as you say, try things. Sometimes ideas don't work. What is worse is not trying new ideas. And I could not care less about something that happened then, except … except … that you failed to be proactive. That attitude marked your career."

Raef shook his head. "You were wrong then and you are wrong today. And about the Friday night event, I have 140 invited guests coming to the Twin Oaks Friday night—about 120 have confirmed; I haven't received your reply, by the way—and I'll not let them down. You can kill it; I know that. But it'll be you doing it, not me."

Fortune held Raef's stare. "You are correct. If I say 'no party' you will have no party. Period." Fortune stood up and walked toward the door, opened it and held up his hand. "You and I will meet at my office at 4:30 Friday evening to discuss your final steps with the company. This discussion is not over. Good day."

Raef nodded and started to walk, but stopped in the doorway. "Technically, you're inaccurate. The Friday party is an R&D gig and it's Brey's party ... but I neither question your influence nor do I challenge it." He stepped through the doorway. "Thank you."

Chapter 31

▼

CLOSING OUT

The Twin Oaks Hotel stood tall enough in the western suburbs to command a clear view of the city's skyline to the east. Perched atop a knoll at the intersection of two major freeways, the hotel guarded a portal to the city, ten minutes away. The center was booked at 85 percent year round. The only reason for openings on the last Friday of September was the confluence of three events: the Gophers played Saturday on the road, the Vikings enjoyed the earliest bye week possible, and the Twins didn't return to the Homer Dome until Sunday. So, like the final piece of a puzzle, Raef's career closeout night fitted itself into September 28, 2001 from 6 p.m. to 9 p.m. in Conference Area NW at the Twin Oaks.

Jake drove up to the house at 4:30 to take Jenifer to the party. "Why'd Dad ask me to pick you up?"

Jenifer shrugged her shoulders. "He said Fortune wanted to meet with him and someone from Employee Services and that he'd join us there … at the party. Actually, all I know is that as of 4:30 today, your dad is retired from WFI and we're starting a whole new phase of our life. Who knows what that means?"

"Well, congratulations. You are now part of a retired team. When should we head out?"

Jenifer looked at her watch. "I'll need a little time to get ready. Let's leave at 5:30."

* * * *

The September sun laid low in the sky when Fortune closed his door and welcomed Raef to the final meeting of his career. "I hope you do not mind, Raef. I took the liberty of asking Lehi Weaver to join us in our little discussion."

"Not at all, Fortune." He turned to see the Employee Services Director walk in behind him. "Lehi, good to see you."

Fortune motioned for his guests to make themselves comfortable, then seated himself in the third chair around the low table. "Some technicalities exist that I want us all to appreciate. First, as of a few minutes ago, Raef, you are no longer an active employee of WorldFoods, Incorporated—you are a retiree. Congratulations on completing your career. Second, this discussion is the continuation of our business left somewhat unfinished on Wednesday. I am hoping we can clear away any confusion that may remain—that is why Lehi is here. Third, a party is scheduled to begin in a little while which may or may not proceed—I will decide that on the basis of this discussion. Now, let us begin."

Raef raised an index finger. "Fortune, why did you make it a point to remind me that I am no longer an employee—that I'm a retiree as of 4:30 p.m. today? Does it make a difference?"

Fortune smiled. "In some ways. I wanted you to appreciate the fact that the ground is now level. Corporate rank is no longer part of this discussion; we are now on equal footing—just two gentlemen chatting. Your benefits are locked in and you are no longer on the company payroll. We are free to discuss all subjects just as though we were not part of the company."

Raef smiled back. "Except that there may or may not be a party … okay. And Lehi's here, why?"

Lehi smiled. "To referee the debate, should it be necessary. And to aid with clarity, should it be necessary. Now, if you are both ready we'll begin. Fortune, your opening statement, please."

Fortune turned toward Raef. "I am a lifer. I love this company. I think we make our shareholders proud every day by providing great products and pleasing our customers so they keep coming back—we make the world better by what we do.

"One way we do that—we hire the best people we can and then provide a broad playing field for them to exercise their skills. We do not bring good people in here to teach them. We bring great people in here to let them perform their magic for our benefit. And we reward them when they perform. That's WFI. And we all know that. And we support each other in getting the job done.

"But once in a while someone we have selected—well, they should not have been selected and we are forced to make a correction. This is our culture. This is what we do. And we all know that. And we support our culture because it makes us strong.

"When one in our ranks who has risen to some level of effectiveness falls out of grace, we are forced to prune the corporate tree so new growth can occur. That pruned branch may get grafted in somewhere in the organization, but we never re-graft the branch in its old spot—it just does not work that way. This is our culture. This is what we do. And we all know that. It keeps us strong.

"Raef—you were a star when you came to WFI and for many years after that—perhaps 15 years or so—a Captain in the U.S. Army, a leader with excellent credentials, and impressive. You impressed the executive wing. When I came to the company in 1977 you had just been promoted to lead a department—one of only two people to reach that level by the age of 35 in the history of R&D. Outstanding. We met and had some interesting conversations. Your aggressiveness impressed me.

"Then I took on other assignments and in the early 1980s we worked together again. At that point, I noticed that you had changed. Your focus seemed ... elsewhere. Other things were more important than the work.

"Soon thereafter you moved back to leading product development teams and never regained your former position. Why? Lack of talent? No. Lack of interest? Possibly. Lack of focus? Perhaps. Lack of results? Definitely. You lost your commitment to our culture and we could no longer trust you to lead in the WFI fashion.

"Your fall from grace was the betrayal of trust; the inevitable career outcome, failure."

Raef shook his head and looked at Lehi. "I assume I can respond to this at some point?" When Lehi nodded he continued. "You weren't here for the early days of that story, Lehi. Some of what Fortune says is accurate, but his views are personal—this is all about personal pique."

Fortune furrowed his brow and leaned forward. "Raef, I am surprised at you—making this personal. I am above that type of behavior and I resent your implying otherwise."

Raef smiled. "I'm not implying anything, Fortune. If you recall, we had a difference of opinion in '82 or early '83 over that technology thing. You wanted to pursue something that I knew to be useless to our systems, any products we might want to market." He turned to Lehi. "By the way, Lehi, I was right: Others tried the system, spent millions on it. We sold the system for salvage eventually." He looked at Fortune. "I told you we were working on the wrong things and you got your nose out of joint—took it personally. And I think, still do. Anyway, we parted company and not too long after that, I was demoted."

Fortune looked at Lehi, "This point is irresolvable," then leaned toward Raef. "No, you did not understand business then and by your current conversation I conclude you do not understand it now. The responsibility of marketing is to run product programs. We try things. You execute the direction provided. In that case you failed to execute. And you showed that we could not trust you to execute in the future. Personal? Not at all. Just basics. Let's move on."

Lehi nodded. "Fortune, what's your point?"

Fortune patted the arm of his chair. "When a person comes to the corporation with leadership skills and technical capability and is hired because those qualities identify him or her to be a person we can count on to lead our business into the 21st century—and that person fails—the impact hurts everybody and that person does not deserve a second chance. To re-promote such a person sends the wrong message. It says that one can do well, fail to perform, and resume the previous path—without consequences—and this simply is not true. Consequences are real—and we need them in order that we may stay strong." He settled back in his chair. "You get one chance."

Lehi scratched a note on his tablet, then looked at Fortune. "Your second point?"

Fortune glanced at the window, then he looked at Raef. "You lost your aggressiveness. Why?"

Raef pursed his lips, took a deep breath, then nodded. "Yep. I was bored." He settled back in the chair and fixed his gaze on some distant point. "I sat back one day and realized that research and development is just a game. Sure, it's played by a fixed set of rules; define a target, make a prototype, develop a formula and system, conduct focus groups, adjust, consumer test, plant test, and market the product. Man, it's cookie cutter." He looked at Fortune. "You know the drill. If you execute your moves well the project matches a timetable and everybody is happy." He raised his index finger just a little. "A mediocre mind can play this game at a pretty high level. A dolt can't do it—the person has to at least grade out at mediocre. Just play the game every day, do what you marketing folks want without kicking up any dust, and even a 'B' level talent can reach some pretty good level—you have plenty examples of that around here. That's my impression—and I think it's accurate. But I quit playing. I quit playing. And no one gets to do that and survive.

"Anyway, WFI rewards stars and those touched by their halos. But if the star quits delivering, the corporation invokes the penalty clause and the player gets removed from effective service; and the game goes on." Raef took a deep breath and looked away. "Yeah, I quit playing the game."

Fortune steepled his fingers. "And you still think I'm wrong?"

Raef shook his head. "Not wrong for taking action—I deserved a spanking. But no warning? Not even a 'heads up'? Yeah, you were wrong, Fortune, to invoke the career death penalty for a single offense that was correctable. Man! Advancement—a one-ticket opportunity? Once lost, never regained? Did you ever look at your programs for transitioning people into new jobs? I've tried to fix your stupid programs—too many people get hurt … just out of ignorance. Can't you people look at the total situation and admit where you blew it?" Raef whisked a backhand. "It happens all the time. Somebody slackens their performance for a little while—a good person, talented, well thought of—and what do you do but take them out of the game … for the rest of their career. Who loses? Everybody. Everybody loses. The person never reaches their level of top performance and the corporation fails to benefit." He raised both hands and dropped them to the arm rests. "Why is this garbage still tolerated? Ego … Ego. Your stupid sponsorship concept … Gutless leadership. No, I don't begrudge you punitive action—corrections were needed. I simply call these personnel practices idiotic, lazy."

Lehi looked at Fortune. "We own part of that problem, Fortune. And we can do better."

Fortune waved a hand, "A small portion," And looked back at Raef. "We must deal with the subject at hand. You lost your aggressiveness because you became bored. In reality, you quit doing the job. You failed to function at the high level we expect of a person with potential. And I think you have just verified that this is true. You earned career adjustment and we employed effective action." He turned. "Now to your point, Lehi. Yes, we can initiate better practices, but sponsorship is how business operates and it's based on trust. Raef betrayed a trust and paid the price." He adjusted his chair. "I have a third point. Religion on the job."

Raef blinked. "Specifics, please."

Fortune stood up and walked over to the window. He turned toward Raef. "You counseled people in your office and openly discussed what you call salvation with people who worked for you. Need I be clearer?"

Raef stood and walked over to the adjacent window. "You're right. I did. They had needs and I knew I had answers, but WFI wasn't paying me to solve people's life problems—guilty. I corrected that as of April 15, 1983—never did it again—never discussed my theological beliefs on company time. But before 8:30 a.m. or after 4:30 p.m.—fair game."

Fortune shook his head. "Raef, that was unacceptable."

"Agreed. And, by the way, once again no one even suggested that my behavior was unacceptable. No one." Raef shook his head. "Not one person. Where do we go from here?"

Fortune turned from the window. "Lehi?"

Lehi tapped his tablet. "I think we have three issues, maybe four. But I'm puzzled. What sparked this conversation? It can't be just this 'he said she said' thing or Fortune's long held pain or about religion on the job some 18 years ago. What's the issue? Why are you two meeting and why was I brought in?"

Fortune ran his hand through his hair. "This is about our company honoring a very average low level manager at the end of a lackluster, failed career—this hoopla is inappropriate and I believe we should cancel his party. WFI does not celebrate mediocrity—it gives the wrong message."

Lehi blinked. "Cancel th ... still?"

Raef held up a hand. "Lehi, it's okay. Fortune and I have a long-standing difference of opinion about what constitutes success—specifically career success."

Lehi scratched an eyebrow. "You see it differently?"

"Yes." Raef walked behind his chair and leaned forward, both hands on the back. "Where is it written that unless a person reaches the goals they set at age 26, they're a failure? Or where is it written that unless you meet someone else's expectations, you're a failure? Life is about change, circumstances and competition—everything's always in flux. Consider these questions: Did you become the CEO? Did your reach the top of your little organizational pile? Did you meet the expectations we imposed on you? If positive answers to those questions are the only criteria used for judging, just about all of us are doomed to fail. Why? Because we can't control all the variables—and we change. So, if we answer 'no' to some of the questions, do I think we automatically grade out as failures? No way."

Lehi looked at Fortune. "Comment?"

Fortune adjusted his shirt cuff to extend the proper amount beyond his suit coat. "Raef lives in a fantasy world. Success is about attaining goals. In the real world we set goals early in life, attain them, and move on to the next set of goals. We work to achieve educational ends, then to enter jobs that offer a challenge and finally to maximize our level of effectiveness in our work. It is called promotion—a system of rewards based on performance. Companies hire us because they see us meeting their needs, fulfilling the goals they set. The company gives us greater responsibility and greater personal reward because more and more they trust us to reach goals. When individuals fail, the corporation suffers and those individuals pay the price for failure."

Lehi tapped his tablet. "How does this bear on Raef and the party?"

Fortune opened his palms to the ceiling. "Lehi, are you so blind? This person came in as a star—we trusted him. Some of us guaranteed his performance—we sponsored him. Along the way he quit on us and hurt the corporation—caused his sponsors to lose face. Then he settled for staying at a level 5 for half his career rather than show the courage to advance himself. This is not the stuff of success. This is weakness. And if we sponsor this party tonight, we endorse the concept that one can fail and the corporation will cheer. It will say that we approve of partial commitment, mediocre performance." Fortune walked over to Raef and stopped. "Frankly, I believe that if we cancel the party right now, it sends our message in ways that words could not. Lehi, take care of it. Cancel the party."

Lehi bit the end of his pencil. "I can't, actually. Brey is the host—it's his party. He's the sponsor, and he's at the party right now."

Fortune spun around and glared at Raef. "This is not over." He crossed the room, then stopped and walked back toward the window and squared face to face with Raef. "Why did you stay? Answer that. Why? If you were any good you would have left and found an even better position—somewhere else."

Raef took a deep breath and let it out slowly. "Simple. My skills suit WFI; that's why I chose the company. My network was intact and I regarded this as a temporary setback—I did think I was that good and that I'd re-establish myself within a year. And it was a bad time to move my family." Raef put both hands into his pockets and leaned with his back against the wall. "And after all the questions were asked and the pride set aside, I felt, deep down, that I should stay and work it out. Whatever was broken in me hadn't been fixed yet and I knew I was too blind to see my lack. So, despite the humiliation I decided to stay. Now, when I consider how much fun it has been to try to work my way back to a level 6—how great it has been to work with all of our people and all the great experiences we've shared and all the growth we've accomplished together—who can call that a bad decision?" He bowed his head, then looked up. "But I've questioned parts of it over the years."

Raef stepped from behind the chair and walked toward Fortune. "I have no fight with you, Fortune. I've been loyal to my bosses over all the years, I've worked hard and well and I've not bad-mouthed the company—now I'm trying to leave quietly, pleasantly."

Fortune slipped a hand into his pocket as he looked out the window. "The question was, 'Why did you stay?' That's not much of an answer, Raef. Is that the best you could do?"

Raef walked over to his chair and stood behind it. "Fortune, I couldn't change my circumstances, so I tried to create a situation that would give me the best probable outcome. I trusted you to do the right thing. Hey, ultimately none of us can save ourselves—we all need help."

Fortune cleared his throat. "This meeting is over."

*   *   *   *

The Twin Oaks reception room looked out onto a sprawling garden with its floral display of reds and browns and golds and a few dwarf maples adding their mixed reds that blended all the way to yellow. Across the middle of the room like a wide angle portrait stretched a 30 foot table covered with a gold and brown cloth where the hotel's culinary artists had begun to show off their autumnal creations. All this surrounded a five foot ice-carved eagle that centered the display. And at the far end, Chap, Goody, Dennis, and Tommy had arranged fourteen tables set with eight per table and created a platform with screen and projectors for the evening show.

Jenifer chatted with Mindy and her family while Jake and his family joked with Raef's sister and brother in law and one of the women from the Portable Foods team.

For the next hour the guests ate and laughed and mingled. Photographers shot stills and videoed the crowd. Raef and Jenifer floated—their term for meeting and enjoying each guest they'd invited. There was no way audio and video could capture all that happened.

In the midst of all the activity Fortune walked in, tall and lean and sun-tanned from an active summer on the links. One of the Portable Foods team nudged the person next to her. "Fortune Montag's here." The other person nodded. "Raef was always well connected. I didn't know he and Fortune were that close."

In the 15 minutes left to him before the program began Fortune managed to introduce himself to each table and befriend all in the room while leaving one minute to pick up some hors d'ouerves as a snack.

Just when Raef moved to spend a moment with the family, Chap grabbed the microphone and said, "Hey, everybody. We have a little thing prepared. It's going to go longer than I wanted, but then, who's in charge? Take a seat, please, and we'll get started."

Chapter 32

▼

PASS IN REVIEW

"We're here tonight to honor Jenifer ... oops ... now that was Freudian. Let me start again. We're here to honor Raef Burnham." Applause broke out. "Well, of course. He hand-picked this crowd so naturally you're on his side." Chap looked at Jenifer. "Jenifer, tonight we complete our caregiving. We've taken care of him as long as we could. After tonight, he's yours ... without the dowry." A corporate chuckle rumbled across the room. "But I'm charged with introducing WFI's Kings of Comedy—our own Dennis and Goody with Tommy at the camera. This will be like no retirement party you've ever attended, so sit back and enjoy."

Each table produced its own level of murmur. Every person made a comment to the person on one side and then turned to respond to the person on the other and the noise grew louder.

"Excuse me ... excuse me." Chap looked at Raef. "We're here to celebrate Raef's career." Chap picked up a six by eight inch card and laid it on the lectern. "Dov Ogden is our first speaker. Dov."

Ogden opened the evening. "Your honor, esteemed counselors, fellow witnesses, and astute members of the jury." Quiet laughter rippled across the room. "We're having fun, but I present my remarks in a spirit of gratitude. Raef, you've touched a lot of lives." He went on to tell a story about a son who worked with his father in the home improvement business. On Saturdays he went with his father to inspect and correct any mistakes the crews had made during the week. The son wanted to be with his friends, but as the day wore on he saw why his father had such a thriving business—he made sure the work was done right. "Raef is that person. He is and has been for 35 years in the right place doing the right things for the right reasons. And we appreciate it." He paused and with a little sparkle in the eye looked at Raef. "Now you go to a better place ..." Laughter exploded. "... To do a better thing ... for a better reason. I'll miss you." Ogden walked over, shook hands with Raef and stepped off the platform.

Chap nodded toward Dov and looked out over the audience. "Our next speaker—Jay Burbank. Jay, some of us here don't know you ..."

"My name is Jay Burbank; I'm WFI's plant manager in Cincinnati." Jay—a 6'3" shooting guard at the Air Force academy 20 years ago, still looked like he could go the 94 feet for 40 minutes if he had to—spoke of friendship. He concluded telling the story of concluding a plant test on January 16, 1992—Raef's anniversary of twenty-five years with WFI. "We finished the day, and Raef said, 'Is there any place we could get a sandwich? We found a place called *The Hideaway* and closed the place after an evening discussing authors, books, leadership, ethics, and how we could all do some things better, and friendship, and sacrificing for the team." He stopped and scanned the audience. "He's one of the few people in my life who, even if we've not talked for months, can pick up the last sentence at the comma. WFI is business. But sometimes what we do creates a friendship. And it's fun when that happens." He turned toward Raef. "Life's a journey—and we're all still on that journey trying to make life a little better for everyone. Raef, I wish you the best in yours."

Chap jumped up and grabbed a microphone. "Jay, do you mind if we make this interactive?"

Jay looked back at the roomful of people. "Does he do this often?"

Applause broke out and a few whistles. Chap waited for the room to quiet. "I have two questions—I think we all do—and you may answer them in any order you wish. First, what does friendship have to do with business? Second, what is the meaning of your phrase, 'sacrificing for the team'?"

Jay nodded and looked at Raef. "The first one is easy. Friendship is about trust. And trust is always a decision. Raef and I decided to trust each other early in our working relationship. I needed to get things done in the plant, but our structure—WFI's structure—and systems made rapid action impossible. Raef had ideas he wanted to implement, but sales and marketing were afraid to make changes, even though the changes improved everything for everybody. We decided to trust each other and work under the radar. And it worked. That was friendship—and it has everything to do with business."

Jay stopped a moment. "The second question is a bit more complicated." Jay smiled at Fortune and nodded. "Let me tell a story that John Russett, a plant manager for one of our competitors, tells about himself. I don't think he'd mind. He tells it like this: 'When I was in high school I played baseball. During a game in my senior year I was hit by a pitch to lead off the bottom of the 7th—in our high school league the 7th was the last inning. Eventually I scored the winning run. After the game our coach gave a rousing post game recap up in our team room. In the recap he declared that our victory was fueled by the heart I had shown by leaning into the pitch—leaning into the pitch—doing whatever it would take to help the team win. He prefaced this by saying that he knew the type of team player I was and the type of tenacity I brought to every game. He also noted he was not even going to ask me if I had leaned into that pitch because he knew I had. I was glad he didn't ask because the pitch that hit me was a high and tight fastball that I had no chance to move on, to lean into or to get out of the way. But I was proud and it made me play even harder the rest of the year and maybe beyond.' And what's my point, you say? Just this: that's how Raef sees the world. But here's the deal: WFI presented a pitch he would lean into and at the same time not be able to get out of the way of … in terms of career choices. Hey, I know this man. I know what he's made of. He leaned into the pitch—got demoted; and took one for the team—he's still here. That's 'sacrificing for the team'."

Chap pursed his lips. "Who's the team?"

From the back of the room boomed the answer, "Everybody in this room, everybody who ever worked for this man, the people who came on Wednesday afternoon and every life he's touched in 35 years."

Chap motioned Jay to wait and looked toward Raef. He nodded once. Then Chap addressed the voice in the back. "Could you introduce yourself, sir, and come forward? Some of us don't know you."

Toward the front of the room strode a trim, 6'4" man with grey hair and mustache who looked like he stepped out of GQ, the men's fashion magazine. He wore a blue blazer with grey slacks, the get-by uniform of every man in the city who had to wear a shirt and tie and didn't feel like going through the selection process—but on him it was style. And he smiled easily as his eyes caught everything in the room—in a single glance. "Detective Sargeant Jeff Byrne, Westphalia Police Department. I'm a friend of Raef's—we work out at the same club. He was kind to me once when I needed some kindness and we've chatted frequently ever since. What's complicated about your question? I just walked in."

Chap smiled. "Could you tell us how you answered that question so quickly not having heard what this was all about?"

Jeff turned his steel eyes on the crowd. "I do this for a living—professional witness. Raef told me about his chat with Jay back when we first met at the club and talked something about 'taking one for the team' and Raef had no clue who that might be." Then looking at Chap, Jeff shook his head. "These guys—guys like this—they never get it. The obvious stuff. It goes right over their heads. It's for the people." Then he looked at Raef. "Get it? They do. And they're showing their appreciation. Thanks for the invitation. Now, do you mind if I just go stand in the back and enjoy this show?"

Chap looked at Jay. "One more thing. What constitutes leaning into the pitch?"

"Whether he knew it or not, he found a way to be free and still be effective—meet his desires and conquer his fears."

Chap thanked Jay, then handed the microphone to Pria Fowler who spoke of Raef's modeling the way to treat people, and read a piece from the late 1800s by Robert Louis Stevenson entitled *Achievement*:

> *Those people are a success who have lived well, laughed often and loved much; who have gained the respect of intelligent people and the love of children; who have filled their niche and accomplished their task; who leave the world better than they found it, whether by an improved poppy, a perfect poem or a rescued soul; who never lacked appreciation of earth's beauty or failed to express it; who looked for the best in others and gave the best they had.*

When she'd finished reading she looked at the crowd. "I believe this man's career was a success for a lot of reasons not measured by the bottom line." Pria looked over at Raef, nodded and stepped to the back of the stage.

As the final three speakers completed sharing their thoughts, Raef looked out over the guests and saw Fortune standing in the back. Fortune returned the look.

Chapter 33

WHEW!

Chap walked over to the lectern and lifted the microphone from its stand. "Raef, before we close this evening, would you introduce your family?"

"Delighted."

After the introductions Chap looked around the room and stopped at Mindy. "Last chance."

Mindy took a deep breath and walked to the lectern, arranged a piece of paper on the surface and stopped. She pulled out a Kleenex and dabbed the corners of her eyes. "Sorry. I get a little emotional. Not like my father. Well, actually …" A wave of laughter spread across the room. "My father is a man who speaks truth …" Five minutes later she turned to Raef and said, "… and may I add my toast to life, health, happiness and FREEDOM!"

Chap stood as the room erupted in enthusiastic applause. "Thank you, Mindy." Raef escorted Mindy to the family table and sat down next to Jenifer. She reached over and touched his hand. Chap grabbed the mike from its holder and walked toward the audience. "The speeches are over. I have a question that requires a voice vote. Answer yes or answer no after I read the question. Do you understand?"

The shout exploded. "Yes!"

Chap waved the paper and shouted into the microphone. "Here it is. Can we consider the career of Raef Burnham a success?"

The crowd rose to its feet and shouted, "Yes! Yes! Yes!" High fives and shouts abounded. Chap let it go for awhile then tried to calm the noise. Raef looked at Jenifer and gave her a hug. He touched the corner of his eye. "Got a Kleenex?"

Jenifer gave him a little squeeze. "I'm using it."

Jake reached over and shook his father's hand. Mindy came alongside with a hug.

Chap gave up. "Thanks for coming, everybody. That's it for tonight. Thanks, Raef. The evening's over."

Raef nodded and mouthed, "The career is over. Thanks."

* * * *

Raef said goodbye to several stragglers and stopped to pick up his gifts when a voice behind him said, "One more thing." Raef turned to see Fortune standing near the doorway. "One more thing for you to consider. There will be packages—you are not on the list."

* * * *

The party was over. The week was over. The month that had started with 9/11 and now concluded with a toast, was over. The career that had begun nearly thirty-five years ago was over—about that, there were no tears.

* * * *

"Thanks again, you two. We'll talk next week. G'nite." Raef waved from the corner of the driveway as Goody and CJ drove away. The Goodwins, Jake and his family, and Mindy and her family had stopped over for coffee and dessert and to close out the evening. Now everyone was gone.

Raef put his arm about Jenifer as they walked up the drive. "Honey, this has been a day. How're you holding up?"

Jenifer laid her head on his shoulder, "Surprisingly well. How about you?"

He shook his shoulders. "I think I'm still on stage. Midnight. But let's go in the living room for a bit before we call it a day, OK? I need to wind down a little." Raef sat down and put his feet on the ottoman, leaned his head back against the chair and exhaled slowly. "I'll tell you what I'm dealing with tonight. We've just completed a thirty-five year career—set out to do something, didn't get it done, and still feel successful—like I accomplished 'the thing.' But why?"

Jenifer moved to her own agenda. "What did Fortune say when he came over after the evening was over?"

Raef completely forgot the question on the table. "Fortune said there will be packages, but that I'm not on the list."

Jenifer just shook her head. "And if you stayed on the fast track you could have ended up like him."

Raef took a deep breath and sat back "Oh, Fortune's OK. He just thinks like a corporation."

Jenifer closed her eyes slowly, let them stay closed for awhile, and opened them slowly. "It's too late to deal with this, and we're pooped. But I'll tell you this. After you've thought it through you'll have to conclude that making the original objectives—whatever they were—and reinstatement to Level 6—why we got stuck on that—isn't the point. It was a good career. You did well. You're successful. I'm going to bed."

"Okay. Hey, we don't have to set an alarm in the morning. How about that?"

EPILOGUE

▼

April 15, 2002

Fortune Montag bounded into his office at his usual 6:30 a.m. arrival time, but this morning was different. The rumor mill was abuzz that WFI was about to make an important announcement and today was the day. Fortune wiped his palms with his handkerchief as he walked to his desk to pick up the daily tracking sheet. Before he could read the top line, he heard a voice from his doorway. "I'd like to visit with you for a few minutes after you've opened for the day—if you don't mind." Dalton P. Harvey, CEO of WFI and the only person senior to Fortune in the organization, smiled. "I'll need only a few minutes."

Fortune nodded. He squared his shoulders, took a deep breath, let it out slowly and walked into the next door office. Dalton Harvey looked up and motioned for Fortune to take the chair opposite him ... across from him ... the chair facing Dalton's desk. *What?* Fortune eased himself into the chair.

Dalton glanced at a piece of paper on the desk, looked up at Fortune, took another quick look at the paper and laid it aside. He rested his forearms on the desk and leaned forward. "That I'm going to retire in the next two years is no secret—we have a mandatory age limit. I've asked Preston V. Conklin, one of the top guys at GE, to join us and to get ready to succeed me. We're flying him in today and he's bringing a few of his people. As part of our agreement with Preston, you will run Southeast Asia for us. The transition people will be in to talk to you at 8."

Harvey said something else, but Fortune couldn't ... couldn't process ... couldn't focus ... couldn't ...

* * * *

Jenifer held up the morning newspaper. "Raef, listen to this. The business section. 'In a surprise move, WorldFoods, Inc. has hired Preston V. Conklin, 46, as executive vice-president, reporting directly to Dalton P. Harvey, CEO. Conklin, considered next in line at General Electric, steps in as the frontrunner to replace Harvey when he retires in two years. Not available for comment were Fortune Montag and Nicolas Penworthy, WFI's homegrown vice presidents and the presumptive favorites to replace Harvey.' Interesting. More coffee?"

978-0-595-46540-8
0-595-46540-4

Printed in the United States
96250LV00004B/1-126/A